HOMECOMING

I'm Your Man Series

Book Two

───────◆───────

Blaine Kistler

Book and cover design by eBook Prep
www.ebookprep.com

October, 2017

www.blainekistler.com

DEDICATION

To my sisters: Joyce, Isabel, Mary, Jane and Wenda, the Fabulous Five. Together even when we're apart. I love you all.

And once again, to Lizzie, mentor and friend. Some debts can never be repaid.

PROLOGUE

If Strom Garrison hadn't gotten stoned at the team's victory party, Jake wouldn't have kissed Lorie Saxton. Sure, he'd thought about it; he'd hankered after Lorie since eighth grade. But she belonged to Strom, and that meant hands-off. He reminded himself of that when she turned to smile at him, her cameo face bathed in moonlight, her hand on his sleeve.

"Thanks, Jake. It would've been a long walk."

She stood close enough the scent of musk drifted to his nostrils. Her smooth shoulders were bare, and his fingers twitched to slide under the tiny straps of her dress, his hands-off policy more strained than usual.

Cut it out, Randolph. You'll make yourself miserable.

She shivered in the autumn air, and he peeled off his letter jacket, draping it around her shoulders. They couldn't stand out on her porch much longer. The autumn air held the bite of the coming winter.

"Thanks," she whispered, and tied the arms of the jacket around her throat. "Strom was in no condition to drive me home after so much beer. I'm still surprised his folks let him have a kegger in their backyard."

"They're out of town. I don't think they knew."

"I guess no real harm was done. Everyone else seemed pretty sober."

Jake nodded, not mentioning the pot smoking that Strom had indulged in along with the beer. The team had made a pact: the less anyone knew about Strom's excesses, the better. Their quarterback's talented arm carried with it the team's chance for the Class C State Championship. More than prestige was involved. A state championship meant that some of them would have a chance at a football scholarship. A college football career meant a later shot at the pros. In a small farm community with money scarce and opportunities few, that was a chance worth protecting.

"You should talk to him, Lorie. If he's caught drinking, he'll get kicked off the team. Coach Gorski would hate it, but he's got a zero tolerance policy toward alcohol. If Strom's benched, we'll lose state."

"He doesn't listen to me. Sometimes I wish Strom were more like you. You know, steady, dependable."

"Boring, you mean."

Jake was Strom's favorite wide receiver, which meant they cooperated for the team, but mutual dislike kept them clear of each other off the field. Jake had never been part of Strom's crowd at Midland High. The fast crowd, the fun crowd. Jake didn't give a damn. He had his own plans. After graduation he'd shake the Kansas dust off his shoes, and not look back, headed for Virginia Tech, a career with computers, and probably the military.

"No, never that. If I wasn't going steady with Strom—I like you, Jake. A lot."

A tremor went through him, and he shifted his feet. She rummaged in her miniscule shoulder purse. He glimpsed her cell, a lipstick, and handkerchief. She pulled out a tin of breath mints and pried open the lid, slipped one into her mouth and held them out to him.

He stared, his hands glued into his pockets. His mind went numb. Lorie Saxton, the prettiest girl at Midland High—was she asking him to kiss her? Swift thinking, Randolph. Obviously, she is. Don't fumble the ball here.

He knew he wasn't good looking. Sure, he was big, six foot with probably another inch or two to go before he quit. And he was in good shape. Weighed in at one-seventy, ran five miles twice a week and lifted weights. He could take the toughest physical stuff that coach threw at them. But the best said about his face was that it wasn't ugly. His brows were thick and almost came together over his nose, a bumpy nose, nothing pretty about it. His eyes were murky brown and so was his thatch of hair. He couldn't even let his hair grow fashionably long. Too many cowlicks meant it stood up in tufts unless he kept it short.

His fingers reached, fished out a mint and popped one in his own mouth, crunching it between his teeth, the fiery taste flooding his taste buds. She rolled her mint around her tongue, and watched him through sleepy cat's eyes as she put the tin back in her purse.

"Swallow it," he said gruffly.

Her mouth made an O. "Wh—what?"

"The damn mint. Swallow it."

He saw her throat work as she swallowed. Doubt flickered in her eyes as he tipped up her chin with his forefinger, but she didn't pull away. His mouth came down on hers, softly, not wanting to spook her, savoring the moment. This might be all he'd ever have of her, and he wanted it for too long to stop. Her breath was hot mint as her lips parted and her tongue touched his. What was left of his brain imploded.

His arms tightened around her and he pulled her against his chest. She sagged against him, returning the kiss. Jake had kissed his share of girls, but none had tasted like this, hot mint and sweet woman, scalding his senses. She melted into him as his mouth hardened, drinking in her essence.

When the kiss ended, she gasped and pressed her fist to her lips, but she didn't pull away. Her hazel eyes were clouded, heavy-lidded. Jake's hands fell to his sides. Should he apologize? That would be stupid when he just wanted to do it again. He cupped her chin and when she didn't resist, fit his mouth to hers. It was even better the second time.

Dimly she realized that she'd asked for this, that she'd wondered for a long time what it would be like to kiss Jake Randolph.

Now she knew. It was wonderful.

A tiny whimper escaped her throat when his tongue slid inside her mouth. Usually she didn't like that. But Jake was taking and she was letting him. Not just letting him, she wanted him to take. She tangled her tongue with his as he pressed her against the shingled porch wall, and she felt the rumble of his growl through her skin. Thought vanished and nothing mattered except the voluptuous melting into him that ended only when he pulled away, shuddering. He pressed his forehead against hers, and gripped her shoulders as they both gasped for breath.

"I—I should go in."

"Yeah." He let go of her shoulders that were trembling under his leather jacket. What now? The next move was hers. He couldn't think of anything to say.

"Your jacket." She fumbled, untied it and slipped it off. He glimpsed the thick, gold ring on her middle finger, the school crest flashing in the moonlight. Strom Garrison's ring. Midland High's star quarterback, All State, first team, the best looking, most popular guy in school and her steady. Strom and Lorie, Homecoming King and Queen, the hottest couple in school, and she had kissed him like she meant it.

His hand closed over hers as she held out his jacket. He didn't have a gold ring to offer, no sporty red convertible to ride around in, just a damn letter jacket and a beat-up pickup truck. "Keep it. But if you wear it at school and tell people it's mine, there's no more Strom."

She stilled, understanding what he was offering. Jake Randolph didn't have a steady girl, although she knew plenty who'd love the job. When he wasn't on the football field he was studying or helping his family out on their farm. He had none of Strom's polish or smooth good looks. But he had a rough honesty and ready laugh, and a lanky body that screamed maleness. And Strom's kisses had never made her skin burn or her body sing. Strom's scent didn't intoxicate and make her dizzy.

Jake was different than the other boys she'd dated in a lot of ways. More adult, more focused. There was an aura of suppressed energy about him. Power smoldered under his easy-going exterior, occasionally lashing out like sheet lightning.

"Keep it?" she whispered, stalling. Her mother would have a fit if she accepted.

That added to the appeal of what her rapid pulse urged her to do. She had never felt like this. She wanted to crawl onto Jake's lap and let him do all the delicious things his mouth and hands promised.

His brown eyes held hers and waited, his hand firmly around hers, and she knew down to her toes that this would be the only time he'd make the offer. She said goodbye to the prestigious ring, the sleek convertible, her date to the prom with the most popular senior boy in school. She took her hand from Jake's, slipped off the ring and dropped it into her purse.

"Lorie, you're sure?" He smoothed his hands over her hair. "I'll be leaving right after graduation. You're headed for K-State. So is Strom. Maybe you should stick with a sure thing."

The purse thumped to the porch boards, and she thrust her arms into his jacket. The size Extra-Large hung to her knees. She stood on her toes and he pulled her into another kiss that was as sweet and sharp in her mouth as peppermint candy. She molded into his body, formed to fit there.

"I—I'd like to give him the chance to break it off," she whispered into his chest. "Let him dump me."

"Yeah," he chuckled without humor. "Let's kowtow to Strom's monstrous ego." And then he frowned. "I'm not afraid of him, or his posse, if that's what you're thinking."

Her mouth curved. "I know. But you're right about his ego." She held up her empty ring finger. "Aren't you getting what you want? What's another few days? We'll have a fight and he'll dump me. Maybelle Gilinsky is hanging around waiting for us to break up and Strom knows that. I've seen him look at her, and he's always telling me how hot she is. As soon as he breaks it off, I'll wear your jacket. Every day."

The front door wrenched open a crack, and Lorie's mother peered out into the darkness. "Lorie, it's after midnight. Where've you been, dear? Is Strom with you?"

Jake stepped into the halo of light that emitted from the bare porch bulb. "It's Jake Randolph, Mrs. Saxton. I brought Lorie home from the party."

The door pulled open and Rose Saxton glared at him. "Where is Strom?"

Lorie rushed in. "He got sick, Mom. Jake was nice enough to bring me home. I'll just be a sec."

"Humph. No messing around out there. You know what I think about that kind of goings on." No mistaking the hostility in her gaze.

"No problem, Mrs. Saxton," Jake said politely. "I'm just leaving."

She slammed the door and Lorie sighed. "I'm sorry, Jake. She can be a pain."

"Nothing wrong with looking after your kid. Guess she doesn't like me much."

"It's not you. She doesn't know you. She just likes it that I'm with Strom."

"How will she react to the news that we're an item?"

"Probably not good."

"She'd rather have her daughter date the banker's son than the son of a dirt farmer. Makes sense."

"To her, maybe. I'll see you Monday, okay?" She reached to give him a quick kiss, and with a gentle stroke of his shirtfront, vanished inside her house.

She wasn't at school Monday. Jake found his letter jacket on the front seat of his truck, a note attached.

"I can't. Please understand. L."

No explanation. He crumpled the note in fury. He understood all right. She'd chosen the banker's playboy son over the farmer's kid. So maybe she had good judgment. At any rate, she was out of his life forever.

CHAPTER 1

Fifteen years later

"Jake, that's pure sin you're looking at. And big trouble. Better back off."

Jake scowled at his brother, and turned his gaze away from the woman who sat on the other side of the barroom, her drink untouched as she stared at him. Lorie Saxton. She had walked in with three other women a few minutes before. He hadn't expected to run into Lorie so soon. Now that he had, he'd attend to the unsettled business between them. Two weeks wasn't much time, so he'd have to move fast.

"I didn't go looking for her, Dex. She's here on her own."

"So maybe she came looking for you; she doesn't hang out much. All the more reason to back off."

Dex reached for the pitcher of beer and poured them both another while Jake looked around. Bullwhackers Grill was a packed house. Not a surprise, given it was one of only three bars in town, and by far the favorite with the party-loving crowd. A smoky haze hovered under the tiffany-style lights. Bullwhackers' ventilation system wasn't topnotch and some of the customers ignored the No

Smoking sign. The dance floor was empty, but the jukebox blared country-western music.

It had been a few years, but the place hadn't changed. The blue neon sign advertising "Beer on Tap" still flashed in the front window. The long, low mahogany bar gleamed with polish, the aroma of grilled burgers and yeasty brew hung in the air. He'd needed this. Not just the familiar setting, but the easy companionship with his brother, the knowledge that he was home. Perhaps while he was here he could escape the nightmare that haunted him, and get some sleep. It was tough to leave the killing fields behind.

He was tired.

If things looked much the same around him, he had changed and it weighed on him, adding a sting to the nostalgia. He'd never fit in here again. A group of people with faces he didn't know entered the front door. Not locals. The women were dressed in fringed cowgirl outfits, the men sported fancy shirts and pristine Stetsons. Drugstore cowboys. The locals were dressed like him and Dex. Jeans faded from hard use. Long-sleeved plaid flannel or tee shirts.

He returned his attention to Dex. "She couldn't have known I'd be here. I just got in yesterday." Jake's intentions were to spend a couple of weeks with his family and then head to the east coast. His mother was demanding information about his plans, but so far he'd evaded her questions. She'd find out soon enough.

Responding to a sharp whistle, Jake waved across the room to Jim Jablosky, the bartender. He and Jim went back to grade school. Jim's folks owned the popular hangout and performed kitchen duty, and left their son in charge in front. Grinning, Jim returned the two-fingered touch to the brow, the standard country salute of friendliness, and pointed the same two fingers like a gun. Every head at the bar swiveled their way.

Dex stood and bowed at the round of whistles and applause that erupted from the townies holding down the bar stools. When the applause turned into hoots and insults,

Jake snorted a laugh. His brother could be counted on to play the comedian. "Sit, you idiot. I'm trying to keep a low profile here."

"Fat chance," Dex said, and took his seat again. "You whiz through town yesterday in that sporty Maserati, and five minutes later the phone lines were on fire. Another thing, Bullwhackers is a popular watering hole, but notice how the crowd is growing? This is a town of twenty-five hundred people remember? Everyone knows everyone and what they're up to. Half the crowd hit the speed dial on their cells as soon as we walked in."

"I fueled up at the Shortstop and drove straight out to the farm. No one noticed."

"Irma Gildersleeve is the cashier there. Ten bucks she called the <u>Nokeah Journal</u>. I think they keep her on retainer. You'll be featured in next week's issue. 'Afghanistan Veteran Returns Home.' They'll interview Mom. Dad will trot out your medals."

Jake sighed and reached for his beer. "I can't believe it. Why would anyone care? What medals?"

"Yeah, what medals? Delta Force doesn't advertise its accomplishments, right?

"Where did you get that Delta crap? I'm a dogface grunt Ranger. Or was."

"Dad found your green beret. With the Delta insignia."

"The hell he did! I left my duffle securely locked."

He groaned and rubbed his face in frustration. His father was an expert with tools and his mother could talk him into anything. Jake made a rapid appraisal of what else his nosy parents might have found. His Berretta, extra clips. Discharge papers, service records. Worst of all, his laptop. All the high clearance files on the hard drive were encrypted. Even his fast-fingered mother wouldn't be able to break into them.

His brother nodded in sympathy. "Everyone in the States knows we sent our Special Forces into the 'Stans to hunt down the al-Qaida. She's been worried sick for the past year."

"I thought what she didn't know wouldn't hurt."

"C'mon, Jake, this is our mom. You won't tell her what's going on, she'll investigate. The FBI could take lessons from the woman, and she uses her PC for more than keeping the books on farm business. She has every website that deals with Special Forces bookmarked, some of them pretty high clearance. She's in and out of a dozen chat rooms a day. Goes by name of Gulliver."

"Mom is hacking into government sites?" Alarm shot through him. His mother was capable of almost anything with a computer, and hacking into secure sites was damned dangerous. No question, he'd have to take steps to curb her nosiness.

"Dad considers her borderline insane, and expects the Feds to come calling any day. He has his shotgun loaded with rock salt and is prepared to die for her."

"You've convinced me. I'll talk to her. But tonight I'm Lorie's, squirt."

"Hey, watch the insults!" Dex shook a fist. "You've got an inch on me on top and nothing down below. If there's one thing I know, it's this town. Except for an occasional visit, you've been gone for fifteen years. A lot's changed."

"Nothing changes in Nokeah, Kansas. What I don't get is why she didn't leave this town after the divorce? There can't be much here for her."

"Lorie has a nine-year-old boy. Matt. Her mother baby-sits while she drives into Blue River every day to her job. How do you think she supports herself?"

"Doesn't Strom pay child support?"

"Strom works at the bank off and on, but word is he has trouble showing up sober. His daddy keeps him on a short leash money-wise. If he weren't working for his old man, he'd've been canned long ago. My guess is Lorie doesn't get much support. And divorced or not, he's made it plain Lorie is off limits." Dex shook his head in disgust.

"No reason I can't test the waters. She's here with her girlfriends and giving me the once-over. Man, she's hot and I'm getting signals."

"Strom is hanging out by the pool table, already half drunk."

"They've been divorced for two years. Any claim Strom had is long gone."

"Don't tell him that. Yeah, she's hot. So why do you think no one asks her to dance?"

Jake pushed back his chair. "Not a problem."

Dex put up a restraining hand. "Jake, he carries a knife in his boot. Go easy."

Jake raised an eyebrow and good-humoredly jabbed at his brother's arm. "That evens the odds. I'll take her for a spin around the dance floor and see what develops."

"The last guy tried that wound up with a pool cue halfway up his ass."

"You think Strom could manage that with me?"

"I think you could take him with one finger. But I don't especially want to spend weekends visiting my brother in the State Pen. Daddy Garrison will see to it they throw away the key if you even ruffle the hair on his baby boy."

"She looks lonely. Her girlfriends are out on the dance floor."

"Whatever. Stay away from her. There're half-a-dozen safer women here looking for some action."

"Then stake your claim brother Dex, and clear out. I have plans for the evening and they don't include you."

"Hell they don't," Dex said. "You're not having all the fun. I hope you have enough cash on you to pay the tab when Jim's bar is trashed."

Jake grunted acknowledgment scraped back his chair and headed across the room to where Lorie Saxton Garrison was sitting.

Dex sighed and picked up his mug to stroll after his brother. "Looks like things're about to get interesting."

CHAPTER 2

The object of Jake's attention held eye contact with him as he moved toward her table. She'd wanted to see Jake again; had ached to see him. Knew she shouldn't. But she'd come looking for him anyway. When she saw him amble across the room—big, solid, his left eyebrow quirked up in the way she remembered so well—her knees went to jelly. She hoped to God she could keep that reaction to herself. She'd never gotten over him, and it would be fatal for Jake to know that.

She hadn't seen Jake since Thanksgiving of their senior year in college, when they'd run into each other after a K-State football game. Immediately they'd both known the attraction between them still raged.

Be honest with yourself, Lorie. She'd searched him out that time, too, and they'd spent a long weekend together. She and Strom were history at the time, permanently as far as Lorie was concerned. She'd had it with his infidelities and drunken, partying ways.

Truthfully Jake had made no promises when they parted, and she'd been foolish to assume so much. He'd left her body sated, with whispered words of gratitude, but no promises. They'd exchanged cell numbers and agreed to meet again during spring break, but when two months passed and he'd made no move to contact her, she realized they'd shared four days of mutual pleasure, nothing more. It was her own fault she'd lost her head and her heart.

Christmas came and went with no word from Jake, and circumstance forced her to accept Storm's marriage proposal. Her calls to Jake's cell number yielded only a mechanical voice citing a disconnected number. In desperation, a week before her wedding she'd called the apartment house Jake shared with three other another Virginia Tech students. She knew if Strom found out it would destroy the marriage before it started, but in fairness Jake had the right to know what was happening.

A woman answered, her voice cool and sultry, a soft southern accent. Haltingly, Lorie had asked for Jake, and identified herself by name. Sometimes during restless nights punctuated by old dreams, she could hear the woman's tinkling laugh. A trill of mockery, tinged with pity. And her words.

"Honey," she'd purred. "You must be the little hayseed loveh. I thought he dumped you hard enough you'd get the ideah."

"Who are you?"

Lorie found the backbone to be angry. Okay, so she and Jake only had four days together, but they were intense. The sex was hot and sweet, and they'd enjoyed being together. She knew that in her bones. Surely he wouldn't have jumped into another woman's bed so quickly?

"Don't worry sugah, I'm taking good care of him. Isn't that an adorable lil' ole birthmark on his cute butt? We're roommates. Want to leave a message?"

Lorie's message had been short and pungent as she slammed down the receiver. She'd surprised herself with the language. Stupid, but ten years later her anger still burned.

Her friend, Shannon, had talked her into coming tonight. It was a given that the Randolph brothers would appear at Bullwhackers to meet with friends and have a few beers. Everyone ended up at Bullwhackers, and Shannon had a major crush on Dex.

Jake approached her, his eyes sharp with masculine intent. Tough. She would never allow herself to be his hayseed lover again.

Jake reached her table and set down his beer, staking his claim. Ten years, he thought, and shoved aside the drink that sat there—some ladies' froufrou cocktail, "Hello, Lorie. Mind if we join you?"

Ten years since he and Lorie had spent that unforgettable four days together in Kansas City. At least he hadn't been able to forget it. Apparently it hadn't meant that much to her. She'd married Strom two months later. After graduation, the NFL came to call. Green Bay picked Strom up in the seventh round, but he'd washed out after one year and returned home to Daddy. The pros demanded more commitment than Strom was capable of. According to Dex, Lorie had divorced Strom for cheating. Big surprise.

Dex hooked another chair with his boot and straddled it, folding his arms across the top to rest his chin. His gimlet dark eyes drilled both of them. The kid was tenacious.

Lorie nodded at them. "Hello, Jake. And Dex. I'm sure Shannon will be delighted to see you, Dex."

Jake hadn't heard her smoky, sultry voice for years, but would have known it anywhere. The smile she turned on his brother was much brighter than the one she gave him. He figured he still could make her smile if she gave him the chance.

"You look good, Lorie."

"You too, Jake. Going to be in town long?"

"A few days."

"It's been a while."

"Ten years." His brother reared back and shot him an incredulous look. As far as Dex or anyone knew, Jake hadn't seen Lorie since high school graduation.

"Ten years," she agreed. Her warm hazel gaze drifted over him with a strange mixture of anger and regret.

She was still beautiful. If anything, age had improved her. Classy. Lorie had always radiated class. She was too thin. The soft curves of her body were more angular than he remembered. Her thick auburn hair lay clipped back at the nape of her neck; an errant lock drifted over one arched brow. His fingers tingled with the tactile memory of that silken lushness against his knuckles. Tiny lines etched the corners of her full lips, and other body parts remembered the feel of their hot moistness pressed against them.

Over the years he'd suppressed the ache to have her, but seeing her turned the sexual heat on with a rush. She owed him one trampled heart and he meant to collect from her gorgeous hide. He sent that silent message and her gaze turned wary.

Dex cleared his throat and interrupted their eye duel. "Am I missing something?"

Lorie bit her lip, and Jake shrugged. "You thought she just dumped me once? Actually, it was twice. Once when we were seniors in high school, and again four years later. Remember that Thanksgiving when I left early to go back to Tech because I needed to hit the books? I was with Lorie. Call me a slow learner, bro."

"Stop it, Jake," Lorie whispered. "It wasn't like that and you know it."

"Here's your chance to set me straight."

"I wouldn't know where to begin."

"How about this?" He stood and offered her his hand. "My car's outside. We'll go somewhere and talk. Dex can find his way home."

She wanted to. In spite of all the cautious warnings she'd given herself when she spotted Jake across the room, she wanted to. Wanted to clasp his hand and walk out of the place with him. To take up where they'd left off ten years before. Why couldn't he have gone to flab and have a receding hairline? Instead he looked better than she remembered. Lean, hard, and very much a man, very much in control. Twice she'd come close to being consumed in his fire; twice she'd pulled away. A third time would be a disaster. For herself, for Matt, for Jake. Strom would see to it.

For a minute Jake thought she would do it. Her hand

hesitantly reached for his. Her expression told him she was torn, but not unwilling. Abruptly she jerked her hand away and cowered into her chair.

"No! I'm sorry."

Jake felt a prickle at the base of his spine and knew Strom stood behind him.

"Well, isn't this sweet? A reunion. Guess you all forgot to invite me."

Jake turned to face the shadow that had silently approached, and detested the man for the fear that flashed across Lorie's face. Strom carried a pool cue over his shoulder, was dressed in tight jeans and hand-tooled cowboy boots. A fancy leather vest hung open to his bare chest, and displayed an impressive six-pack and flat gut.

"Lorie and I were just leaving, Strom. We'll catch you later."

"Seems I heard the lady say no. Guess that means you're leaving alone, hotshot. She only goes out that door with me. Got that?" He pointed at the bar entrance with his cue stick and then reversed its direction to roughly poke Jake's belly.

Jake shrugged and brushed the stick away, letting his contempt show. "Got it. You use that as a substitute for the limp excuse in your pants?"

Strom reddened. "I'll be glad to demonstrate, piss-ant."

Lorie straightened in her seat. Her face had turned white; the lines around her mouth tightened. "I'm not going anywhere with either of you. I'll leave when I'm ready."

"Guess you boys have both been turned down," Dex drawled, still slouched in his chair. Jake understood his brother, and knew the drawl and slouching posture were a sham. Dex stood up in a lazy motion, coiled for trouble. "What say we adjourn to the bar and drink to the good judgment of the fair sex? I'm buying."

Dex, the peacemaker.

"Nice try, Dex," Jake nodded. "But I don't think so. The day Strom and I have a drink together will be a snowball's day in hell. Right, Strom?"

"Damn right. You and your wimp ass brother go

somewhere else to drink. Or I'll have Jablosky haul you out of here with the rest of the trash."

Before Dex could leap in front of him, Jake laid a restraining palm on his brother's chest. "It's me he wants, Dex. Keep out of it."

"Stay away from my woman, Randolph. I'll cut you into fish bait and smile."

"Hey." Jake spread his arms. "Have at me. Way I hear it, she divorced you, and about time."

Swearing, Strom took a step forward. Jake braced himself, his weight on the balls of his feet, his eyes on the pool cue. Strom was big and tough, and physically fit despite the signs of dissipation in the puffy jowls and bloodshot eyes. And he was a mean infighter. The way he held the cue balanced in one hand signaled martial arts training.

It dawned on Jake that this was what he needed to shake the black mood he was in. He needed to smash his fist into something and Strom's leering grin would do just fine. The idea held the added appeal of revenge for what had happened between him and Lorie. Revenge for the way Strom had messed up her life. Maybe this was why he'd come back. Before he could get on with a new life, he needed closure to the old one. He wanted to see Strom bleed; even the knowledge that his own blood would flow was welcome. There were all kinds of pain, and physical pain wasn't always the worst.

"Stop it, both of you!" Lorie shot to her feet. "This is childish and stupid. I don't want either one of you. Get over it, Strom. You too, Jake."

Dex put a gentle hand on her shoulder. "It's gone too far, Lorie. It isn't much about you anyway."

Dex wasn't worried his brother couldn't handle Strom Garrison in a fight, but he was a little concerned about the repercussions. Garrison Senior owned a chunk of the town and since he'd backed Sheriff Gould in the last election, the sheriff tended to remember that when the time came to allot jail cells. Likely he and Jake would end up in the drunk tank, while the sheriff would tenderly carry what was left of Strom back to the Victorian mansion where the Garrison family resided.

Jim Jablosky pushed his way through the crowd gathered around the two snarling men. "I don't care what it's about. Take it outside. Strom, you're an idiot if you take Jake on. The man must know a dozen ways to kill you."

"That's a bit exaggerated," Jake protested mildly.

Strom prodded the bartender's chest with the pool cue. "The bank owns the mortgage on this place, Jablosky. Best remember where your bread's buttered. Toss Randolph's ass out of here and everything settles down nicely."

Jim stepped back. "What I remember is the last time you pulled this stunt my front window got smashed and a load of tables and chairs were turned into firewood. I've no quarrel with Jake. Take it outside, boys."

"Hey, I'm cool," Jake said, smiling that easy smile Dex knew was fair warning that his brother was extremely pissed. Jake held his hand out toward Lorie again. "Not to worry, Jim, we're leaving. Ready to go, Lorie?"

Dex held his breath. This was twice Jake had asked. If the woman had any interest in his brother—and he was pretty sure she did—she better make the choice now. Jake wouldn't ask again. He'd walk away. Quiet settled over the room. Even the sound of the jukebox died, indicating someone had pulled the plug.

Dex figured the room was divided fifty/fifty. Fifty percent would like to see Strom get his butt stomped; fifty percent considered Jake an outsider and still remembered Strom as the high school football star who'd brought fame and the Class C State Championship to their town.

Without a word, Lorie stood and took Jake's hand. Dex could feel the heat six feet away. Likely Strom wouldn't have dropped it anyway. The man was just drunk enough to be dangerous and stupid. He moved toward his brother; his eyes swept the room looking for Strom's allies.

There were three of them. They'd been lounging beside the billiard table taking it all in, and rushed over to array themselves around Strom. Each of them carried a pool cue, and they parted the crowd like Moses before the Red Sea.

"Dammit," Jim yelped. "Outside, all of you. I'm calling the sheriff." He backed to the bar and grabbed the house phone.

"Which two do you want?" Dex asked his brother.

"I've got a better idea," Jake said, and handed a trembling Lorie over to Dex.

"Take care of her. I'll just be a minute here."

He plucked an empty metal tray from the hands of a waitress who stood nearby, her mouth agape. "You heard Jim, Strom." He gestured toward the door with his head. "Outside. Let's see what you and your boys have got."

Strom charged with a roar, using the cue like a spear, but his target dodged and Strom kept on going. Jake pivoted and smacked the flat of the tray squarely against Strom's butt, sending him flying. Strom howled as he slammed into a nearby table. The crowd scattered for a safer vantage point. As a unit, Strom's buddies moved toward Jake.

"Help him!" Lorie pulled away from Dex's grip. "There're too many. They'll really hurt him."

This was her fault. She knew Strom and his bullying ways, had known he would try to stop her from leaving with Jake. But she was sick of it, sick of having to walk on eggs all the time, sick of being afraid. She wasn't proud of it, but a part of her wanted to see Jake smash Strom's face in. A part of her needed Jake's strength to give her courage to do what she should have done months ago. To confront Strom and defy him. She hadn't counted on Jake facing an army.

Dex stood beside his brother. Strom struggled to his feet.

"If you want a piece of this, watch their sticks," Jake ordered coolly, crouched and ready for the attack, the tray held in front of him like a shield. It was a good idea, but might be a bit difficult to accomplish. Dex had a fleeting vision of what his brother would be like leading a combat patrol. Ice. Very dangerous ice.

The bravest of the attackers bellowed and charged, the cue

raised over his head. He was beefy, with powerful arms that sported a barbwire tattoo around each bicep. Again the tray slashed, sideways this time, and caught the attacker square in his considerable gut. The man gushed air like a punctured tire; his stick tumbled to the floor. When Jake's hard fist connected with his jaw, he went down and didn't move.

The two other men charged Dex as a team, swinging their weapons. A sharp blow slammed into his shoulder, another grazed his skull. He throttled the stick on the next vicious jab, planted his feet and used the man's momentum to send him airborne. The attacker rammed smack into a support post and slowly oozed to the floor. The last man dropped his weapon and grabbed Dex in a sweaty bear hug. The two of them tumbled across the barroom floor, bluing the air with curses.

His opponent down, Jake gave a quick glance to check on his brother. Dex had rolled onto the back of his attacker and straddled him, forcing the man's arms into a wrestling restraint. Dex was holding up nicely.

Jake dropped the tray and turned to face Strom.

Fifteen feet away, Strom came to his feet and shook his head like a wet dog. He crouched, the pool cue discarded and forgotten. "Come get me, hotshot," he growled and motioned with his fingers. "You're dead meat."

There was a collective hush from the crowd; the air was taut with expectation. Jake had experienced that hush before, on the football field before kickoff, at the ringside of a prizefight, awaiting the opening bell. He was briefly irritated. He intended to beat the crap out of Strom, maybe play with him a little, but didn't need the audience. This couldn't be a good thing for Lorie, and she'd have to live here after Jake was gone. Maybe he should suck it up and walk away. Let Strom have his little victory.

His slip in concentration proved disastrous. Strom was on him. A sidearm blow clipped Jake's jaw and sent him reeling. He tasted blood. A steel-toed boot swept him to the ground, as Strom cackled in triumph. A brutal kick landed against his gut and he felt something give in his ribcage.

No surprise. Strom wasn't interested fair play. Come to it, neither was he. He ignored the agonizing flash of pain, focused on his opponent, and forced training to take over. Waiting. When Strom's foot slashed out again, aiming for his face, Jake rolled and grabbed the booted ankle in both hands, and yanked hard. Strom pitched backward; his head slammed to the floor and rocked the room. Even a man with a skull as hard as Strom's should be down for the count. Jake labored to sit up, clutching his throbbing ribcage. Strom didn't move again. Jake's ribs were grateful.

Dex hollered at him from his straddled position. "Jake! You okay?"

"Yeah. You?" He watched his brother get to his feet. The man Dex had bested lay moaning in defeat, the fight out of him. Dex looked okay. Jake swiped at his mouth and stared at his own blood.

"Need a hand, big bro?" Dex grinned down at him and held out a muscled forearm.

"Don't mind." Jake hauled himself up, managing to keep his wince to a minimum. "Nice going, kid."

Lorie screamed.

They whirled to see Strom crouched low; his right fist held a knife. Palm up, in the expert fashion of a skilled knifeman. An upward knife thrust would do fatal damage to the internal organs. The onlookers scrambled back and cleared the area between the two men. All jocular catcalls and verbal bets on the fight's outcome hushed.

Jim leapt the bar and came up with a metal baseball bat. The other bartender grabbed and held him back. "Garrison's lost it, Jim. Wait for the sheriff."

His attention riveted on Strom, Jake's knee squat mirrored that of his opponent. He tamped his rage and forced his temper to cool. He'd learned to detach himself from emotion after months in the killing fields. Emotion had no place in a firefight. To survive, you let training and instinct take over.

Strom was maybe thirty feet away. Twenty-one feet was the magic number. Any closer than twenty-one feet and an

Blaine Kistler

opponent with an edged weapon could easily kill an unarmed man.

Strom's teeth drew back in a snarl. The steel blade flashed. To hell with staying calm. Jake shoved Dex aside. Blood rage gripped him and time slowed. Strom didn't care which brother the blade sliced into. He and Garrison had an ugly history, but Dex was only defending himself. His baby brother. At that moment, Jake was ready to kill. And Jim was right; Jake knew a lot about killing.

Roaring a challenge, he seized Strom's wrist and chopped with the calloused edge of his other hand. The bone snapped and the knife flew to the floor. Strom's scream of agony cut short. With the full power of his two-hundred pounds behind the stiff-armed punch, Jake slammed the heel of his hand into Strom's cheekbone. Coldly choosing his spot. Two inches to the left and the blow would have splintered the cartilage in the nose, driving the fragments into the brain, killing instantly. Strom folded like a busted flush, spewing the contents of his stomach onto the polished dance floor.

Lorie hadn't expected World War III to erupt. Never underestimate the stupidity of men rutting after a woman. When Strom lunged at Jake with his knife, Lorie's heart had gone to her throat. Only Shannon's tenacious hold on her shoulders kept her from leaping into the fray.

It was over quickly. Jake had put Strom down in seconds. She'd never seen anyone move with such vicious swiftness. Strom writhed on the floor as Jake staggered back, clutching his gut. His lower lip was bloody. Her eyes streamed tears of guilt. She gasped his name and started toward him.

He held his palm up to halt her approach and spoke to Shannon. "The sheriff deputies will be here any minute. Get her out of here."

"No! You're hurt." God, what had she done? She knew Strom would never allow her to be with Jake again.

"Not too bad." His voice dropped to a husky murmur. "I don't want you involved."

That made her wild. Involved! How could she be any more involved? She shook off Shannon's persistent grasp.

"Lorie!" He kept his voice low, but there was no mistaking the command behind it. "Go home. I'll see you tomorrow." A flash of humor crossed his face. "If I'm out of jail."

Shannon shoved her toward the door, dragging her, clucking in distress. They passed the sheriff and his deputy on the way out.

CHAPTER 3

The sheriff hauled the sorry lot of troublemakers to the town clinic and woke Doc Jensen to patch them up. After Doc's taping treatment, Jake's ribs fell into a steady throb, which he ignored. The adrenaline still pumped.

Dex was largely unscathed, as he cheerfully pointed out. "Too bad he didn't kick you in the head, bro. It's the hardest part of you."

"Runs in the family. You seem to have settled in." He looked around the cramped cell. "All the comforts of home. When did Deputy Dawg say we could get out of here?"

"Gould called the judge while doc taped you up and put a cast on Strom's arm. We're stuck here until court tomorrow morning. If we plead guilty, it'll be four hundred bucks plus costs for disturbing the peace. With five of us to pay up, the city stands to pick up some nice extra revenue."

"No question we're guilty. I'll pay your fine and whatever bill Jim comes up with."

Dex snorted. "Want me to bruise a couple more ribs?"

"Not on your best day. Where'd Gould put Strom?"

"Our fair city only boasts two cells. We're in one, Strom's buddies in the other. Gould toyed with the idea of locking Strom in with us. Man's a touch sadistic."

"So where is he?"

"Strom? Home with Papa. The old man has an in with Gould."

"Does that mean he's off the hook?"

"Not if you press charges against him for coming at you with a blade." Pain flashed across Dex's face. "Do it, Jake. I'm not kidding. He could've killed you."

"I'm not that easy. Strom's vicious when he's backed in a corner. That's why he was so dangerous on the playing field. Did you call and tell the folks where we are?"

"Yep." Dex grinned. "Mom says we can rot in here. She's whipping up one of her chocolate sludge cakes. Probably with a file baked inside. Dad asked how the other guys made out. He plans to take us both to the barn for some fatherly discipline."

"Ouch. Like the old days, huh?" Jake said, chuckling. When they were growing up their father had a swift and effective method of dealing with his ornery, disobedient boys.

"You got it. You're oldest, so you drop your pants first. Hopefully his arm will be tired by the time he gets to me."

"Think he can still catch us?"

"I wouldn't bet against him."

They both lay on the lumpy cots provided and stared at the ceiling. Jake had refused the pain pill Doc had offered, and the physical discomfort served as a reminder of his stupidity. He scratched at his day-old beard in frustration. There were no grooming facilities in the jail cell. The only amenities were the cots and a stainless steel sink and toilet. Well, he'd suffered through worse.

He couldn't believe how badly he'd wanted to stomp Strom into jelly. And how close he'd come to killing the man. He'd never lost his temper that fast and reacted that violently, ever. Not even when he and his squad were pinned down by al-Qaida crossfire and had to fight their way out.

Dex propped himself up on an elbow. "You figure Strom knows you had a fling with Lorie before they were married?"

"What do you think?"

"Seems like." Dex sighed and flopped back onto the cot. "Maybe she told him?"

"That'd be my guess. I certainly didn't."

"You plan to roust her about it?"

"Oh, yeah."

The silence stretched. Jake knew Dex had more to say. His brother cleared his throat. "She's had a rough time the past couple of years. Wouldn't hurt to go easy."

Jake sat up and swung his feet to the concrete floor, ignoring the white flash of pain. "What do you mean rough?"

"Strom has a temper. Past few years he's been drinking steady. Some say he took his temper out on Lorie."

"Hell! Has Strom been beating on her?"

"There've been rumors."

"Damn. Not the boy?"

"Grampa Hy wouldn't stand for that, he worships that kid. Just Lorie. And she's afraid of Strom. That's obvious."

Jake swore viciously. "If I'd have known that—"

Dex stirred uneasily. "Jake, you thrashed him pretty good. Could be he'll keep his hands off her now."

"Yeah. Maybe. Could be I've made it worse. Likely Strom and I are not done."

"Get some sleep, bro. It'll look better in the morning."

"Yeah. I'll check on her tomorrow." Jake didn't think he'd be getting much sleep.

The cold autumn wind blew through the stadium. Wind cold as his heart. Four years since high school graduation, since he'd last seen Lorie, and not much had changed.

In a bitter mood, Jake washed his face and hands, slicked back his wet hair, and left the men's room. The stadium was rapidly growing deserted; the crowd of 52,000 fans crammed into the Bill Snyder stadium exiting in record time. Still high on K-State's latest victory, Dex and his buddies were off to Aggieville for an after game celebration, but Jake had begged off. It was an hour's drive to the family farm, and the twists and turns on the backroads meant driving with a snootful was a bad idea. Plus he'd be rotten company. Jake regretted that he'd come. But he was home for the Thanksgiving holiday, and his brother had found an extra ticket.

By the fourth quarter K-State held a sizable lead, and as second-string quarterback, Strom took the field and put on his usual flashy pass plays. Lorie was on the front line of the pep squad, cheering her heart out. Wherever she'd been on the field, Jake's eyes had followed. Damn, he was a first-class idiot.

Outside it was dusk. Night came swiftly to Kansas in late November. A whiff of pending snowfall hung in the air. He'd missed the Midwestern climate, the harsh winters, the blistering summers. The seasonal changes were elemental and a reminder of the passage of time, of the fragility of existence. He took off for the east end of the stadium, toward the general admission parking area. Dex would catch a ride with his buddies, and Jake wanted to get on the road and put the day behind him. The car lot was close to deserted. No one wanted to stick around with the game over, and a snowstorm predicted.

A soft female voice spoke from the shadows. "Hello, stranger."

He stopped mid-stride. She was leaning against the Randolph family sedan, still in her cheerleading outfit, hugging her arms together, her hair blowing in the gathering wind. Jake itemized dispassionately. The purple sweater lay loosely across her breasts to allow for the arm movements required of a cheerleader. The matching short skirt displayed flashes of white during flips and leg kicks. The silk panties were purple; he hadn't missed that. Purple and white, the school colors. Lorie Saxton, his lost love.

He thrust his hands in the pockets of his leather jacket. "How've you been?"

"Pretty good. How is Virginia Tech?"

"I'm done next semester. Then a career in the military. It's going okay."

"I saw Dex earlier. He said you were in town for the game and told me where you parked. I wanted to see you."

Genuinely puzzled, he wrinkled his forehead. "Why?"

"To apologize."

He didn't bother denying he knew what she meant. "Four years past due, don't you think?"

"You're right, but could you make this a little easier?" She bit her full lower lip, and his sex stirred.

He leaned against the sedan, folded his arms and scowled. "I'm listening."

"Jake, I was seventeen years old. You scared me. No, that's not fair. I scared myself. I couldn't handle my feelings. Strom was—comfortable."

His lip curled. "Sex with Strom was comfortable? Sounds pretty dull."

Her head jerked as if she'd been slapped. "We weren't having sex. I'd never even wanted to. Until you kissed me, I'd never had those feelings."

"Yet things haven't changed. The cheerleader and the star quarterback. Together in high school, together four years later at K-State. The perfect match. Why look me up?"

"Because," she ducked her head and her smoky voice dropped to a whisper. "Strom's been a habit for years. Everyone expects us to be together. But he drinks too much, and he cheats. I broke it off last week." She pressed her palms against the smooth leather of his jacket. The auburn tumble of hair splayed against his chest. Her bare legs rubbed against his jeans and he was immediately, painfully hard.

He grasped her shoulders and roughly reversed their positions, pressing her against the car door. "Don't play games with me, Lorie. I'm not a kid anymore. You'll get more than you bargain for."

"Jake, it's not a game. I'm not sure what it is, but it's not a game."

She lifted her face and even in the dim light he could see the desire. His mouth came down on hers, brutal with his hunger, with his anger. Being forced to watch her cavorting on the field had brought on his rotten mood. He'd wanted to leave the stadium during the game, to ignore her presence, but hadn't managed the trick of that. Now she was here, in his arms, moaning as his tongue dove into the warm recesses of her mouth. He kissed her until she went limp, until her legs collapsed and his strength was the only thing that kept her upright. It was the same magic between them. Except it was different. They weren't the same people, and neither of them was a sexual novice. And they were both at flashpoint.

The parking lot was deserted now, as the last fans exited onto Denison Avenue.. He pulled the car keys from his pocket, beeped the automatic locks and opened the backdoor. There was only one way to handle this. "Get in the car, Lorie."

"Jake, I needed to talk to you, but I—I—"

"It's freezing out. Get in the car and we finish this. Or leave. Your choice."

She ducked her head and climbed in, and he swore he saw a smile curve her lush mouth. He climbed in beside her, hit the locks and reached. He didn't have to reach far. She was astride his lap, her mouth open and needy. "Put your arms around my neck, and hold on," he said thickly, reaching for his billfold and fingering out the condom he kept there. "If you wanted to stop this, you should have left."

"God, Jake, don't stop. I've wanted this for four years."

He stripped off her panties, parted the moist tangle of curls between her thighs and dove into her in one hard thrust. He was maddened. Obsessed. Nothing would have stopped him from taking her. She was as crazed as he was and dug her nails in his back, biting his neck, urging him on. He cupped her bottom and surged into her, stifling her cries of pleasure with his mouth. She came hard, bucking against the car seat. He sucked her scream into his own throat and exploded inside of her, the spasms rocking his body.

The condom had split, but it was too late to worry. Whimpering, she lay limply against his chest. He caught her and lifted her with one hand, and zipped himself back up with the other. She began to cry. What the hell was he going to do now? His own legs were shaking, his emotions stripped to the bone. He sat against the backseat and held her until she stopped sobbing. Only she wasn't crying, she was purring.

"God, Jake. Why did we wait so long?"

He'd never be able to look at the family sedan in quite the same way again.

CHAPTER 4

Jake woke disoriented, his sex fully aroused. As erotic dreams went, this was his favorite. All the more because it wasn't just a dream. It was a memory.

The aroma of coffee brewing wafted through the bars, along with the first rays of daybreak. The cot was lumpy and uncomfortable, but he'd slept some. Dex was still snoring. The throb in Jake's ribs reminded him of how they'd landed here.

Many times in the past the dream had cursed him, causing him to wake with a hard-on the size of a crowbar. He didn't suppose there was a man alive who hadn't fantasized lifting a cheerleader's skirt and removing her panties. It had been crazy and he wouldn't do it again, but damn, it had been fun. She hadn't gotten the purple panties back easily. It had taken her four days. And nights.

Lorie sat at her breakfast table, sipped black coffee and nursed a ferocious headache, watching dawn seep through the gingham-curtained windows of her tiny kitchen. She'd been up for hours, unable to sleep. She deserved the headache after her foolish actions the night before. The need to see Jake had overridden her good sense.

Life wasn't just about herself anymore; there was Matt.

Her son had accepted the reality of his parents' divorce. He had his own room, his own special things. He was happy in third grade, had friends to play with, and his life was stable in a way it never had been. Lorie worked hard to give him that. With Strom behind in his child support, she darn well had to work hard just to put food on the table.

The two-bedroom bungalow she rented was cozy, and it was home. Paint and a scrub brush helped with the cosmetics, while she'd learned to cope with the erratic plumbing. Best of all, it was theirs. Hers and Matt's. Quite an improvement over the misery their life had been two years ago when they'd moved in with her mother. At the time there'd been nowhere else to go. Strom gave her no money and she had none of her own. He'd never allowed her to work.

She reached for a pad of paper to write her Saturday list. It was errand day and grocery day. She divided the paper into four sections. She wrote milk in the diary section, and ice cream bars. Yogurt for herself. Matt wouldn't touch it. She laid down the pen.

She no longer tried to convince her mother that Strom was an abusive alcoholic. "Go back to your husband, Lorie. He'll take care of you" was her advice. Lorie heard it frequently. But her mother meant well. She always did.

It seemed to Lorie that she was surrounded by control freaks. Strom. His father, Hy. Her own mother. At times the feeling of being trapped overwhelmed her. If she could, she'd take Matt and live somewhere else. But the courts forbid either parent to move Matt from its jurisdiction without permission. Strom would never agree her to leaving town with Matt. Driven by a need she couldn't control, she'd gone last night to find Jake, knowing Strom would be hanging around. Knowing he hated Jake.

With reason.

Jake was the only man she'd ever loved, and Strom knew that. Knew it because she'd confessed it once—no, she'd thrown it at him—during one of their interminable quarrels about his drinking. She'd quickly learned never to mention

Jake's name again, but Strom hadn't forgotten. Last night proved that.

Shannon's brainstorm to visit Bullwhackers had led to the trouble. "Aren't you curious?" Shannon demanded. "This is Jake Randolph! All the unattached females in town—and some who aren't—are panting for a chance at him. C'mon, gal pal. I need some backup here with Dex."

Still, Lorie refused.

Her mother's phone call followed Shannon's. "Don't go near that man, Lorie. Strom wouldn't like it."

Lorie had lived with her mother's dictatorial ways all her life. What kind of lame excuse for a woman was she, allowing her mother to boss her around at her age? Inspired by a spurt of rebellion, aching with the need to see her son's father again, she'd called Shannon back and signed on for the night out.

No one, not even Shannon knew about Lorie's brief, scorching affair with Jake. Confronted with the need to wed quickly, Lorie nursed her secret fiercely and admitted nothing. Not to Rose. Not to Strom. For Matt's sake. God knew she wasn't sorry that of the two men, Jake was Matt's father.

She'd lost her train of thought. What else did she need from the store? Salad stuff. They were almost out of bread and peanut butter. Matt couldn't survive a day without peanut butter. She really should jot things down as she thought of them during the week. Right, Lorie. You should be so organized.

She rubbed her eyes, the words out of focus, her brain splintered and foggy. Lack of sleep had caught up with her; she couldn't even write a grocery list. How had the situation last night exploded so quickly? What could she have done to stop it? She should convince Jake to leave town. She knew Strom's temper, and the way he nursed a grudge.

And Strom kept guns. His friends kept guns.

The last year of her marriage had been total hell. Most of the marriage had been hell, and she'd gone into it with such hope. Except for a few teenage dates, she and Strom had been an item for as long as anyone could remember. Their friends would have been shocked if they hadn't gotten married. And yet, she wasn't sure. Through all the celebration, all the hoopla of the biggest wedding ever seen in Nokeah, doubt nagged.

About Jake. Their short time together and its consequences. Not just the sex, fantastic as it had been, but the joy they found together. The laughter. She really missed the laughter. She laid down the pen, remembering.

Maybe if Jake had called or written her after they parted, her life would have taken another path. But her attempt to contact him had resulted in anger, and reinforced her decision to marry Strom. Sometimes she wondered if she'd jumped the gun. She had only the word of a female voice on the phone that Jake was living with someone else.

No question, Strom had been the better match for her. Jake attended college on a ROTC scholarship and would serve at least four years in the military after he graduated. Besides the fact that Jake had never asked, she'd doubted the lot of an army wife was the comfortable lifestyle she wanted.

She winced and picked up the pen. She'd chosen what looked to be an easy life and ended up alone, with no man to warm her bed. A single mother in a rented house, struggling to make ends meet. It was near the end of the month; she had to keep the list to necessities. She crossed out ice cream. Next week, she'd get ice cream. After payday.

You were one shallow cupcake in those days, Lorie Anne. You got what you deserved. The idea of marriage to Strom had been glamorous. The richest boy in town with a great future in pro football, he'd painted an appealing picture of what their lives would be. Lots of money, parties, visiting exotic places and mixing it up with celebrities. It had turned her head and what little brain she'd had at the time.

Her mother had been behind her, ecstatic at the prospect

of her daughter's match. Rose Saxton was socially ambitious, and saw her daughter as a way up the ladder. Lorie would be rich, her husband famous. Her own friends would be green with envy.

Rose hadn't had much to crow about in her life; her husband had vanished when Lorie was a baby. Left Rose high and dry for another woman. Lorie didn't remember her father. Her mother had struggled to keep her daughter in style, had worked hard to buy her good clothes, to provide dance lessons, to see her fitted in braces. No question, Lorie now had nice straight teeth. She owed her mother, if only Rose would quit reminding her.

She looked at her list again. She wasn't that broke. She could afford to buy Matt ice cream bars, darn it. She'd hold off on the hair appointment another week.

When Green Bay cut Strom, the trouble really started. Oh, she'd wondered about the road trips, the ones she wasn't allowed to go on. She'd heard tales about the groupies, about the drinking and the orgies, but she'd discounted the tales. Strom wouldn't do that to her. Those were the days he couldn't get enough of her in bed. Their lovemaking was quick and not always good, but it was frequent.

They returned to Nokeah. The heavy drinking kicked in; Strom's slide into ruin started. The gambling. Women. Staying out all night. She should have left their second year of marriage, left him and taken her chances that she could find a job and support herself and her baby. Because of Matt, she'd stayed. She knew she'd stayed too long.

"Mom?"

Lorie turned to see her young son in the hall doorway, rubbing sleep out of his eyes, his red hair in bedhead disarray. "Hi, tiger. What are you doing up so early?"

"I heard you talking to somebody." He yawned.

She was squirrelly. Talking out loud at six in the morning. She picked up her cup and walked over to the coffeepot for a refill. "Just muttering to myself."

Matt yawned again. "I'm hungry. Can I have pancakes?"

"Pancakes are Sunday fare. You get cereal. I might be talked into cocoa, after you make your bed. You can watch cartoons for half an hour, after you get dressed."

Her son grinned at that. Saturday cartoons were strictly rationed. "Deal. Is Dad coming to take me to karate lessons this morning?"

Lorie hid her stab of pain by taking a swallow of coffee. The brew turned to ashes in her mouth and she poured it in the sink. It had been Strom's idea for their son to take a martial arts class. He swore he'd pay for the lessons and accompany Matt to class on Saturday mornings. The dojo policy was strict. Until the student reached age twelve, a parent had to sit in and observe. No dumping the child off and picking him up later. More often than not, Strom sloughed his responsibility, although Hy paid for the lessons.

She knew better than to expect Strom this morning. He wouldn't be in jail; Hy would have bailed him out. But he'd be nursing a major hangover and licking his wounds somewhere. Probably already started on the day's drinking.

"'Fraid not. I'll be going along this morning. I washed your karate outfit and hung in your closet. Don't you have to practice your new form? Where are the instructions?"

"In my backpack. Dad isn't coming? That's three Saturdays in a row. He promised to drill me before class."

"I can drill you. I've got the hang of this martial arts stuff. I'm a Kung Fu Mama."

She took a mock karate stance and her son hooted at her form. She couldn't blame him. Despite sitting in on Matt's lessons, she had only a vague idea of how the forms were done. The instructor called Matt a natural, and thought her son would be a good martial artist someday. The one thing Lorie really liked about the dojo discipline was they emphasized the importance of anger control. Strom served as a terrible example of that, and Matt needed some male guidance.

She got a bowl out of the cupboard and filled it with cornflakes. "Come slice your banana, mister. I'm not the scullery maid."

"Can I phone Dad?"

Matt shuffled his feet and looked at the floor. As frequently as Matt's father disappointed him, he never gave up hope. Fury for her son shook her. Seeking to calm down, she closed her eyes and mentally repeated the First Step. *'We admit we are powerless over alcohol.'* Al-Anon meetings had helped her understand that, but hadn't relieved the stress. Maybe she had caused her own troubles, but Matt deserved better.

"Sure, but it's too early yet. Get dressed and have your breakfast first. And talk to Gramma Garrison while you're on the phone. She wants you to come for Sunday dinner tomorrow after church. Fried chicken. Your favorite."

"Can you come too?"

Lorie rinsed her cup and loaded it in the dishwasher. She should eat something. Maybe she could get some yogurt down. "I wasn't invited. Get dressed, okay?"

"Okay," Matt sighed and headed toward his bedroom.

"Sheriff, you're supposed to keep the peace. I want Jake Randolph locked up. His brother, too. You shouldn't have let them go. Getting drunk and starting a bar fight is something folks around here don't appreciate." Hy Garrison's salt and pepper moustache quivered with indignation.

The sheriff shook his head in regret. He usually tried to accommodate Garrison's wishes. "Can't do that, Hy. According to more'n thirty witnesses, your boy's the one that started it and when things went sour, pulled a knife. He's lucky Randolph's refused to press charges. Attacking a man with a knife—that's assault with a deadly weapon and goin' too far for me to overlook. The Randolph boys paid the fine and settled their share of the damage with Jim Jablosky. That's about all I can legally do. And neither of them was drunk. Can't say as much for Strom."

"The man's a trained killer and Strom is in serious condition. His mother is extremely upset."

The sheriff snorted and tipped his chair onto its back legs, careful to conceal his glee. "Strom has a broken wrist, a beaut of a shiner and a few bruises. Has to smart, but the injuries don't look fatal to me. Jake Randolph's got sore ribs and a fat lip. Let Strom be happy with that. And the fact Randolph didn't kill him. He could've easy enough. Then I'd have an excuse to put him in jail."

Hy Garrison sat his stocky body in the opposite chair, obviously settled in until he accomplished his mission. Strom didn't look much like his dark-haired, ruddy-complexioned father. The son's blonde, blue-eyed good looks came from his mother's side of the family.

Hy pointed an angry finger. "The man has no business coming back here and stirring things up. Strom's still not over the divorce, and this has added to his personal problems. My son was looking after his woman, same as you and I would."

"Now, Hy. Lorie isn't his woman no more, and Strom's a pure fool not to accept that. Problem is you spoiled that boy since he was born. Thinks he can have whatever he wants. He's needed a whopping for years and Jake Randolph dished out a good one. Maybe Strom'll settle down a little now."

"You don't know Strom if you think this is the end of it. Get Randolph to leave town. Convince him it's for his own good."

John Gould sighed. "Hy, you and I go way back, so let me hand out some advice. Jake Randolph's got a right to visit his family. He's been overseas for a year, fighting a dirty war. Put his life on the line every day. Plenty of folks around here consider him a hero for that."

"Plenty of folks around here owe me their loyalty. Including you. Especially you. Best remember that."

The chair legs crashed down. "Care to explain, Hy?"

"Could be I won't find the funds to back your campaign this fall. Could be we need new blood. I've been thinking Storm might do a good job as sheriff. He's young and smart and not about to let anybody get away with the kind of horse manure those Randolph boys pulled."

"That's an interesting thought. But there's nothing I can do for your boy now."

Hy Garrison glared at him, speechless. John supposed he hadn't bucked the senior Garrison since they'd been boys together. He was amazed how good it felt. And if Hy thought he could railroad Strom into the sheriff's job, he was in for a shock. Plenty of people knew Strom for the bully he was. John had worried for months about the way Strom continued to harass his ex-wife, but until Lorie Garrison filed a complaint, his hands were tied.

"This isn't the end of it, John."

"Didn't 'spose it was."

CHAPTER 5

Jake parked in front of Lorie's house. The bungalow was modest compared to the brick two-storied homes that rose on either side of it. The front entrance stood ajar, barred by a shabby screen door, and curtains billowed from the open windows. In their small town, people left their windows and doors unlatched without fear of being robbed or assaulted. He climbed out of the car and sniffed lilacs. Purple blooms hung heavily from the bushes that lined between the bungalow and the neighboring properties.

The house was neatly painted white, but the yard looked neglected; muddy bare patches sporadically punctuated the wiry grass. The sycamore tree in the front yard was dead; its bare limbs stretched toward the sky like gnawed bones. He'd have thought Strom could have done better by her. Given the price of real estate in their town, Jake's Maserati had cost twice as much as the bungalow. She was listed in the phonebook as L.S. Garrison, so she'd kept Strom's name. Probably because of the boy. Jake had phoned ahead and she'd been cool when he'd asked to come over.

He'd rather confront an al-Qaida death squad than knock on the door and face Lorie after last night's fiasco. He was headed for the front stoop when he spotted the boy zooming toward him on a fancy two-wheeled scooter. Must be today's version of the skateboard. He wore a bike helmet and knee and elbow pads, and at the speed he was traveling that seemed a wise precaution. A homemade ramp blocked the sidewalk in front of the cottage, a wide, flat board hoisted up on a stack of bricks. The kid hit it at warp speed and with the grace of a natural athlete, went soaring, making a clean landing some six feet from the take-off point. He wheeled onto the driveway and reversed smoothly, coming to a stop. He faced Jake, a sturdy little sentry guarding his territory.

Jake leaned against his car while they took measure of each other. The helmet hid a lot of the kid's face. Jake glimpsed brown eyes, a freckled nose and stubborn cleft chin. Lorie's chin. "Nice jump," Jake offered.

"Thanks."

A man of few words. "Neat scooter. Fast."

"My grandpa bought it for me."

Jake nodded. "I know your grandpa."

"What happened to your face?"

"Ran into something. Forgot to duck." Hopefully the kid wouldn't find out it was his father's fist Jake had run into.

"Bummer. Mom's inside. I'm Matt."

"Jake Randolph. I knew your mother a while back."

"She told me. You played football with my dad."

"A few years ago. You want to let her know I'm here?"

"Okay." He dumped the scooter on the driveway and hustled toward the front porch, banging the screen door behind him, bellowing. "Mom! Mr. Randolph's here!"

Mr. Randolph. Jake was impressed. So Lorie wasn't one of those modern parents that encouraged their offspring to use an adult's first name. He wondered what kind of mother she was. Being a single parent these days couldn't be easy. She'd been raised by a single parent. Maybe that had provided some job training. He waited on the front porch.

Lorie opened the screen door. She did a double take at the sight of him, but was too polite to mention his battered face. Jake had never considered himself pretty, but he usually looked better than he did today.

"Come in, Jake. I just going to pour myself some iced tea. Would you like some?"

"Sounds good." He wiped his feet on the doormat.

"Thanks for that. I have to remind Matt to wipe his feet every time he comes in. When I can catch him."

She chuckled, and the sound was a relief to his ears. Maybe it would go okay. "I learned pretty fast when I was his age if I didn't want to scrub the floor, I'd better not track in dirt. Some things stick with you."

"Not a bad idea. How about that, Matt?" She pointed to muddy tracks that led from the front door to the refrigerator.

"Aw, Mom. I mostly take off my shoes." He took a gulp from the milk carton and wiped the moustache from his mouth. His helmet was tucked under his arm and his red hair stood up in sweaty peaks. Red hair and freckles and all boy. Jake felt an unfamiliar tug of envy. He'd once thought he'd have kids of his own. Somehow the years had slipped by and it hadn't happened.

Lorie tapped her foot and pointed again. "Looks like you forgot this time, son."

The kid sighed and returned the carton to the refrigerator. "I'll get the mop."

"Never mind. I'll take care of it later. You can go over to Jeff's if you want. He called and I talked to his mom. He has a new computer game."

"Really! I can play on Jeff's computer for a while?"

"Supper in two hours so come back at six. I made you some peanut butter and crackers to tide you over. In the plastic bag on the cupboard."

Matt gave a whoop and scooped up the snack. "Bye, Mom. Bye, Mr. Randolph."

Lorie blew him a kiss. "Just don't bang—"

Too late. The boy tore out the front door at a run. The screen door slammed behind him, his whooping war cry following him down the street. Jake could see why the door was in such bad shape. And probably the yard. He stifled a grin.

"Funny, huh? I just wish I had that energy."

"Is he always like that?"

"Pretty much. Why do you think I'm getting gray?"

There wasn't a gray hair on her head. It was the same rich auburn he remembered, and tumbled down the back of her neck, held in place with a blue ribbon. She wore a simple white tee shirt tucked into baggy jeans. No lipstick, no makeup of any kind. Obviously she hadn't dressed to entice.

It wasn't working. He was as enticed as hell.

He reached and pushed aside the stray curl hanging over her eyebrow. It sprung back. His fingers tingled.

"Stop it, Jake" she whispered.

"What?" He stroked her smooth cheek; his thumb brushed her lower lip.

"You know what. Stop it."

"Okay." Reluctantly he let his hand drop.

"Sit down, please." She motioned toward the kitchen table, an old picnic table painted green. "I'll get our tea."

She reached for drink glasses, yanked open the refrigerator door, and he took the opportunity to look around. When the house was built, this part had probably been two rooms, but a wall had been torn out and one large room now served as a combination living room-dining room-kitchen. A colorful kilim-style rug covered the living room portion of the scarred wood floor. The furniture looked like garage sale pieces that had been painted white. Toss pillows in bright primary colors were thrown about with abandon; a few framed museum posters decorated the walls. The scent of apples and vanilla lingered in the air.

It had been done economically but in good taste, and looked extremely comfortable. His gaze wandered to the large television set that squatted in the far corner of the room, and imagined sprawling on the couch with a beer, catching a ballgame. A simple fantasy, but appealing. He embellished. Lorie lying beside him on the couch, her head in his lap. Damn!

His lap found that part of the fantasy more than appealing.

Ice tinkled as she set a glass in front of him. She'd

garnished the drink with a sprig of fresh mint. "Sugar?"

"No. This is fine. Thanks."

She sat across from him and sipped her tea. The silence stretched until they both spoke at once.

"Lorie, I—"

"Jake, we need—"

She flushed, laughing. He joined in and reached across the table to take her hand. "Me first, okay?"

She nodded. "Okay."

"I'm sorry. About last night. If you want to kick my butt, I've got it coming."

She looked at him in disbelief. "You're sorry! I'm the one who should apologize. You have a right to go into Bullwhackers and have a beer with your brother. But when Strom is drinking, there's no reasoning with him."

"Yeah, well," He shrugged. "Dex tried to warn me. I didn't listen. Truth to tell, Lorie, I was in a rotten mood last night, so I'm not blameless. And why in the hell should you apologize? We're big boys and we never liked each other. But I hate to think I might have brought you grief. Maybe made your situation worse."

"Jake, I was sure you'd be there. You need to know that."

She removed the sprig of mint from her glass and twisted it in her fingers, its herbal aroma permeating the air. Something primal stirred in him; the memory of mint. The sharp scent tripped his libido into overdrive.

"You came to the bar last night because you thought I'd be there?" he asked, keeping his voice neutral.

"Yes," she whispered. "I knew Strom would probably be around, but I wanted to see you."

"Because?"

She scowled. "You're going to make me say it, aren't you?"

"Uh-huh. Like it when you blush."

She turned an even brighter shade of scarlet. "I'm thirty-two years old and a mother. I don't blush."

He laughed softly, his left eyebrow quirked up, and her insides turned to mush. He could do that. Even after all these years, he could laugh, lift an eyebrow and she wanted to roll on her back and yell *Take Me*. She had to get a grip.

She gulped a swallow of tea, hoping to chill the internal heat. One side of his face bore evidence of Strom's heavy fist and the guilt returned. But he was right. Damned if she should apologize because two territorial men had come to blows. Hopefully they had knocked some sense into each other.

"This is silly. You're leaving in a few days. I won't let you do this to me again."

He rat-a-tated his fingers on the table and slit his eyes. "Do what?"

She got to her feet and walked over to the refrigerator for more ice. Sedately. Completely in control, as she replenished the ice in both of their glasses. Two could play this game. "What do you think I mean?"

"Why don't you tell me?"

She really wanted to dump the iced tea on his head. Anticipating her, he reached across the table and took the glass from her fingers. "That wouldn't be a good idea," he said mildly. "Sit back down and behave yourself. We're having a discussion here."

"I'm having a discussion. You're too slippery to contribute anything of value."

"What do you want me to contribute?"

"Awk! I don't know how you do it. Ten minutes with you and I'm ready to scream. You are the most obstinate, the most aggravating—"

"Cut it out, Lorie. We both know what's going on here."

She licked her lips. "You intend to sit there and let me make a fool of myself?"

"Much as I'm enjoying that, I would've had you stripped naked on the couch by now, except for a couple of problems."

"Not if I have anything to say about the naked part. What problems? Overlooking that I might have a different idea."

"The battered ribs are bound to hamper my technique."

She closed her eyes, trying to think back. Mostly she remembered the knife flash and her paralyzing fear. Before that there had been a harsh jumble of boots stomping and fists thumping, bodies crashing into furniture and vivid male cursing. Then the fight was over and Shannon had shoved her out the door. From what Lorie knew about it, bruised ribs were extremely painful.

She clenched her teeth. "Take off your shirt."

"Ah, Lorie?"

"I mean it!"

He nodded and slowly unbuttoned his khaki shirt, letting it hang open. He was taped from under his nipples to his navel.

"Strom did that!"

"He didn't go down easy."

"What kind of injuries does he have?"

"Broken wrist. A pretty good shiner."

She blew out her breath. "You're right. You have made it worse."

CHAPTER 6

"Great pizza, Mom. Right, Jake?"
"Terrific."

Jake and Matt were now on a first name basis, and they'd been chattering like old pals throughout supper. He liked the kid and the feeling seemed to be mutual. Matt was fascinated with the fact that Jake served in the military, and was full of questions about his adventures and future plans.

"I'll be reporting in in a couple of weeks," Jake said. "And getting a new assignment. I'm not sure what, yet." Which wasn't true. He knew exactly what, he just couldn't discuss it.

"My dad's in the militia, you know," Matt said, proudly. "He's on maneuvers this week. That's why I can't see him for a while."

"Maneuvers? You mean he's in the National Guard?" He looked to Lorie for an explanation.

"Not the Guard," she said, reluctantly. "They call themselves the New Sons of Liberty, and have a training camp in the Flint Hills. They play soldier on the weekends."

Jake's alarm antenna went up. This explained the knife in Strom's boot, and the martial arts stance. It wasn't good, and would bear looking into. Self-styled militia groups were hotbeds of political intrigue and violence. Even more alarming, Lorie's stony face shut off any further discussion.

"Dad has a camouflage suit and guns and everything," Matt said, taking a last bite of pizza. "What's for dessert?"

Camo and guns? Definitely bad news.

Again, Lorie shot him a back-off glance. "Ice cream bars. Get a couple out of the freezer for you guys. I don't want one right now."

Matt fetched the frozen treats, handed Jake one and tore off the wrapper of his own, looking at his new buddy for approval. "They're chocolate-chocolate. My favorite."

Jake took an appreciative bite of the creamy bar. "Mine, too. Way I look at it, a meal isn't over until dessert."

Matt beamed. "Hey, me too."

"It's been a long time since I've had homemade pizza, Lorie. You went to a lot of work." Tasty pizza was among the foods he'd missed the most. The best that could be said for field kitchen food was it was nutritious and filling.

"You guys are easy. Better get on your homework, Matt. You don't want to leave it for the last minute, and tomorrow you'll be with your grandparents most of the day." She gave her son a hug and an affectionate tousle of his red hair.

Jake hadn't put any special significance to the invitation to supper. Country hospitality usually included an offer of a meal. He watched Matt excuse himself and carry his dishes to the sink, then disappear into his bedroom. She began to clear the table and Jake took the dishes from her hands.

"Let me do this. You cooked."

"Wasn't much. Pre-made crust, bottled sauce, packaged cheese. Lots of fresh chopped vegies. It's about the only way I can get vegetables down Matt. Put tomato sauce and cheese on anything and he'll eat it."

"He has good manners. Minds you, too."

"Don't let him fool you, he's on his best behavior because you're a big guy and he wants to impress you. He can be a handful."

"He's a great kid, Lorie."

Her face sobered as she nodded agreement. "The most important thing in my life."

"What about your personal life?" He was beyond being subtle at this point. He was pretty sure she wasn't involved with anyone, but wanted to be certain.

She snorted, rinsed the dishes he stacked in the sink and began to load the dishwasher. "What's a personal life?"

"You were out with friends last night."

"A rarity. My life is pretty much Matt and my job."

"I didn't recognize any of your friends."

"Two of the girls I work with. They live in Blue River and are unattached and fun. Shannon is four years younger than me, about Dex's age. She's Strom's cousin, and we became friendly a couple of years ago at—ah, she's been a good friend. Once in a while we take in a movie."

Lori bit her tongue before too much came out. Janice Garrison Miller, Strom's sister and Shannon's mother, had joined AA and unlike Strom, was fighting her addiction. Lorie and Shannon had met at Al-Anon, but one of the precepts of the organization was secrecy. You never discussed what went on at meetings with anyone.

Jake had a way of getting her to open up about things. Some things that were better avoided. Strom's militia group, for instance. She didn't know much about the group, just that Strom's connection with it made her uneasy. That, coupled with his alcohol addiction and affinity for violence, was downright frightening, and she avoided going there in her thoughts.

Jake handed her the last of the soiled dishes from the table. "Where do you work?"

"At a medical clinic in Blue River. Records and billing. There aren't many decent jobs in Nokeah. It's not a bad commute. Half an hour each way. Mediocre salary but topnotch medical benefits."

"Your mom watches out for Matt?"

"Before and after school. Mandy, the teenager next door, sat for me last night."

She dumped in a soap cube and started the dishwasher,

sliding the throw rug under the appliance door. Right on schedule, the machine oozed suds and hot water and soaked into the rug, but the leak was still manageable. Lorie dreaded the day what it went completely. That would mean doing dishes by hand for a while.

Jake stepped back from the puddle and raised that eyebrow, the one that drove her nuts. "Looks like the gasket is shot."

She cocked her head and lifted an eyebrow in mockery of his. "Ya' think? I kind of like it this way. Saves scrubbing the floor."

He chuckled. "Your plumbing is eccentric. When I flushed the john, Niagara Falls erupted."

She used her foot to vigorously swipe the rag rug at the puddle under the sink. Usually after the fill cycle, the leak slowed down. "Forgot to warn you about that. Sometimes you need to take off the tank top and jiggle the chain or the water runs indefinitely."

"The chain was too long. I fixed it."

The dishwasher leak was getting worse. The need for a plumber loomed. What with the dishwasher and the toilet needing repair—damn, a plumber cost a fortune. She swiped away the lock of hair that had tumbled into one eye and muffled a curse. Jake leaned against the refrigerator, hands shoved into his jean pockets, his shirt still hanging open, exposing a chest with muscles that even the white adhesive tape couldn't disguise. What was it he'd said? Something about fixing the toilet.

"Excuse me?"

"I said your screen door is barely hanging by its hinges."

"Thank you, Mr. Home Improvement." She wadded up the wet rug. It would have to go into the washing machine.

He squatted and opened the cupboard door under the sink, frowning at the spaghetti junction of hoses and pipes. "Why don't you call a repairman to fix the leak? Someone who does general repair work?"

"I'll have to do that. How did you fix the toilet?"

"Hooked the chain up a couple of notches. It works fine

now. You're not Miss Fixit, I take it?"

"Two left thumbs and a mind that boggles at anything mechanical."

"I could come tomorrow afternoon and take care of a few repairs for you. I promised Mom and Dad I'd go to church with them in the morning, but nothing's scheduled for the afternoon."

She gaped. "You could fix the dishwasher? The screen door?"

He looked annoyed. Obviously she'd insulted his manhood. "I was raised on a farm. I can fix almost anything."

Oh, it was tempting.

But there was that distracting chest. And the biceps and lean hips and long legs, the sensual mouth, not a bit less appealing because it was bruised on one side.

Forget the sexy body. She hadn't had sex in twenty-six months, one week and three days, but who was counting? Nothing was sexier than a man who could fix things. After two years of coping on her own with everything from car repair to snow shoveling, she'd learned to seize help when it was offered, no questions.

"Don't tell me you own a tool belt," she asked, feeling a little faint.

"Not at the present time, but Dad must have one around I could borrow. Why?"

"Leather?" The fantasy of Jake wearing a tool belt and nothing else flooded her mind, weakening her moral fiber.

"Tool belts are usually made of leather."

"Oh, my." She fanned herself with her hand. "Is it a little warm in here?"

He straightened up from his squat and chuckled. "Tool belts turn you on?"

"Of course not! How ridiculous would that be?"

"They do! Sonovabitch." He clutched his gut; the chuckle burst into full, rollicking laughter. She hoped his ribs hurt like hell.

CHAPTER 7

Lorie answered the door Sunday afternoon to find Jake on her front porch, wearing a fully equipped tool belt and a Cheshire cat grin. Fortunately he had clothes on. Sort of. Khaki shorts that showed off hairy masculine legs, topped by a sleeveless tee shirt. He spread his arms. "What do you think? Turned on?"

He had no idea. "I don't know what you're talking about. Did you come to show off, or to work?"

"If he didn't, I did. Work, I mean. And I'm in a lot better shape than he is." Dex appeared beside Jake, a slightly shorter but no less devastating version of his brother. Also wearing a tool belt, shorts and a tee shirt. Dex's grin was even wider than Jake's, probably because his face wasn't battered.

Lorie folded her arms and glared. "Jake Randolph, you blabbed."

He pulled a sheepish face. "It was too good to keep. Besides, it cost him."

"How do you think he got me here?" Dex patted his tool belt with affection. "The scoop on one genuine female sexual fantasy in exchange for an afternoon's labor. I have a date next Saturday, and I'm giving this baby a trial run."

"The least I can do is warn her," Lorie said. "Who do you have a date with?"

"Classified. Want me to start on the screen door, Jake?"

"Let's yank out the dishwasher first. I need to be sure the gasket I brought will fit. Lorie, I'll have to turn off the water valve under your sink."

"It kind of rusted, the plumbing's so old. You'll probably need a wrench."

"Not a problem."

Lorie stepped aside and the two large males entered, filling her small house with vitality. They had the water turned off and the ancient appliance heaved out of its under-counter niche and into the middle of the kitchen floor in five minutes. If that wasn't sexy, she didn't know what was.

They were attaching a new gasket, when a horn blast sounded from the driveway.

"That'll be the other half of Team Randolph," Jake said. "You might want to give Mom a hand, Lorie. She's toting a huge pan of lasagna, and God knows what else. Dad'll be unloading his chainsaw and toolbox."

"Your parents are here?" Panic gripped her. She'd straightened up the house but hadn't dusted or run the vacuum, and the place needed a thorough cleaning. There hadn't been time that morning, what with attending early church, and getting Matt fed and ready for Hy to pick him up for the scheduled afternoon visit. "Jake, I wasn't expecting your mother and father! I didn't clean the house. Or fix anything nice to serve company."

Both brothers sat back on their haunches and stared at her. Dex scratched his head and took a quick glance around the room. "Looks fine to me. There're chairs to sit in. And plenty of space at the table to set down a cup of coffee. Whoa! Look at the size of that flat screen TV. Satellite hookup?"

Perplexed, Lorie nodded and looked at Jake. "What does that mean? A place to sit? Why wouldn't there be?"

"Angel, there are a dozen things our mom would rather do than clean house. She relies on kid power and husband power to get the loathsome chores done, and we're not always on top of things. We usually have to clear magazines, bills and dust bunnies off of the table before we eat. Right now I'm pretty sure the sofa is heaped with clean clothes that need to be folded. Believe me, your place is pristine."

"Well, okay, I guess." She'd have to set him straight. An angel she was not. It was a typical country gesture to help out a neighbor, but she was uncomfortable with the surprise. What else had Jake said? His parents brought food? Again, typical of country folks. But a chainsaw? "Why did your father bring a chainsaw?"

"To cut down the dead tree in your front yard. He'll haul it away in his pickup, unless you want the wood. If you do, we'll saw it into pieces and stack it by your backdoor. A dead tree can be dangerous. Might uproot in a storm and take out part of your house."

Speechless, she sat down at the table.

"Hello, there." Jake's mother peered in the screen door, holding a large flat pan. "Lorie, this is such fun. How long has it been since we've gotten together?"

"Quite a while, I guess. Come in, Mrs. Randolph," Lorie said faintly. "Let me get the door for you."

Either Mary Randolph's memory was faulty or hers was. As far as Lorie could remember, they'd never gotten together. They visited sometimes at church, but that had been the extent of their acquaintance. As soon as she sued for divorce, Lorie had gone back to the First Methodist church she'd grown up in. The Randolphs attended there, too, while Garrisons were Episcopalians.

The roar of a chainsaw resonated from the front yard. Jake and Dex didn't raise their eyes from their task, and continued to tape and reattach hoses.

Mary stepped in the door, beaming as she looked around. She was a small woman, probably three inches shorter than Lorie, and had baby blue eyes, a button nose and a rosebud mouth. She would look like a cherub when she hit eighty. Her hair was cut short and artfully tinted blond. She exuded bouncing energy, which explained why her figure would have been the envy of a teenager.

"We should refrigerate the lasagna and heat it in the oven later. What a nice place. You certainly are neat and tidy. Don't know how you do it. Working fulltime with a little one to look after."

"Matt's not so little, Mrs. Randolph. He'll be in fourth grade next school year."

"Call me Mary. Where is your son? Jake says he's a lively one and I'm dying to meet him. I hope he likes lasagna and chocolate cake."

"He loves both. But he's not here this afternoon. He went to visit the Garrisons."

The older woman's face fell. "Oh. Well, we'll save him some. The Garrisons are lucky to have a grandchild. Wilber and I don't have any grandchildren, you know."

Lorie felt a pang of guilt.

Jake and Dex didn't bother to look up. "Don't start, Mom," they grumbled in unison.

"Humph. Both of you go out and bring the rest of the stuff in from the pickup. Your father's busy."

Jake was working with a wrench. "Later. We're in the middle of something, here."

"Not later. The gelatin and eggs need to be fridged right away."

"It'll keep," Dex said, holding the dishwasher hose while his brother worked.

"I'll just mention it to your father, then."

Jake dropped the wrench. Dex let go of the hose. They were out the door in thirty seconds.

"Works every time," Mary said with satisfaction. "I learned when they were young that Wil got results faster than I did. Not that I ever tattled to their father unless they'd been really bad. Thank goodness they never caught on to me. I suppose you use the same trick. All mothers with growing sons do."

Ask Strom for help with Matt? Not likely. A far as Strom was concerned, Lorie was the disciplinarian and his job was to indulge their son. He was cavalier about paying his child support, but lavish presents were the norm. Hence the fifty-six inch television which had been delivered last Christmas. Things like the hundred-dollar tennis shoes Matt wore. At age nine, Matt had no concept of money. He'd lost the first pair of Nikes after he'd had them for a week. Strom just bought him another pair.

Lorie evaded Mary Randolph's friendly questioning gaze. When she got Jake alone she'd skin him alive for not warning her his family was arriving. "This is really so very nice of you all. I hope you didn't go to a lot of trouble with the food."

"Not a bit. Lasagna, snap beans, deviled eggs, and strawberry gelatin mold. It was all ready before we went to church. We're just sharing a light Sunday supper."

Good grief, Lorie thought. That's a light supper?

Jake and Dex reentered the front door, quarrelling with each other, Jake particularly vocal. "The Royals don't stand a chance this year. Their pitching sucks."

"Wrong, bro. They're bringing up this guy from Omaha. Has an arm like a semiauto."

"Ten bucks they get blitzed the next three-game series."

"You're on. Where should we put this stuff, Mom?"

"On the table here. How's your father doing?"

A shouted male warning came from the front yard, and the thunderous sound of a falling tree answered her question.

"Wow," Lorie said, catching her breath. "I hope it didn't crash into the neighbors' yard."

"Mercy no, child," Mary said. "Wil knows what he's doing. But we'll go check if you'll feel better."

They trooped outside to find the dead tree on its side, the stump cut through clean as a whistle. Dead branches hung into the street, but no damage had been done to the neighbors' houses. Obviously the man behind the chainsaw was an expert. She supposed the Randolph boys' father was mid-fifties, but other than some gray hair at the temples, age hadn't touched him much. His sons were younger versions of him, dark-haired, dark-eyed with lanky, muscular bodies.

Will Randolph removed his headgear, a hardhat advertising a well-known farm machinery company, and swiped his brow. He grinned at all of them, but his eyes were for his wife. The affection Lorie saw there startled her. What would it be like to have a man love you that much after thirty-odd years of living together?

"Mary, we have an early start on our winter firewood. Unless the young lady here wants it." He reached out his hand and Lorie took it. He had a warm, firm grasp. "Wil Randolph. You must be Lorie."

"Yes. This is so nice of you. I've been wondering how— I mean, I knew the tree should come down. Yes, please take all of it. I'm delighted someone can use the wood."

"Probably measure out to almost two cords. I see you have a fireplace. Why don't I cut some into usable pieces and stack it by your backdoor?"

"No need. I don't use the fireplace. Something's wrong with the chimney. I found that out the hard way."

All three men pivoted and stared. Jake and Dex at her, while Wil's narrowed glance shot up to the chimney. Oh, oh. Lorie knew that contemplative look. She'd seen it from his older son when he'd examined her leaking dishwasher. It was a measuring Okay We Have a Problem Here Let's Fix It" stare.

"Chimney mortar seems to be in good shape," Wil said. "No brick falling out."

"What's the matter with it?" asked Jake.

"Just old, I guess," Lorie said. "I tried a fire once, and it wouldn't draw. Smoke poured back into the room. I had to get a shovel and carry the burning logs outside. Good thing there was snow on the ground, so they fizzled out. I haven't tried a fire since."

Jake moved closer, his thick brows lowered in a frown. "Let me get this straight. You carried actively burning logs from the fireplace, through your living room and out the front door? On a shovel?"

"Well, yes. One at a time of course, there were too many to carry all at once. But I couldn't think of another—"

"Are you crazy? Don't you have a fire extinguisher?"

She bristled. "Yes, but the smoke was awful. I had to get the fire out of the house before everything was covered with soot. So I used the tongs and loaded each log on the shovel. I was careful."

The three men were obviously appalled. Mary clucked sympathy. "It makes perfect sense to me. No woman wants her house to reek of smoke. She would have had to wash every curtain in the place, and all their bedding and clothes."

"Right." Lorie folded her arms and stood next to Mary, and glared at Jake.

"Better give up, son," Wil said. "You'll never win this one. Why don't we check out the chimney? You boys done fixing the dishwasher?"

"Almost, Dad," Dex said. "I'll go up on the roof. You have a ladder, Lorie?"

"The Dannenbergs next door do. I can borrow it, but really, you shouldn't bother."

Wil shook his head. "No bother. I'll take off the tree branches while you boys finish up inside. We can dump 'em into that ditch on the north forty. Might stop the erosion from getting worse."

"Lorie and I will drag the branches to the truck," Mary said.

"Of course," Lorie chimed in, glad to do something useful.

The Randolphs went to work with oiled efficiency. Jake and Dex disappeared inside the house. Wil revved up the chainsaw and began to slice the fallen tree into sections. Mary dug in the pickup's glove compartment and came up with two pairs of dingy work gloves.

"Put these on, Lorie. No need for us to have hands like leather just because our men do."

Oh, oh. Our men? "Ah, Mary, Jake and I are just—"

"Just friends. I know, he told me. But I've got eyes, child. He likes you a lot."

"We've known each other since we were kids. That's all

there is to it. There's nothing serious going on here."

Mary nodded, her eyes vague. "I always hoped he'd find a local girl and settle down close by. But he chose a different path."

"He's leaving again soon, isn't he?" Lorie ached with that knowledge. God, how much worse would the pain be if she gave in to her overactive libido and slept with him? She couldn't let it happen.

The vagueness on Mary's face became shrewd intelligence. "It would seem so. Did he tell you he resigned from active duty?"

"No. We haven't had much time to talk about his plans. I mean, aren't you glad? He was involved in some dangerous stuff."

"I'm glad he won't be gallivanting around the globe playing cowboy. But he won't tell me his plans and that worries me. Maybe you could find out?"

"I certainly wouldn't pry."

"Of course not. But a man will tell a woman most anything under the right circumstance, don't you agree?"

Great day. Another manipulator. And a slick one. Lorie set her jaw. "If that means what I think it means, those circumstances aren't about to happen and I told Jake that."

Mary chuckled, as if at a private joke. "Looks like Wil needs us to get busy."

Despite Mary's small stature, she appeared to have no trouble heaving the heavy branches into the bed of the truck. Dex and Jake joined them in their efforts and the pickup was soon loaded. Wil laid the screaming saw aside. "We'll finish this up later and load the rest of the logs into Dex's pickup. Jake, why don't you get on the screen door, while your brother and I check out the fireplace?"

Jake shook his head. "I can go up on the roof, same as Dex. This was my idea."

"Son, you're nursing banged-up ribs. You were idiot enough to get 'em, don't make it worse."

Dex grinned and flexed his biceps. Jake snorted an insult and stomped toward the front door, muttering to himself.

He had it off the hinges in a matter of seconds.

Team Randolph, Jake had called them. A functional family, working as a unit. What struck Lorie was the deep respect the family members had for each other. Despite the horsing around between Jake and his brother, the affection between them was fierce. What would it have been like to grow up in a family like that? A brawling, rowdy, loving family that supported each other through anything that came along. Something she could never know, but she held out that hope for Matt. So, Lorie, why don't you find a nice man to take you and Matt as a package deal? She wasn't too old to begin again, but Strom would never allow it. Again, the feeling of being trapped overwhelmed her.

Two hours later, Lorie and Mary put the food on the table while the men drank iced tea in front of the television set, chortling over the array of sports channels available via the satellite hookup.

"Whoa!" Dex said. "Australian soccer. Awesome."

"My turn for the remote," Jake said. "There's got to be a baseball game on somewhere."

"Turn it off," Mary ordered. "No television during supper. You know the rules."

"You heard your mother, boys," Wil agreed.

Lorie set the table in a state of semi-shock. The dishwasher was back in place and in working order; her screen door hung straight and square from new hinges, and the dead tree had been eradicated from her front yard. Dex and his father had pulled several bushels of ancient bird nest material from her chimney, which appeared to be drawing fine again. A neat pile of firewood was stacked by her backdoor. It might be April, but she was ready for winter in the firewood department.

CHAPTER 8

"Come eat," ordered Mary. "While the food is hot." Lorie found herself seated between the two older Randolphs, while Dex and Jake sat across from them. Will muttered a quick blessing and Mary cut the lasagna. To Lorie there seemed to be an enormous amount of food, but the way it began to disappear showed Mary knew what she was doing. Matt's appetite hadn't reached that capacity yet.

Lorie looked doubtfully at the slab of lasagna in front of her. It was enough for breakfast, lunch and dinner. "Smells delicious, Mary, but it's way too much."

"Nonsense. Someone pass Lorie the beans. And the gelatin salad."

Lorie took a bite of the pasta and chewed. And chewed. Chewed some more. Instead of the bite getting smaller, it seemed to be growing. Alarmed, she chewed harder. Across the table, Dex and Jake attacked their food with gusto. Mary was daintily cutting her pasta into tiny bites. Maybe that was the trick. Discreetly, she put her paper napkin to her mouth and spat out the half-masticated wad of rubbery cheese. Now what? Maybe the gelatin salad. A bite revealed it to be tasteless pink fluff, but at least she could swallow it.

Next to her, she could feel Wil's body shaking. She

slanted him a look. Yep, he was barely holding it in. Obvious where Jake got his warped sense of humor.

"Mary's lasagna is special, don't you think?" His eyes twinkling, Wil popped in another bite and chewed vigorously.

"I'll get the rest out of the oven," Mary said, tossing her napkin aside. "Good thing I made a double batch."

As soon as his wife left the table, Wil whispered an aside. "Trick is to swallow tiny bites. Chewing is optional. You probably figured out I didn't marry her for her cooking."

Dex peered under the table. "Sure you don't have a dog, Lorie? At home I rely on ole Bonaparte, our beagle."

"Can it, you guys," Jake said, methodically shoveling in the pasta. "It beats army chow all to hell."

"Sure," Dex said. "A Ranger will eat anything."

Jake nodded, giving it some thought. "Actually, snake's not bad if it's cooked. Raw, it's jungle sushi."

Dex made a gagging sound and gulped his iced tea.

Jake grinned and took his last bite of lasagna. "Weenie."

"Boys, behave yourselves," Wil said. "Ladies present." He took the hot pan from his wife and set it on the table. "Sit down, sweetheart. I'll dish it out. Who wants more?"

Despite the grousing, the lasagna pan soon emptied. Ditto the dishes of green beans, deviled eggs and jellied salad.

"Chocolate cake," announced Mary. "Then you guys can load the dishwasher while Lorie and I get a turn at the television."

Ten minutes later, that was the scene Matt and his grandfather walked into. Hy Garrison did a double take as he entered the front door and found her tiny house crowded with Randolphs. "What's going on here, Lorie?"

Matt gave a whoop and tore over to Jake, skidded to a stop and offered an exuberant high-five. Jake returned it with enthusiasm. Lorie's heart dropped to her toes. The only good thing about the delicate situation was that Strom was nowhere in sight.

Hy Garrison lit a Cuban cigar and tipped back in his desk

chair, brooding. It had happened, what he'd feared for the past two years.

His ex-daughter-in-law had found another man. Not that Hy gave a whoop if the tramp took up with someone. It was the thought of losing Matt that terrified him.

Strom had visiting rights, but Lorie held full custody. If she remarried, the chances were good that the court would allow her to relocate. The judge might be amenable to Matt having a mother and a father in a stable home. Strom's track record as a father wasn't the best, and unfortunately Hy had little influence with the district judge, who had been reelected year after year for an ice age.

This specific man held double danger, because Strom hated Jake Randolph. There couldn't be anyone bedding his son's ex-wife that would infuriate his son more. Even worse, from what Hy had seen of Matt's reaction, his grandson was fond of the soldier boy. The situation was almost comic, if Hy were up to appreciating the irony.

He considered his options. Confront Lorie and convince her to discontinue the relationship? He'd leave that up to Strom. Strom was good at handling his ex-wife.

Bring pressure on the sheriff again? Possible, but John had been strangely unwilling to cooperate. That could be rectified. His old friend had a few skeletons rattling around in the closet, and a reminder of that might prod him off the fence. But however much pressure he put on John, the sheriff had to operate within the system. That left Randolph himself. Was bribery a possibility? Pay him a few thousand to leave town? Hy didn't think so. The man reeked self-righteous honor.

Where was Randolph vulnerable? Of course, his family! Unfortunately, Nokeah Federal didn't hold the paper on their land, or Hy could apply some financial pressure. But all farmers needed money these days, particularly owners of small family farms like the Randolphs. Probably their loan was held at Blue River First National. He'd approach the bank's lending department and see if it was possible to purchase the paper. It was likely a callable loan, and would be renegotiated on a yearly basis. But that solution would take some time, and Hy was anxious to move quickly.

He puffed on his cigar, enjoying the smooth taste. No need to smoke unless you could afford the best.

What about the brother? Dexter Randolph was a bit of an enigma. He helped out at the farm and did some auctioneering and rodeoing on the side. Unmarried, and never a scandal in the female department. Same with the father. Wilber Randolph was as faithful to his wife as an old shoe. Maybe hire a detective to look into the family background, try to unearth some dirt. Again, too slow an approach.

The best bet was Lorie. She had to drop the relationship before it became serious. And that meant turning the matter over to Strom. He reached across his desk and dialed the phone. His son always kept his cell handy, but turned off. Part of the New Sons of Liberty militia business he was so hopped up on. Important to be available at a moment's notice, he'd informed his father. In case something big breaks, but you never know who's listening. All of which was pretty silly in Hy's opinion. Bunch of grown men running around in camouflage, shooting guns at bales of hay and blowing up woodpiles. But not particularly dangerous, as long as the members kept their games confined to their mockup camp in the Flint Hills. Hy even contributed money to the cause from time to time. It enabled his boy to let off some high spirits in harmless soldier playacting.

Impatiently, Hy drummed his fingers on the arm of his chair, listened to three rings, and hung up. Strom would return the call from a land phone. More of his son's paranoia. He was sure the FBI eavesdropped on his cell phone calls.

Ten minutes later, Hy's private line rang.

"Strom? Sorry, boy, but you better cut your stay short and get back as soon as possible. We have a problem."

Strom hung up the phone, infuriated, his mind whirling.

His father was right. The return of Jake Randolph in his ex's life needed to be dealt with. Randolph would get his, and Lorie was due a lesson. His father didn't need to worry about losing his grandson; very soon Matt would be leaving Kansas with Strom, joining the Sons' cause. With Matt gone, Lorie would lose what she loved best in the world. Certainly she loved the kid more than she ever had Strom. His ex-wife needed to learn who was in charge.

The Sons of Liberty had made plans that would shake the country, and Strom would play a big part in them. First things first. To assume his place of leadership with the Sons, Strom needed a quick infusion of cash. His sis, Janice, should be good for a few grand, His father held tight to the purse strings, but Strom had access Matt's college fund. Yeah, it would all come together soon. Like the saying went, revenge was sweet.

CHAPTER 9

◆

"Lorie, it's Jake."

"Oh, hi." She cradled the phone against her ear as she added diced potatoes and carrots to the hamburger hash she was cooking for Matt's supper. Not his favorite, but he couldn't have pizza every night. "I meant to call you, but I just walked in the door a few minutes ago. I want to thank your family again. It's wonderful to have things fixed around here."

"We were glad to do it. My mother hasn't stopped talking about how much she enjoyed the day with you."

"I like her, too. She's a special lady."

He chuckled. "You have no idea. Don't get me started."

"I'll write her a note. Tonight after I get Matt settled down to his homework."

"She'd appreciate that. Lorie, Matt is why I called. I didn't want to do something without checking with you first."

Apprehension grabbed her stomach. But Jake didn't suspect the truth, and would never know. "What about Matt?"

"Nothing's wrong. But we have a mama cat on the place that's in the process of weaning her kittens. They're litter-trained and cute as the devil. Mom wants to keep them all, but Dad says no way. I wondered, would Matt like a kitten? And would you mind? I'd pay for the shots and neutering. Mom won't let just anyone have one of her babies, but she's approved of you and Matt."

"My goodness. It's a thought." Lately she'd been considering that Matt needed a pet, but a dog was too much responsibility. A kitten was possible. They more or less took care of themselves and it wouldn't matter if it were alone most of the day. She made the decision swiftly. "Matt would love it. But male or female? Describe the kittens."

"They're five of them and it's a little early to be sure of the sex. There are two calicos and calicos are almost always female. There's one honkin' yellow fur ball, the biggest in the litter. I'm pretty sure he's male. Tell you what, I'll come by after your supper and bring Matt out to the farm. Let him pick. How does that sound?"

"Like a little boy's dream." Actually, she felt warm and fuzzy herself. "How nice of your mother to think of it."

"I'll be by at seven."

The phone clicked. She turned the stove to low and replaced the receiver on its cradle. Her son lay sprawled on his stomach in front of the television, totally absorbed in <u>Animal Planet</u>. If only he would use that kind of concentration on his schoolwork. He was going to be so excited. That the kitten came from Jake would make it even more wonderful.

"Matt, get busy on your homework. I've got a surprise for you."

As usual, Strom entered Lorie's house without knocking. Strolled in like he owned the place, rudely kicked the door and left it standing open. He never waited for an invitation, just assumed it was his right.

Tonight the timing couldn't have been worse. She'd invited Jake to supper and he would be there any minute. Lorie set aside the pan of biscuits she'd readied for the oven, and wiped her hands on a paper towel as her ex swaggered toward her.

"Strom, you really should knock and wait to be invited."

"Why should I? I pay for this place."

That was so not true, Lorie didn't even bother to argue. She had a flash of uncharitable pleasure at the sight of the cast on his right forearm, and his face was in far worse shape than Jake's. For once, Strom had been the one to take the physical punishment. He carried a can of beer and slurred his words, which meant he was well started for the evening. She held her temper because if she got testy, he would dig in his heels and hang around to argue.

"Would you please leave? I'm busy, and Matt's not here."

"When I'm ready, and I'm not ready."

So much for keeping her temper cool. "I mean it, Strom. You have no rights here and never will."

He snorted. "Where's my kid?"

"Down the street at Jeff Roblie's house. Jeff's mother asked him for supper and the boys are playing Nintendo together. He'll have to go to bed when he gets home. Leave him a note. Or you could run over to Jeff's house for a hello if you want. I can call Jane Roblie and tell her you're stopping by."

He set the can of beer aside and lifted the lid of the pot on the stove, taking a sniff of the simmering contents. "You're cooking fancy tonight." His face split into a nasty smile. "Plenty for two. Happens I'm free. I'll even stay the night if you make nice."

He moved into her space, the beer fumes and scent of male sweat overpowering. It had gotten so the smell of him gagged her. She stiffened when his good arm slid around her waist and pulled her closer. "Stop it, Strom."

"Why? Way I hear it from my dad, you're passing it around. Guess I'll just take what I want this time."

He bent to kiss her and she twisted away. Ordinarily she couldn't have managed it, but with one arm in a cast, he wasn't at full strength. Again, she had a stab of satisfaction at the uselessness of his right arm. He wouldn't be bullying her anytime soon. "You have no right to touch me. Next time you walk in my house without being asked, I'll get a restraining order."

He narrowed his eyes and color flushed his neck and cheeks. "Yeah, right. Try it and you won't get out of bed for a week."

She lifted her chin and ignored the pounding fear. Her ex was building up to one of his rages. The only way to cope with a bully was to stand up to him. Her mind knew that, but her strength of will always failed against Strom. This time she meant to stand her ground. She reached for her cell and held it up like a shield. "Leave now, Strom, or I'm dialing 911."

Chortling, he wrenched the phone from her fingers. "We're going to have some fun. You've needed a lesson for a long time, missy."

Lorie pressed against the wall to protect herself. It was too late to run. She would scream when he hit her. Scream her lungs out and hope the neighbors heard. And this time she would press charges. Naked determination smothered fear. He could hurt her body, but that was the worst he could do. She would no longer cower and give him control over her mind and spirit.

"I'm calling my lawyer, whatever you do. I mean it."

He barked a derisive laugh. "Who cares? I can hurt you and the marks won't show. You know that."

Oh, God, she did.

She hid her face in her hands, quivering despite her intent to stay strong, sensed him towering over her, heard his rapid breathing. Giving pain excited him.

The blow never fell.

Strom's yelp of surprise was echoed by a feral snarl. Lorie uncovered her face to see her ex-husband flat on the floor, belly down. Jake was on him, Strom's good arm jammed against the small of his back. With every kick and curse, Jake twisted higher and harder.

"Raise a hand to her again, I'll break you into so damn many pieces, they'll never put you back together."

"Bastard! I'll kill you!"

"Yeah? I'm not as easy a victim she is." Jake jerked Strom onto his feet and slammed him against the nearest wall, grasping the fabric of his shirtfront. His right fist doubled and drew back; his face was a savage mask. "Hell waits for both of us, but you're going first and you're going screaming. Just give me an excuse, you worthless piece of crud."

Lorie had never seen fear on Strom. She saw it now.

"Jake! For God's sake, calm down. I'm okay."

"Back off, Lorie. This time I finish what I started."

"Jake, he's not worth it." She tugged at his sleeve and grasped his shoulder. "Please," she whispered. "Matt will be back soon. Please, let him go."

Slowly Jake's muscles relaxed and his fist fell to his side. He released his grip. Strom leaned against the wall, wincing and nursing his shoulder. He glared murder at both of them, settling his venom on Lorie. "I knew it! You're doing him! You effing whore, you're doing him. Swear to God, I'll take Matt away from you for this."

The guttural sound from Jake's throat raised the hairs on Lorie's head. He twisted Strom's good arm backward, and frog-marched him to the front door. "The lady asked you to leave. And she will get that restraining order, I'll see to it. Anytime you want to discuss it, you know where I am."

He shoved the cursing man out the door. Strom staggered and barely managed to keep his feet under him, turned and shot both of them a look so full of malice that Lorie took a backward step. If visual hatred could be projected as a bullet, she and Jake would be dead on the spot.

Jake laughed.

Folded his arms, rocked back on his heels and laughed.

CHAPTER 10

The words tumbling out of Strom's mouth were pure sewage, as he lurched off of her front porch and out into the night. It was the worst scene he had instigated since their divorce. She could only thank God that Matt hadn't been there.

Jake shut the front door, threw the lock and turned to give her a searching look. "Are you okay?"

She rubbed her face. "I'm okay. Thank you. He meant to really hurt me this time."

"You are going to get a restraining order? Promise me."

"Yes. I've held off because of Matt, but this time he went too far."

A muscle moved in Jake's jaw as he approached. "Any idea what set him off?"

"Hy told him I was sleeping around. I'd guess it had to do with you and your family being here Sunday. I knew Hy was upset when he saw you here."

"Lorie." Jake stroked her face "I'm sorry. I've brought trouble on you."

She shivered under the delicate touch. "The trouble was already here. I let him bully me too long, but no more."

"You're to tell me if he pulls anything like this again."

She turned away and picked up the bottle of Merlot she

had opened. "Yes? Well, that will be a problem for you, won't it?"

She poured a goblet of the wine and handed it to him.

"Problem?" He raised an eyebrow as he took the wine. "Why a problem?"

She poured herself a goblet and took a sip before she answered. "Your mother said you were leaving in a few days. Isn't that right?"

He grunted acknowledgement and set down the wine. "I'll talk to Dex before I go. He'll take care of it."

"Don't bother. I've learned the only person you can depend on is yourself."

"Lorie, I wish it could be different between us."

"No worry, Jake. I'm not your responsibility. I'm an adult and there's no reason we can't take what we want from each other without regrets."

His face registered astonishment. "You backed off before. Made it plain I was to keep my distance."

"Strom just changed my mind."

She stuck out her chin and glared. Head unbowed, ramrod straight and defiant, surprising him. Lorie had grown. She had always been sheltered and a bit naive, a bit shallow, loved parties and a good time. She'd never been this cynical, or this strong. She took care of her son and played the laidback mother, but she would defend her cub to the death. Jake admired the woman she had become. And God help him, he wanted that woman. To taste that vibrant sexuality. To dive into her female heat. He shoved his hands in his pockets to prevent himself from grabbing her.

"Seems like a poor reason to have sex," he hedged, his heart hammering. "Like you said, I'm leaving in a few days. Hit and run isn't my usual style."

"Oh? Soldier boy doesn't have a girl in every port? No, that's sailor boy, isn't it? Every city, then?"

"Lorie, I'm wary about this. You should be too."

"Don't tell me you've turned into a monk, Jake Randolph, because I know you better than that. Sooo, put up or shut up, soldier. I know you want me." She took a deliberate swallow of her wine and licked the rim of the glass, grinning at him impishly.

He took the glass from her fingers and set it beside his. "Remember, you asked for this. And you better not be teasing, because you'll regret it."

He didn't need to pull her into his arms; she just melted into him, her face lifted for his kiss. He thrust his fingers into the lushness of her hair and tipped her head back to take her mouth. He intended to kiss her hard, hard enough to warn her of what she was asking for. Afterwards he'd back off. Give her a chance to renege. Because while he might occasionally indulge in a one-night stand, Lorie didn't.

He knew that in his bones.

Then his lips were on hers and settled in, found the right angle. She gasped, her mouth opened and she went up in flame. His reason, all sanity vanished.

Her knees buckled and he pushed her against the refrigerator, his mouth plundering. They descended into fire. They dipped and soared, their tongues doing delicious things together. He tasted wine. Sweeter than wine. Honeyed nectar. He dived deeper, drinking from her mouth, taking her sweetness for his. When the kiss ended she gasped for breath and began a slow slide toward the floor. He caught her. She licked swollen lips and lifted her face to his.

"God help me," she whispered.

He took a shuddering breath.

"God help us both," he echoed, and roughly yanked her against him, fisted her hair and kissed her again. When he pulled away, their hearts were hammering in erratic cacophony. This was a complication he didn't need, but if he didn't take her now, his heart would burst.

"Do you want me?" He grated the question.

She nodded and buried her face in his chest. He smoothed her hair and it sprung to life under his fingers. She shivered under his touch.

"Matt," Jake asked. "Where is he? Right now."

"With his friend, Jeff. He's staying for supper."

"How long will he be gone?"

"A couple of hours. He's supposed to be back at nine."

He looked at his watch and grunted. "Not enough time, but it'll do for a start. Your bedroom. Where?"

She wrapped her arms around his neck, her body trembling. "The right door, across from the bathroom. Hurry. Please, Jake, hurry."

He didn't remember walking to her bedroom. Just laying her down, stretching beside her, both of them pulling at each other's clothes. His shaking fingers managed to undo the buttons on her blouse. The front hook on her bra parted with a flick. Her breasts were full, larger than he remembered, and the rosy buds were taut with desire. He cupped them in his palms and bent to suckle. She flung her arms back and bowed under him.

"Yes! Oh, God, that's wonderful."

He propped himself on his elbows, shoulders heaving, breathing deeply to stay in control. "Lorie, are you on the pill?"

"No, of course not. Don't you have something?"

"Not with me. You mentioned supper, not the possibility of us knocking boots."

She tugged his shirttails from his pants, bit her lip in concentration, dragged her fingers across his stomach and began working on his belt buckle. "It'll be okay. I'm at the end of my cycle. Go back to what you're doing."

His erection pulsed painfully, and he stilled her hands with his. "I take it it's been a while for you."

"I can barely remember. They say it's like riding a bicycle."

"Angel, it doesn't even resemble riding a bicycle," he said, holding her hands firmly under control. She was too good with those searching hands.

She sighed and slumped against the bedcovers. "Are we going to do this or not?"

"Not unprotected, we're not."

"Damn it, Jake Randolph. Do you always have to be so reasonable?"

"It'll be six months before I can get back here. This new job will take all my energy for a while. I can't be worrying about whether you're pregnant. I'll be back at Christmas. That will give us time to think about this. About where it could lead."

Her lower lip went out in a pout and reminded him of the old Lorie. The spoiled, teenage I-demand-instant-gratification, Lorie. "Don't concern yourself," she sniffed. "Now that you've got me warmed up, I'm sure I can find a man who's more willing."

"Don't even think about it," he said through clenched teeth. The stab of jealousy almost knocked the wind out of him, it was so unexpected. Even knowing she was goading him didn't help. He really wanted to chew on that pouty lip. And roll her on her back and ride her so thoroughly she'd never forget it.

She made a derisive raspberry with her tongue. "Ha! You won't be around to stop me, buster."

She pushed at his chest and he moved, swinging his feet to the floor, reflecting it was a good thing the ribs were healing nicely. Except for an occasional twinge, he usually forgot about them. He could certainly move well enough to shut Miss Sassy Tongue up. "I'll make a quick run to the drug store. Put supper on hold."

She looked up from refastening her blouse, her face horrified. "Supper! Oh, no!"

Her blouse still hanging off her shoulders, she leapt up and sprinted for the kitchen. The shriek of fury that echoed through the house made him grin. One thing about Lorie, she didn't hide her emotions.

He tucked in his shirttails and ambled into the kitchen. "Problem?"

Pulling on oven mitts, she jerked a pot off the stove, marched to the sink and dropped the metal container into the basin. "It's ruined, and it's all your fault. Do you have any idea how much work goes into preparing beef burgundy?"

"How is it my fault? You jumped me." He checked the pan's contents. He would have named it beef stew, and it did appear a little brown around the edges. "Looks okay to me. Mom would call this a good do."

She clenched her teeth. "I am not serving that. And I did not jump you."

"Yeah? Could've fooled me."

"Ohh, if I weren't a lady!"

"The lady needs to get laid. The spoiled brat needs her butt paddled. I'm not sure which I'm dealing with here, but I'm willing either way."

She doubled up her fist. "I'm about to send a message to those sore ribs of yours."

He laughed and pulled her close, cradling her chin in his palm. "I'll pick up a pizza on the way back from the drugstore."

Her lower lip went out again and this time he did chew on it. Then kissed her, spiraling into the feverish magic. He drove his tongue deep, teasing them both with the rhythm of intimacy. God, the taste of her drove him crazy.

God must have disapproved, because before things got out of hand, someone pounded on the front door.

"Mom! Open the door!"

"Matt!" She froze, her eyes flying open. "Oh, look at me. Half the buttons are off this blouse! My hair's a mess, makeup shot."

He patted her butt. No way would he paddle that sweet ass. He had other plans for it. "Go do your thing. I'll keep Matt at bay."

Jake took his time getting to the door, letting Lorie escape to the bathroom. "Hey, kid," he said, greeting the boy who tumbled over the doorstep. "What's up?"

"Hi, Jake. How come the door was locked? Mom never locks the door."

"Beats me. You'll have to ask her, but she's in the bathroom right now."

Matt wrinkled his nose. "What's that smell?"

"Burned stew. I wouldn't mention it to your mother."

"Gosh, she cooked all afternoon. Said it was a special dinner for you, 'cause you gave me Roly-poly and took him to the vet for his shots and everything."

Jake cleared his throat, momentarily at a loss. "Well, I guess accidents happen. You should try my mom's cooking sometime. Now that's an experience."

"Mom's a real good cook. Even when she pours that stinky red stuff on things."

Stinky red stuff? He took a stab. "You mean the bottle on the cupboard?"

"Yep. Stinky red stuff. What are you guys going to eat now?"

"I was just on my way to pick up a pizza." And it looked like that was all he was going to pick up.

Matt brightened. "Really? Pepperoni's my favorite."

"Mine, too. I'll get an extra-large. Didn't you have supper?"

"Oh, sure. Jeff's dad did hamburgers on the grill. But that was a long time ago."

Remembering his appetite at that age, Jake figured it was probably all of an hour ago. "Extra-large, it is. Aren't you home a little early?"

"Yeah," Matt sighed. "Jeff's mom is 'lergic to Roly-poly." He held up the shoebox he carried tucked under his arm. The box had once housed a pair of lady's boots, and was punctured with air holes. Matt set it on the floor, and lifted the lid. A yellow puffball leapt out mewing his disapproval at being confined, and pounced on Matt's nearest shoestring. Two tugs and he had it unlaced, and immediately attacked the second one.

"He's real smart," Matt said proudly.

"Matthew Lloyd Garrison!"

Matt cringed guiltily, and the horror in Lorie's voice even made Jake wince. It was his own mother's Go to Your Room immediately, and I'll Speak to your Father about This voice he remembered from childhood.

Lorie placed her hands on her hips and glared at her son. "Didn't I specifically tell you to leave your kitten in his box in the laundry room? That you were under no circumstances to take him to Jeff's house?"

Matt hunched his shoulders and frowned. "He would've been lonesome."

"Then you should've stayed home with him. Take Roly-poly to his box. Be sure he has fresh water and clean litter, and go straight to your room."

"Aw, Mom. I don't wanna. Jake's going for pizza."

"I mean it, mister! You're grounded for three days. Two for disobeying and one for arguing. Forget about the pizza."

Matt's lower lip went out and he lifted his chin. The resemblance to his mother was eerie. "That's not fair."

Jake cuffed him on the arm, chuckling. "You're busted, kid. Take it like a man."

The pout disappeared. Matt snickered and cuffed back, man to man. "Okay, I guess. I really, really love Roly-poly, Jake. And he would've been lonesome if I left him. Wanna pet him? He won't mind."

The kitten had turned his attention and sharp little teeth and claws to the kilim rug in the living room. "Oh, oh," Matt said, sprinting and snagging the yellow menace one-handed. "Sorry, Mom. I'll put him away. G'night, Jake. Are you coming over tomorrow? It's Sunday and Mom doesn't have to go to work."

"Sure, if she asks me."

"She will. Maybe you can sleep over. She likes you a lot, I can tell."

Jake smirked in Lorie's direction. "Oh, really? I'll remind her of that."

"Oh, God." She hid her face in her hands. "Now you've done it, mister big mouth. Go to bed or you're grounded for a week."

Matt scurried away. Jake folded his arms and leaned a shoulder against the front door frame. He dropped his voice to a husky drawl. "Now, about that sleepover, angel."

After Jake left, Lorie puttered around the house doing unnecessary chores, straightening the sofa cushions, washing up the few dishes in the sink. Thanks to Jake, the dishwasher functioned perfectly, but there were too few dishes to bother loading the machine. Already missing him, she locked the house, showered and pulled on an old nightgown.

She'd known seeing Jake again would be tough, just hadn't been prepared for how tough. God, he'd looked good. Older of course, but so was she. She knew what her mirror said, and she hadn't aged as gracefully as Jake had. She looked at her reflection as she brushed her teeth, and sighed. Using her fingers, she stretched her skin to smooth out the lines that etched her mouth and forehead. *There you are, Lorie*, she thought, and smiled at her own whimsy. There was no turning back the clock.

After an hour of tossing in the sheets, she gave up and turned on the light, reaching for the book she kept on her bedside stand. It would be another one of those nights. She touched her lips, the memory of the sizzling kiss he'd given her when he'd returned with the pizza and his drugstore purchase, still burned her mouth. A kiss of fire and promise. Promise of the kind of ecstasy she'd only known briefly in her lifetime. With Jake.

They'd shared a pizza and talked like old friends do, but they hadn't made love. Her fault. He certainly had been willing. While he'd been gone on the drugstore errand, sanity returned and she remembered the high cost of sex with Jake. He'd accepted her decision, a slight flare of his nostrils betraying his disappointment, but he hadn't pressured her. That wasn't Jake's style. He'd let her know he was eager, but the invitation had to come from her.

She was afraid. Afraid to allow herself to be with him. Because she still loved him, and knew he would leave her again, and this time she might never recover. A sad commentary on her lack of gumption. She wanted him, but couldn't forgive the past. Underneath the sensual pleasure of his kiss and touch, the old anger was still there. Her man had done her wrong, and left her with a broken heart and under the circumstances, with no options.

She had Matt.

That would have to be enough.

CHAPTER 11

"How're you doing today, angel? Got time for a chat?" Jake's husky drawl could curl her toes even over the phone line.

Lorie glanced around. The woman who worked with her in Billing and Records was out to lunch. So were the doctors and the rest of the staff. "It's pretty deserted around here. Everyone is on lunch hour."

"Let me guess. You take a sack lunch."

"Yogurt and an apple. How did you know and how did you get this number?"

He chuckled. "Uncle trained me in espionage techniques. Also, Matt told me."

She polished the apple with a paper napkin and took a bite. "Ha. Should I be impressed? My kid's a blabbermouth." She munched. "So what do you want, soldier boy? I thought you were mad at me."

"What gave you that idea? Just how deserted is the place?"

She munched again. "Just me and the front desk gal. Why?"

"Anywhere you can go to take a private phone call?"

"Well, Doc Symondson is out today. Guess I could use her office. All the doctors have their own private line. Is it that important?"

"Call me back on the private line. I'm at the farm."

The phone clicked off. Lorie stuffed the remnants of her lunch in the wastebasket and headed for the absent doctor's office, wondering what there was about Jake that prompted her to obey such a mysterious order without question. A trait that probably made him a great leader of men, but it was darned irritating.

She was in deep trouble.

Just the sound of his voice was enough to start her pulse pounding and her libido twanging. She felt a little guilty. She hadn't meant to tease him Saturday night, had intended to let him make love to her. Had wanted to. But Matt barged in at a crucial time and things never settled down after that, and while Jake was gone she'd reconsidered and lost the mood. He'd left when she asked him to, didn't even argue. She knew the bulge in his pocket was a box of condoms and the bulge under his zipper had to be downright painful. Strom would have been furious.

He answered on the first ring. "Okay," she said. "I'm here as ordered, at attention and saluting."

"On a private line?"

"Uh-huh. But why?"

"Is the door locked?"

She frowned. "I shut it, but it's not locked."

"Lock it."

She set the receiver down and did as asked. What in the world could be so important? "Okay, it's locked."

"I have to leave Friday, Lorie. I didn't get a chance to talk to you about it before."

Friday. Four days and he'd be gone. Her skin chilled, as if winter had arrived in April. Perhaps it was a good thing they hadn't made love. The memory of his kisses, the pleasure of his skillful hands roaming her body, had kept her tossing for two nights. She knew once he took her completely, the ecstasy would brand her forever.

"Friday," she repeated faintly. The pain in her chest was surely her heart breaking.

"Yeah." A stretch of silence, as if he searched for words.

She pictured him running his fingers through his hair, like he did when he was frustrated.

"Okay, here it is, Lorie. I don't have the right to ask, but could you take the next two days off? Maybe get your mother to watch Matt? I'd like it if we could go to KC. Have some time together before I leave. Just the two of us. What do you think?"

She didn't think about it for long. There would be regret either way. But better regret after two days in Jake's arms, than brood over what she had missed because she lacked courage. "Yes," she said. "I'll arrange it."

"Great. I'll pick you up tomorrow morning around nine." The soft timber of satisfaction was audible even over the phone.

"Okay." Her cheeks went warm with excitement as the full import hit. Two days with Jake. Oh, God. And two nights. "What should I pack?"

"Casual. We'll stay at the Plaza, take in the art museum and a show, whatever you want. Maybe one dressy outfit. There're some nice places to eat on the Plaza."

"'Kay," she agreed absently, already running lists of things to do through her mind. "I'll be ready."

"And Lorie," his voice dropped.

"Uh-huh?"

"Don't bother to pack a nightgown." He hung up.

Lord. She fanned herself with the doctor's memo pad. That was one sexy hunk of male. She hoped she was up to handling him. She could hardly wait. She put the memo pad down and started a list. Call her mother. Ask Mandy Dannenberg to come over to feed and check on Roly both days. Call the school.

The phone rang, and she picked it up without thinking. "Lorie Saxton."

"Is the door still locked?"

"Jake, how did you get this number? I don't even know it."

"I'm good. Well, actually, we have caller ID. I forgot to say I won't be able to come over tonight."

"Okay. Just as well. I'll be busy."

"Hmm. Ever have phone sex?"

"Ah, no. It's a little tacky, isn't it?"

He chuckled, an evil chuckle. "Don't knock it 'til you've tried it."

"Oh, my God. You're going to do me on the phone. That's why you had me lock the door." A mixture of horror and anticipation lifted the hair on her head.

"Uh-huh. You owe me after Saturday night."

"No need to get drastic. I'll make it up to you later."

"Hmm. You will now, I think. Put the receiver tight up against you ear. Tuck it under your chin so your hands are free. I want you to hear my voice humming through your body, feel it scorching your skin."

Oh, my lord. Something wild would to happen if she let this go on. His voice was dark, ripe with seduction.

"Done that?" He chuckled again at her gargled affirmation. "That's good. What does the air smell like?"

"It's a clinic," she said, blowing out her breath in exasperation. She should hang up right now. "Ozoney, I guess."

"I smell mint. Like you grow by your backdoor. Like you put in your tea."

"Mint." She sniffed, and the tantalizing odor hovered just out of memory.

"Rub a piece of mint between your fingers. Hold it to your nose. That's right. Close your eyes. Smell the greenness? The sharp aroma?"

"I almost can. Give me a minute."

"I love the smell of mint. It reminds me of you. Fresh. Clean. A little wild."

"W-wild?"

"Mmm-huh. I'm sucking on your fingers, tasting you. Tasting mint. First the middle one. Now the pinkie. I'm practicing before I suckle your breasts, angel. Feel my mouth tugging?"

Her fingers tingled. Oh, lord.

"Where are you sitting? Are you comfortable?"

She wiggled and the chair rollers slid a bit to one side. "At the desk chair. It's leather. Cushiony."

"Lean back. My arms are around you, holding you in my lap, cuddling you against my body. You're so soft. You fit snug against me."

She leaned back and sighed. Nothing felt as good as Jake's arms around her.

"Look at your hands. Hold them in front of you."

She gulped. "Okay."

"They're my hands now. Do what I tell you with them."

His voice was a silken command. There was no question she would follow it. "J—Jake—? About the other night—"

"Hush. I'm going to kiss you now. Turn your face to me. Ah, good. I'm taking your mouth. Soft, gentle at first. Our kiss goes on and on, until you're boneless and melt into me. Dig your fingers into my neck, sweetheart. How do you feel?"

She shuddered. "Hot," she muttered. "I'm burning up."

"We're both burning. In a few minutes I'll be inside of you. My teeth are nibbling. Such soft skin. Arch your neck for my love bite. Mmm. There, right there. The hollow of your throat. You like that."

"There," she gasped. "Right there."

"Unbutton your blouse. I assume you're wearing one of your starchy cotton shirts? Are you wearing a skirt or pants?"

She fumbled at the blouse buttons. "A skirt," she gasped.

"Good. Hike it up over your hips. Way up." He sighed. "I really love your ass. Is your blouse unbuttoned yet?"

"Yes!" The chill of the office air conditioning hit the heat of her skin. She could hear her own breathing; feel her heart thud in her chest.

"Ah, nice. Unfasten your bra to let your breasts tumble loose. Your breasts are incredible. I'm touching them now. They're so firm, so warm." His voice was a husky narcotic, impossible to resist.

She gasped. Her hands weren't her own anymore. They were his. Hard and calloused. A little rough. Cradling her breasts.

"That's right," he crooned. "Feel me touch them? I'm cupping the right one in my hand and stroking the nipple with my thumb. Now the left one. The nipples harden where I stroke. Mmm. And so sweet to the taste. I'm suckling. Do you like that?"

"Yes! Oh, God, yes. Jake—"

"Hmm?"

"You may have to come over tonight after all."

He laughed softly, and it was a husk of wickedness against her ear. "I'm hard and getting harder. I want you in the worst way. Dying for you, angel. Do you want me? You don't have to answer. Just a little sound from your throat."

She gasped for breath. The memory of his spicy male scent clogged her lungs. A small whimper escaped her.

"Do you want me? Say it now."

"Yes." She swallowed. "I want you."

"How bad do you want me?"

"Bad. Real bad."

"Spread your legs!" He snapped the command.

She squeaked and obeyed.

"Feel my hand stroke between your thighs. Slowly, fingertips, caressing, stroking. I can hear you breathing. Hard and fast. You're more and more excited, aren't you?"

She couldn't stand much more. She wanted to pull him through the phone line.

His coaxing changed to a growl. "Enough teasing. You're going to get what you're asking for. I'm grabbing the elastic of your panties. Pulling down. They're around your ankles. Kick them off."

The leather of the swivel chair was smooth and cool against her bare bottom. She fought for sanity, for some judgment for God's sakes. She was a mother! She was thirty-two years old! She was a responsible adult!

"Good girl. My middle finger is exploring your sex now, sliding inside of you. Hmm, you're so wet, angel. Your sweet little nub is hot and hard. I'm using my thumb on it, circling gently, gently."

"No!"

"Oh, yes." The rough growl was merciless. "You're really going to get it now. Spread your legs wider. I'm doing you harder and faster. Deeper."

Warmth suffused her abdomen. A bolt of lightning shot from her belly to her toes. She quivered like a tuning fork, the wild music oscillating through her bones, expanding, exploding. "Jaaaake!"

She came back to earth, shaking in disbelief. What was she doing in Doctor Symondson's office? Half-naked, her skirt hiked up, her blouse open and her panties dangling off of one sandal. My God, she'd gone insane. She supposed she'd moaned when she'd climaxed, maybe even cried out, because he knew what he'd done to her, the gloating bastard.

He was humming the Star-Spangled Banner. *The rockets' red glare, the bombs bursting—*

She took a deep breath. "I-will-get-you-for-that! You are going to pay."

"Oh, I'm counting on it." He was still laughing when he hung up.

CHAPTER 12

Jake replaced the receiver and checked his watch. A two-hour drive to KC and the hotel where he'd reserved a room. By this time tomorrow they'd be checked in and he'd have her in the sack. He was pretty sure she'd be ripe and ready. He'd damn near driven himself nuts in the process, but she'd earned a taste of teasing.

A sharp whistle.

"Whoa! Am I in the presence of the Kama Sutra master?" Dex stood in the doorway of their mother's computer room where Jake had placed his call to Lorie, looking like he'd been slugged with a two-by-four.

Jake scowled. "How long have you been there?"

"Long enough." Dex fell to his knees and clasped his hands in supplication. "Teach me, oh, master."

"Very funny. How much will it cost me to insure you never mention this to Lorie?"

"Cost you? Everything I have is yours! My bank account. My IRA. All yours." Dex scrambled to his feet and emptied his pockets. "Fifteen bucks and change. Do you want my watch?"

Jake laughed. "All right, jackass, that's enough. I thought you and Dad were planting milo today."

"It's starting to rain. You're lucky I got in ahead of him,

Don Juan. I have to make a call. After that scenario, I need a woman bad."

"I didn't know you had a woman."

"For your information I have several. Maybe none as hot as yours, though. Ah, aren't are you leaving for DC soon? You'll be gone a while, right?"

"You want trouble? I can arrange it. Broken bones, land in the hospital, painful trouble."

Dex grinned and jabbed his brother in the arm. "Buy you a beer? You look like you could use one." They ambled toward the family kitchen.

"It's a little early. Besides, we're out of beer. I checked the fridge last night."

"Guess it's milk or iced tea, then. I haven't had time to talk to you. How did supper with Lorie go? From the sound of that phone call, it must've been pretty good."

"Yeah," Jake sighed. "Good and bad. I need to fill you in."

"Shoot, bro," Dex said, pouring a glass of milk. "Want some? All we have is skim. Mom's on a cholesterol kick again."

Jake shook his head. "Nothing, thanks. Strom was there ahead of me last night."

Dex stopped drinking and set down his glass. "How bad?" he asked cautiously.

"Couldn't have been much worse. He's out of control, Dex. I'm scared shitless for her. And I have to leave in a few days. I have no choice."

Dex nodded. "Then we better make some plans."

Lorie drove home from work, a smile on her face. No one questioned her request for a couple of days off. She had plenty of vacation days piled up. She'd stopped at the mall and splurged on new lingerie. A lover of Jake's caliber deserved sexy lingerie. And a nightgown. Jake was getting her decked out in a nightgown whether he wanted it or not. A black silk and lace confection that she looked really hot in. Probably she wouldn't have it on for long, but hey! Some things were money well spent.

Her mother had been a bit difficult.

It was the same old, same old. What will Strom think? Strom's a drunk, mother. He was a rotten husband, is a rotten father, and I'm going on with my life. So is your grandson, whether you've noticed it or not.

And what will you tell Matt? Her mother asked.

A bit of a problem. Lorie experimented with a couple of tacks. Jake has to leave soon, so he and I are going away for a couple of days. Won't it be fun to stay with Gramma Saxton? Sigh. Pretty lame. How about, Jake and I are going to Worlds of Fun? Huh-uh. Matt would want to come along. It would be worlds of fun all right, but not the kind Matt would envision. Darn. What did you tell a nine-year-old about sex? Matt knew about babies, just not how they were made. At least she didn't think so.

She wheeled into her driveway and began to unload packages. She'd overextended her Visa a bit and shook off a pang of guilt. Her watch said six o'clock. Time to pick up Matt from her mother's house. She'd take him to his favorite fast-food place for supper and break the news to him over burgers and fries. She'd even let Roly-poly sleep with him tonight. Now that was a plan with merit.

Her mother was watching television, and looked up with a frown. "You're late."

"I know. Sorry, Mom. I had some shopping to do. But I brought you a present. An early thank you for keeping Matt."

"Really? What?" Her mother smiled and looked downright pleased. If there was one thing her mother liked, it was presents.

"A pretty robe. It was on sale. I didn't have time to wrap it." The next best thing her mother liked was getting something on sale. So a present on sale was just about the ultimate.

Her mother peered into the sack and pulled out the flowered seersucker robe that Lorie had selected. "Well, my gracious. It is pretty. Thank you, daughter. That's real thoughtful."

Lorie gave her a hug. "You're a good Mom. I should tell you more often. Where's Matt?"

Her mother shook out the robe and slipped it on over her blouse and slacks. "This will be so cool and nice for summer."

"Matt, Mother?"

"Matt? Oh, with Strom."

"With Strom?" Lorie shook her head in puzzlement. "Why? It isn't the weekend. Strom never wants him during the week. Where did he take him?"

"Well, I couldn't say. Strom called and said no need for me to pick Matt up after school. That he would get him and bring him home later."

"When did he call?"

"Call? Oh, right after lunch. I remember my soap was about to come on."

"Mother." Lorie kept her voice under control, even as her temper soared. "You didn't tell him I was going away with Jake for a few days?"

"Well, I might have mentioned it. After all, he was your husband, and you owe him a little consideration."

"My God, Mother, how could you? Especially after I asked you not to! Strom would never have had to know."

"Don't use that tone with me, young lady."

Lorie was out the door and running. She'd go to Hy's place first. That was likely where Strom had taken Matt. She prayed that's what had happened, because Strom kept himself under control when around his father. She'd tell Strom it was all a mistake. That her mother hadn't understood. After all, Rose was getting on in years and her hearing wasn't the best. Plus she was forgetful.

Rose heard just fine and had a memory like an elephant, but Strom would buy it because it would suit him. Whatever happened, Lorie wouldn't let him beat on her again. She owed it to herself and to Matt. What kind of message would it send her son if his father abused his mother? She'd call Jake. Beg off. He'd understand. He had to.

CHAPTER 13

Three hours later, Lorie hung up the phone. She'd talked to every one of Matt's schoolmates on the list the school principal had given her. Strom had picked Matt up after lunch and told the school secretary that he was taking the boy for a dental appointment. How could the woman have been so stupid? Strom had never taken their son for a dental appointment.

No one had any idea where Matt was.

It was a prank. Lorie was convinced of it. Strom just wanted to scare her. He'd threatened to take Matt away from her when he'd seen her with Jake. But her ex meant a legal battle, surely. He'd hire one of the bank's hotshot lawyers and take her back to court. That had to be it. Claim she was an unfit Mother.

She'd like to see him prove that.

She pressed her hands against her face and laid her forehead on the kitchen table. Strom knew he couldn't prove she was unfit. If he took her to court, his heavy drinking would come out. And the abuse. And the fact he wasn't paying his child support regularly. He could end up losing the privileges he had now.

Strom wasn't stupid. He would know that.

She rubbed her eyes and reviewed the contacts she'd

made that night. Strom's parents. The school. Matt's school chums. Jeff's family and all the neighbors. She'd called the movie theater and had Matt paged, in case Strom had taken him there. She'd even gotten in touch with the dentist at his home. Not a soul knew where her son was.

At the jingle in her ear, she picked up the phone on the first ring. It would be Strom of course, with a perfectly logical—-at least to him—-explanation.

She'd been an idiot to get so worked up.

"Lorie, its Shannon."

Not Strom. The knot in Lorie's stomach tightened. "Shannon, I'm sorry, I can't talk right now. I need to locate Matt and Strom."

"I know. Listen, I just talked to my mother." Shannon's mother, Janice, was Strom's older sister. Lorie had called Janice earlier, and the woman professed to know nothing. "It's about Strom. And Matt."

"My God, Shannon! What do you know? I've been worried sick. Was there a car accident?" Please, God. Not an accident. Not her son.

"Nothing like that. But Mother lied to you, Lorie. I'm so sorry, but Mother has spoiled Strom, just like their parents. He's her kid brother, and she's always been protective. Her conscience finally got to her and she called me. Too embarrassed to talk to you herself, I guess."

"Shannon, for God's sake, what do you know?"

"Strom came by her house earlier in his van. Matt was with him. He told Mother that he and Matt were going on a fishing trip and for his family not to worry. Wanted her to call Gramma and Grampa and tell them, but not to say anything to you. Said that you'd raise a fuss if Matt missed any school. They left about two o'clock, Mother said. Strom didn't say where they were going or for how long."

A fishing trip. Lorie felt a surge of relief. Strom had no right to do such a thing of course, but it was something he would pull. A trick he knew would terrify her and furnish him with a future method of intimidation. Also to very effectively cancel her plans to leave town with Jake.

"Thanks, Shannon. You can't imagine how frightened I've been. I called everyone I could think of to locate Matt, and was just about to notify the sheriff."

There was a pause and a sigh, as if Shannon was reluctant to continue. "Lorie, you still might want to do that."

Five minutes later, Lorie hung up with the full story. Not only was Strom's van packed to the ceiling with gear. His sister had glimpsed a tent, camping equipment and a large cooler. Way over normal supplies for a fishing trip of only a few days. What had alarmed Janice, and finally caused her to call Shannon and confess to her duplicity, was the weapons. Strom's sister had glimpsed a high-powered rifle, an array of knives, a and a professional huntsman's bow. Strom knew how to use the bow. He'd brought an elk down with it during the last hunting season.

Tiredly Lorie got to her feet. Her mother was off the hook. Strom's plans must have been made before Rose had told him about the getaway plan with Jake. The packed vehicle indicated an established scheme to take Matt and leave. None of her son's belongings were missing, which meant Strom had driven straight from picking him up at the school to his sister's house. It was after eleven p.m. They'd been on the road for over eight hours.

It was time to contact the authorities.

She'd drive to the sheriff's office and file a complaint. Make it official. If Strom appeared at her doorstep in a few days with Matt in tow, she'd cancel it. She clung to that hope. But right now she had to do something. Anything. She'd sit in the sheriff's office all night if need be. In the morning she'd get in her car and drive the streets. Stop at every store, every gas station. Show them Matt's picture.

A pitiful meow came from the laundry room. Roly-poly. Wherever he had gone with his father, Matt would never want to leave Roly-poly for long. He'd only had the kitten for a few days, but the bond was strong and Matt was enchanted with his own furry buddy. He hadn't been happy to leave Roly even for a few hours to go to school.

Wherever the father and son were, Matt hadn't gone willingly. Maybe at first, but not for long. He'd want to come home to his pet, his own room, and his friends.

She couldn't bear to think about it.

Lorie opened the laundry room door and the yellow fluff ball bounced out, skittered across the wood floor in the hall and headed for Matt's bedroom. "Here, Roly," she said softly, making kissing sounds. "I'll get you a treat. C'mere, baby."

The kitten ignored her. Cats were notorious for refusing to obey unless it was their idea, and Roly was following the feline code. His mother had probably fed it to him with her milk. He batted his little paw against the bedroom door, meowing pitiably.

Lorie sighed. "He isn't here, baby. See?" She opened the door and Roly cat-walked in, tail up and nose twitching, meowing in irritation, ordering his playmate to appear. He made a bounding circle of the room, and sniffed suspiciously at the closet door.

"All right, go ahead and look." Lorie slid open the door. Roly darted in and rooted among the jumble on Matt's closet floor. Shoes, dirty underwear, broken toys, old school drawings. She really had to get her son to clean up better. The kitten pounced on a grungy old sneaker and tugged at the soiled laces, growling, intent on the kill.

"All right, that's it." Lorie scooped him up and held him at arm's length, palms cradled under his fat little belly. The kitten blinked his blue eyes, stretched and yawned.

"Okay, so you're adorable. Don't think you can get to me, buster. I'm on to your cuteness trick and it won't work." The kitten blinked again, then stuck out his tiny pink tongue and licked her hand.

It knocked the legs out from under her.

She sank down on her son's bed and cuddled the soft bundle in her arms, her body rocking in agony. She'd kept the fear at bay for hours and handled the crisis as best as she could. Released by the furry sprite's pink tongue, terror rushed at her, mowing her down with the power of a freight train. Unmanageable, paralyzing terror. She might never see her son again. The tears started. For hours she'd held them in, and now they wouldn't stop.

"Oh, God, Roly. Where is he? Where is our little boy?"

CHAPTER 14

Jake stormed into the sheriff's office, ready to tear a strip off of someone. Anyone, since he couldn't get his hands around Strom's neck at the moment. He slammed the door behind him and stalked over to the dispatcher's desk. "Where is she?"

The woman flinched and glared back. "Mind your manners, mister. You can't come in here and yell at people."

Jake made an attempt to rein in his temper. "Sorry. Where is she?"

"If you mean that Garrison woman, she's back in a cell."

The temper roared and this time he made no attempt to control it or to lower his voice. "You have her in a cell! Why in the hell would you arrest her?"

John Gould stuck his head out of his office door. "Calm down, Randolph. She's not under arrest; she's in the back sleeping. She's been here all night, and the only quiet spot we have is in a cell. I just got her to lie down a bit ago."

Jake pushed around the sheriff and struck off down the hall. He was familiar with where the cells were.

"Now hold up, Randolph."

She was in the same cell he and Dex had recently occupied, lying on her back with her arm flung over her head. Fully clothed, probably in what she'd worn to the office the day before. A beige linen skirt, a rumpled white blouse. Her discarded sandals were on the floor beside her. He entered quietly, not wanting to wake her if she slept.

She stared up at him, her lovely eyes swollen and blank of emotion.

"Lorie? Angel?"

"He took him, Jake. He took my baby."

"I know. I'm so, so sorry."

"It's my fault, you know. Knocking me around wasn't working anymore. I wish I'd let him hit me. It didn't hurt like this. However much it hurt, it wasn't like this."

"Lorie don't say that. This isn't your fault."

"Yes, it is. He knew about you, and punished me this way."

"We'll find Matt, Lorie. I swear it." And they would, if Jake had to dedicate the rest of his life to the search.

She turned her head away. "What can you do?"

"You should've called. I would've come."

"Go away, Jake. There's nothing you can do." Her voice was wooden, totally without expression.

"I can do this much." He sat beside her on the cot, gathered her in his arms and pulled her into his lap.

She had thought there were no tears left. They leaked silently down his shirtfront as she absorbed his strength. For a few moments she allowed herself the luxury. He was as dressed up as she'd seen him, except for Sundays in church. He wore a tan sport coat, a white, open throated shirt, and brown, loose fitting trousers. He was close-shaven and smelled of soap.

She placed her palm on his strongly beating heart. "I'm sorry I didn't let you know, but things got complicated. You're all dressed up and we made plans. Maybe you can get someone else to go with you."

He gave an exasperated sigh. "You know better."

"How did you find me?"

"I got to your house and caught your next-door neighbor backing out of his driveway on his way to work. He stopped and told me what happened. Said that you'd asked them to call here if Strom showed up."

"I talked to everyone in the neighborhood, in case someone had seen Strom. No one had."

"The sheriff said you've been here all night."

"There was nowhere else I wanted to be. They won't let me file a complaint for twenty-four hours, so I'm waiting."

"I'll talk to Gould. Get him to speed up the process. He'll notify the State Patrol and issue a bulletin on Strom's vehicle. You need to go home to rest, and get something to eat. I'll stay with you until they find him."

"Sheriff Gould won't do anything until ten o'clock tonight. He says it's the law."

"Why the hell not? What's so special about ten o'clock?"

"They wait twenty-four hours after being notified someone is missing, before they take any official steps. I should have called them sooner, but it wasn't until after I talked to Shannon that I realized Strom wasn't coming back."

"Maybe he is. Maybe he just wanted to scare you."

"No." She shook her head. "He packed his van full of survival gear. And raided the college fund."

"College fund?"

"He told Janice that he cleaned out Matt's savings account. Hy Garrison established a college fund for Matt when he was born, and both Strom and I were on the account as legal guardians. There was over fifty-thousand dollars in it. And Strom talked Janice out of one of her credit cards. His was maxed out."

Jake swore vehemently and held her tighter. "All right, so he's on the run. I can do something about that. I know people with enough clout to get on this right away."

She didn't allow herself to hope. Jake knew a lot of military people, but this was a civilian matter. "I can't see how anyone in the army can help, Jake."

"Not the army. My new boss is a heavy hitter and he's federal. I'll make a phone call or two. But first, I'll take you home."

"I have to stay here. To be sure they do something."

"Being here won't budge Gould. Has he talked to Hy? They're buddies and go way back. Maybe Hy knows where they went."

"Hy claims he doesn't know, and the sheriff believes him."

"Do you?"

"No. Hy Garrison would say anything to protect Strom."

"My take, also. C'mon." He scooped her to her feet. "You're going home."

Jake dialed the fifteen-digit number and punched in his security code. He'd only used the code once before, and it was changed frequently, but it was the quickest way to get to Cavetto. He hoped the number was still operational. A bored female voice came on line, claiming to be the representative of a fictional computer facility, and asked Jake's business.

"Les Cavetto, please. 66503."

"You're Randolph?"

"Yeah. I need to get to Cavetto."

"What's the name of the family dog?"

Last time it had been his favorite baseball team. The question changed every time, was always personal and Jake never knew what it would be. For the tenth time he wondered why he was involved in this clandestine garbage. He was a soldier, not a spy. Oh, yeah. Cavetto had convinced him it was his patriotic duty. After Les Cavetto left Delta, he'd joined the DIA, Defense Intelligence Agency, to head up HUMINT, Human Intelligence Collection, where predictive intelligence was his responsibility. Jake admired the man almost as much as he admired his own father.

"Bonaparte."

"The one before that. The one who died when you were in college."

How did these people find out this stuff? "Missy."

"I'll put you through."

Les's suave voice came through the wire. "I hope you're on your way to D.C."

"No, sir. Something's come up."

"I heard about your dustup at the local bar. We're low key, remember? That's the way we operate. If I have to put you in the field, I want you to be Mr. Anonymous. You knew the drill, Jake, when you signed up."

"Yes, sir. No excuses. I let a personal matter get the better of me. It won't happen again." How in the hell Cavetto kept up with everything his men were doing was something Jake didn't want to know.

"When can you be here? I needed you yesterday. Hell, I needed you last month."

"Sir, this is the deal." Quickly Jake explained the situation. "I have to hang here a few more days. Until they locate the bastard. I wondered if you might speak to one of your contacts. Maybe light a fire under the feebs on this one. The sheriff refuses to contact them. Says there's no evidence of a kidnapping."

A pungent pause. "He's right. I doubt our friends in the FBI will want to get involved in a family squabble. And there's nothing I can do from here. We have limited domestic jurisdiction, you know that."

"Yessir. I'm talking unofficially."

An even longer pause. "You've got balls, Randolph. You haven't reported yet and you're muscling for favors?"

"I'd appreciate it, sir."

The rumble that came over the wire could have been a chuckle, but it wasn't likely. Cavetto wasn't known for his sense of humor. "Anything else?"

"Something maybe the feebs will have a line on. Have you heard of a quasi-military bunch who call themselves the New Sons of Liberty?"

For the first time, Cavetto sounded interested. "No. What about them?"

"They have a base camp somewhere in the Flint Hills. Garrison is a member, and the man is hauling a small arsenal around in his van. That's about all I can tell you."

"Hooker might know. I'll find out."

"Appreciate it. I have a gut feeling about this, and it's not good. Who's Hooker? One of ours?"

"Dan Hooker. He's the senior field agent for the feebs in the Midwest. Based in KC last time I heard. Doesn't have the gigantic ego some of them have. A good man, but you never want to cross him. He'd have you for lunch and spit out the bones."

"If you say so, sir."

A snort came across the phone line. "That damned Delta arrogance. Why do I admire it so much?"

Les Cavetto had joined Delta from the 82nd Airborne, and distinguished himself during the Afghanistan War, where his eight-man unit aided in the takeout of several SCUD missile sites. He was a man capable of outside the box thinking, and possessed extraordinary skills. Never publicized, Cavetto's exploits were spoken of in hushed tones, even among the Delta elite.

"Probably because you're Deltoid yourself, sir. And you recruited me."

"Don't cause me to regret it. It's good you speak fluent Arabic, Randolph, and know how to handle yourself. Otherwise, I'd can you before you even show up."

"I speak Farsi, too, sir. And Spanish." This time Jake was sure he heard a chuckle.

"I'm aware of your language skills. But your ability to think on your feet interests me more. That, and your expertise with covert eavesdropping equipment. I've got a dozen handpicked men prepared for infiltration of Arab militant groups. They've volunteered to put their lives on the line, and you're an important part of their training program. Don't let us down."

"I understand what you expect, sir. I'll do my job."

"Okay. I'll call in a favor or two. See what I can do. You'll get a phone call. But I want you here at Langley in two weeks at the latest. Understood?"

"I'll be there as soon as possible, sir."

"You better be. The president has made this project a number one priority."

"Yes, sir."

"Jake, you're not military any longer. No more sir, understand? We'll be a tight-knit group. Just Les works fine."

The line went dead.

If there was one man who could make Jake sweat, it was Les Cavetto. But Jake trusted the man to keep his word. Help, however grudgingly, would be furnished.

CHAPTER 15

The Rocky Mountains loomed to the west, silent and overwhelming in presence, extending north and south as far as Lorie could see. From the window of the passenger aircraft, she watched the massive elevations come closer. This morning they were shrouded in mist and mystery, befogged, much like the past few days. The mind-numbing bureaucracy she'd encountered had frustrated her to the point of insanity. It seemed no one would assist her in locating her son. In fact, many of those she'd turned to had thrown obstacles in her path.

Neither the sheriff's office nor the Kansas State Patrol had located Strom and his missing van. And while Sheriff Gould had put out an all-points bulletin on Strom's vehicle, he refused to track Strom's credit card, or to get a court order to tap the phones of people her ex might contact. Hy Garrison stuck to his story that Strom had taken Matt on a fishing trip, and the local law enforcement community refused to issue a warrant for Strom's arrest.

With every hour that passed, her ex-husband was going deeper into hiding and would be more difficult to find. She knew the odds. In desperation, she'd contacted the National Center for Missing and Exploited Children. They'd agreed to post Matt's picture on their website, but warned that every week, every day that followed a child's disappearance, decreased the chances of a safe recovery.

Which was why Jake's information was so crucial, and why the two of them were on an airplane, ready to debark at the Denver airport. How far would fifty-thousand take Strom? What would he do when he ran out of money? If he nursed the funds, they might last a while. The enormity of it washed over her again, along with the pain. Months or years without Matt? Unthinkable. She and Jake had to find him.

She eyed the landscape below. A meandering highway and fallow fields and the sparsely-populated outskirts of the city rushed into view. "We're almost there. The FBI is sure Strom's phone call originated from Denver?"

"The feebs don't make mistakes when it comes to tracing phone calls."

"The sheriff said Strom called Hy from Oklahoma. I just can't imagine Strom had the nerve to lie to his father."

"Well, he did. Or Hy lied. Take your pick. The information is unofficial, Lorie. The only reason we know where Strom is, is because my boss put pressure on Dan Hooker to check the phone records."

Lorie bit her lip. "Will the FBI help us when we get in?"

How much should he tell her? She was near the breaking point.

"I have a number to call. I don't expect much assistance, and nothing hands-on at this point. A warrant on the charge of kidnapping a minor child has to come from our local authorities. So far, Gould insists it's a custodial dispute and a family matter. And the feebs won't get involved unless there is proof of a physical threat to the child."

She paled. "Strom has a van full of lethal weapons in his possession. My God, doesn't that prove Matt's in danger?"

"That fact caught Hooker's attention. Lorie, do you think Strom would hurt Matt?"

She shook her head, and if it was possible, turned even whiter. "No. That's one thing I'm sure of."

"The FBI can't get involved until they're convinced it's a

problem. Or until they receive a specific request from Gould and the Pottawatomie County Attorney. But Hooker wants to learn more about the militant group Strom belongs to, and I'd bet the farm he's looking into it. Not that he'd admit it to anyone outside the agency."

The *Fasten Your Seatbelts* sign blinked on. The stewardess's dulcet tones came over the loudspeaker. "Ladies and gentlemen, we're approaching the Denver International airport—"

Lorie buckled up. "Jake, I can never thank you for what you've done. Not really."

"Save it for when we get some results. All we have is an address of the motel where Strom made his phone call. It's been a day since he made it. We'll rent a car and drive to the address. Maybe we'll get lucky."

"I wouldn't know what to do if it weren't for you. This is costing you time and money and taking you away from your new job. Maybe I can make it up to you in bed."

For a minute, Jake doubted his ears. A look at her face and he knew he had not. She looked bruised and beaten. Where was the sassy, tough woman of a few nights ago?

"Lorie," he said, keeping his tone neutral. "Do you realize you just insulted the hell out of me?"

"I—I didn't mean to. It's just—I'm sorry. It was a stupid thing to say. I thought you wanted to make love to me."

"Hell, yes, I'd like that fine. But don't you ever suggest trading your body for my help in finding Matt. He's a great kid. I like him more than I do you at the moment."

She turned away, as the wheels of the airplane hit the ground with a jarring bounce. "In my experience, there's a price for everything. Strom taught me that. I offered the only coin I have."

"Damn, that infuriates me. You're worth more than that and you owe me nothing. You're done with the man. Get over it and get on with it."

"How easy you make it sound," she said quietly. "I'll never be done with him, don't you understand? Even after we find Matt, I'll always know that Strom could do this again. And next time you won't be around to help."

Her pain pierced him. And frustrated him. What if she was right? "You're the legal custodian. Strom faces a punishing fine and possible jail time. That should chill any further stunts like this."

Five minutes alone with Garrison, he'd pound some basic facts into him. And if Strom put a single bruise on the boy, Jake would hunt him down and there wouldn't be enough left to bury.

Strom would be aware of that.

Strom would be very cautious, very alert, and he had a cache of weapons. Jake had no gun. If it came down to it, Jake knew he'd take a bullet for either Matt or Lorie, but he'd rather be armed and even up the odds. Security regs at the airport precluded his packing the Beretta. No way would the local feebs furnish him a weapon. Even Cavetto couldn't help, so Jake would have to locate one on his own.

He mentally listed the ex-Deltoids he knew to call on for assistance. No one in the Denver area, but Puma was in Colorado Springs working for the US Forestry. Fletch Ansari was part American Indian, known as Puma because of his lithe physique and ability to move soundlessly. The NCO had been as dependable a man as you could ask for in any situation, and he'd have weapons at his disposal. It was a source Jake could tap. When they found Matt, the boy would willingly go with Lorie. Maybe they could wrest him away from Strom without a firefight, and the gun wouldn't be necessary. Jake wasn't counting on it.

CHAPTER 16

L orie showed Matt's picture to the desk clerk again.
"Please, be sure. He's nine years old and has red hair
and freckles. About four-feet tall."

The woman took another disinterested glance and shook
her head. She obviously had more important things on her
mind. "Huh-uh. Haven't seen him. Cute kid. I 'spect I'd
remember if he'd been around. Sorry, but I've got to get
back to work."

"He would have been with a man," Jake's voice rumbled
behind her. "A big guy, six feet tall, weighs in about one-
ninety. Blonde with blue eyes, around thirty years old."

Lorie fumbled in her purse. The only picture she had of
Strom was a photo of him in his K-State football outfit,
looking cocky and young. Matt kept it in his bedroom.
"Here." She thrust the photo at the woman. "This was taken
twelve years ago, but it's still a good likeness. His hair is
cut butch now, with a skinny ponytail in back. He probably
wore jeans and cowboy boots. He—he drinks and gets a
little obnoxious at times."

The woman snorted a laugh. "Like fifty percent of the
guys that check in here. This is a biker and construction
worker motel. Plenty of troublemakers. I don't pay any
more attention to 'em than I have to. Sorry, he's not

familiar. Come back tonight at six and ask the night deskman. Name's George. He's seventy-five years old, but he has a good eye."

"Thanks," Jake said, and slid a twenty-dollar bill and his credit card across the desk. "We'll book a room. Put the charge on the card. The twenty's for you, and twenty more if anything helpful comes back to you. We'd like to take a look at your register for the past three days."

The twenty disappeared like snow in June. The woman's manner became much friendlier. "Wish I could help. Against the motel policy to show anyone our register. Guests deserve their privacy, know what I mean? This guy a friend of yours?"

"No," said Lorie. "Well, sort of."

"Not a friend," said Jake. "The boy is her son."

"Oh." The woman's shrewd face puckered in understanding and she stared at Lorie. "You worried about him, hon?"

"Terribly." Lorie held the woman's eye in silent plea.

"Room's seventy-five a night for a double," the woman said, swiping Jake's credit card in her machine. "Or eighty-five for a king."

"We'll take the king," Jake said.

"Figured you would," the woman grinned. "The size of you. I need to answer the phone, then I'll sign you in." She gave Jake a broad wink and walked to the other end of the counter. The computer screen blinked, as the clerk turned her back and picked up the phone. Which Lorie was sure she hadn't heard ring.

The two of them scanned the screen of past registrations. "Nothing," Jake muttered. "Not that I thought he'd be dumb enough to use his own name. He probably paid cash in advance and used a phony credit card."

"Jake," Lorie hissed, pointing. "See this entry from two days ago: J. Miller. Strom's sister is Janice Miller. She gave him her credit card before he left Nokeah."

Jake took a quick look. "Room three-eighteen. Let's check it out." He raised his voice. "Ah, Miz?"

The woman hung up the phone. "You still want a room?"

"Is room three-eighteen available?"

The woman glanced at the array of keys on her pegboard. The day of electronic card entry hadn't yet arrived at the Boomer Inn. "Checked out this morning before I came on. King size with a foldout couch and kitchenette. Hundred a night. Six-hundred a week. You want it?"

"Yes. We'll need the key, please."

"Room's not been cleaned yet. Why don't you run across the street to Burger World and catch some lunch? I'll buzz housekeeping."

The woman began to laboriously type in their information on the screen. "Name and car registration?"

"The name's on the credit card. And the registration number is on the key ring." Jake pushed both at the foot-dragging clerk. "No need to wait and have the room cleaned. We're in a bit of a hurry if you don't mind."

"Everyone's in a hurry." She grumbled, handing back his car keys, and giving Jake an appreciative up and down. "Ya'll have fun, now."

The elevator was out-of-order. They climbed the three flights, Jake sprinting and Lorie hustling to keep up. The door opened with a regular key, not one of the coded cards the more modern hotels used. Jake pushed the door open cautiously, held Lorie back, and flicked on the wall switch.

The room was a mess.

A gamy smell wrinkled her nostrils. Bedding was tumbled and hung onto the floor. Crumpled burger wrappers were strewn on the dresser top. The wastebasket was piled with empty beer cans, plastic milk containers and soiled wrappers that had once held a children's meal prize. Strom and Matt were living like pigs. Lorie was heartsick.

"This is disgusting."

"Yeah." Jake grinned as he shoved the key in his pocket. "We caught a break."

"A break! He's filling Matt up with junk food while he holes up in a shabby motel room guzzling beer. You call that a break!" She didn't know when she'd been angrier.

Matt needed good nourishing food. He needed his own bedroom, his friends, and his pet.

He needed his mother, damn it!

"Hey." Jake touched her face tentatively. "Welcome back. I prefer the furious female to wimpy waif. It's a break the room hasn't been cleaned, because maybe we'll find something that will help locate them. While you're good and pissed off, let's sort through the trash."

"Fine." She upended the trashcan on the floor. "I doubt anyone will even notice. What are we looking for?"

"Anything that will point us to where they're headed. These wrappers came from the fast-food joint across the street. We'll check there to see if anyone remembers them. Matt's a gregarious kid. He must have talked to someone. See if you can find a phone number or an address. I'll check the bathroom."

"Okay." She began sorting. A nasty job, but she didn't even want to see inside the bathroom.

"Lorie?" Jake called to her. "Come look at this."

She got to her feet and joined him in the bathroom. It was ugly. Wet towels strewn all over the cracked tile floor, hair and crud in the sink. "What in the world is that black goop? Shoe polish?"

"Hair dye," Jake answered and held up the empty bottle. "Ebony black. Strom dyed his hair. I'd guess Matt's, too."

She fought the tears. Jake was right. She couldn't help her son by wimping out. "Damn him. He had no right."

"We'll find a copy center. Alter the photos to show dark hair. Maybe they can age Strom's photo if they have the right computer equipment."

"Couldn't the FBI do that?"

"Sure, if they were so inclined. Find anything in the trash?" He followed her into the bedroom.

"This," she hissed, holding up a crumpled plastic container. "Chocolate milk cartons. And candy wrappers. Matt only gets sweets on special occasions. Too much sugar and he goes postal. When I get a hold of Strom Garrison—"

Jake helped her sort through the remaining greasy food

wrappers and empty beer cans. "Lorie, does Matt like to draw? Make pictures of things that interest him?"

"Oh, sure. Airplanes and cars. Sometimes it's hard to tell them apart, though."

Jake smoothed out a paper napkin on the monkey's nest of a bed. "Like this?"

She looked over his shoulder. "Not Matt's work. What is it?"

"Maybe a map."

"Doesn't look like any map I've ever seen. More like cat scratches."

"If you'd ever seen a map coordinates sketch you might recognize this."

"You mean like in the military?"

"Yeah, we used them on maneuvers. Strom is headed somewhere specific, and this might help us find him."

She pointed. "4/19. That must be a date. April 19th. But what does 12C/Hr mean?"

"Military time. Twelve-hundred hours. Noon."

"And this?" She pointed to a scrawl line of numbers and letters on the back of the napkin. "A shopping list. Bologna and bread. And Fruity ABC's are Matt's favorite cereal. But why would Strom buy two tons of fertilizer? What does this means? $NH4NO3$ and three cans of fuel oil? Food and fuel oil, okay, if he's camping out, but—"

"Let me see that!"

Jake took the crumpled paper from her fingers, swearing viciously. She had never imagined some of the words. His face turned ashen as possible, given his tanned skin. "Jake, what's wrong?"

"I need to get to a pay phone right away. I can't risk my cell."

"Why don't you use this phone? You paid for the room. I suppose after it's cleaned up, it won't be so bad. Or you could use my cell phone. It's in my purse."

"A pay phone. Now!" He grabbed her hand and hustled her out the door. "If this is what I think it is, the FBI will be all over this place within the hour. And we won't need to beg them for help in finding Strom. They're going to want him as much as we do."

CHAPTER 17

————◆————

Dobie Knox prowled the motel room, restless and angry. "Where the hell have you been, Garrison? We're five days from countdown."

"I hadn't planned to bring my kid, Knox. And I had to make sure we weren't followed," Strom said, attempting to placate the short, thick-necked man who paced the narrow space between the bed and the dresser. Strom had used Janet's credit card to rent a room in one of the smaller motels off The Strip. The rooms were old and seedy, but cheap. Also, the place was nondescript. Guests came and went without fanfare.

Knox stopped pacing and pointed a hard finger. "It's Major Knox to you, soldier. Until the mission is over, we follow strict military discipline."

Knox's ability to rally men to a cause had attracted a group he named the New Sons of Liberty. The Sons shared his hatred of the government and its anti-gun policies. Knox didn't believe in paying income tax or in public schooling, and despised the way the courts catered to criminals. People needed to wake up! Women, minorities and gays were undermining the freedoms of this country, destroying the very fabric of America.

Knox was a strutting rooster, but Strom acknowledged

his beliefs were solid. Strom mumbled an apology.

Knox frowned. "Do something about your sloppy appearance. No excuse for it."

"Yessir, Major. I'll take care of it." He'd have to hunt up a dry cleaning establishment and drop off his soiled wardrobe. Knox kept his own fatigues starched and his boots spit-polished and expected the same of his men.

"What happened to your arm? Your face is a mess."

Strom recited the lie he'd settled on as plausible. "Wiped out on the Harley. Wasn't going fast, but hit some gravel and spun out. Don't worry, I can drive a car just fine, and I shoot just as good left-handed as right."

Knox grunted acknowledgement. "Where's the boy?"

"I gave him ten bucks and sent him to the lobby gift shop. Told him to pick up some snacks and a comic book. He'll be gone a while."

"This is a mission soldier, not fun and games. Remember, Strike first, strike hard, and never leave an enemy alive!"

That old bromide again. Knox's personal mantra, and boring as hell after the hundredth time.

"I had personal reasons," Strom said.

"We've no room for personal feelings. If you've set the law on our trail, I'll take you out myself. Don't doubt it."

Strom shifted and felt a shiver of fear. You didn't mess with Dobie Knox, but no way Strom was going to admit to the thirty-grand he had stowed in the lining of Matt's backpack. If things went south, that was his getaway cash.

"No, sir. My old man has the clout to stop any investigation. The kid's good cover. I didn't leave tracks. Never used my name or credit card, or stayed in one place for over two days."

"Good man!" Knox dropped his voice to a conspiratorial whisper. "Trust no one. The government bastards planted a microchip in my buttocks before I left the service. Tracking device. Had to cut it out myself with my combat knife."

"Yessir. I never relax my vigilance, sir."

A few of the Sons bought the microchip story. Strom's

personal opinion was the Knox had excised a giant carbuncle. Still, slicing open your own butt took a particular kind of cold-blooded nerve.

Knox waved him into a more relaxed position. "I don't trust kids. You sure your boy will stay put?"

"I'll get him a burger and he'll watch television for a while. Probably fall asleep. He's a good kid. Knows better than to disobey his old man."

"You damn well keep him under wraps or there'll be severe consequences. That's an order, Sergeant Major."

"Yessir, you have my word." Strom was careful not to let his hatred show. Under the guise of military discipline, Knox walked all over his men. Plenty of them resented it.

Knox flung himself into a nearby chair. He ran his hand over his cropped hair. It was cut so short he appeared almost bald. "I'll hold you to it. What about your cargo?"

"I picked up my quota and spread out the purchases. Plenty of ammonium nitrate available in feed and grain stores in the small towns. Didn't buy enough at any one place to rouse suspicion. You told me to bring all the money I could lay my hands on, so I raided the kid's college fund. I've got almost twenty-grand."

For the first time, Knox smiled.

Strom knew he was sucking up, but Frederick Knox was a man he wanted to keep on the good side of. At least for now. Nicknamed Dobie, because of his boney musculature and a wedge-shaped head reminiscent of a Doberman police dog, Knox had a dog's vicious temper when crossed.

Knox had joined the regular army at eighteen, and was sent to the Mideast as company clerk, but he'd never seen battle. When he applied for the Special Forces, and washed out, he'd gone AWOL and holed up on his uncle's farm, licking his wounds and nursing his hatred of the government.

The bitterness grew.

And hardened into the core beliefs that ruled his soul.

"Can't argue the money won't come in handy, soldier. We're not flush with cash right now. Our sponsor is out of touch until we accomplish our mission."

Their multi-millionaire sponsor, the mysterious shadow creature they all referred to as Four Star. Only Dobie had seen his face, and then only briefly. Feeling foolish, Strom straightened up and snapped off another salute. Knox expected that from all his men, but still the resentment burned. "My boy is proud to be a part of it. The stuff's in the back of my van, covered with a tarp and a mattress. The kid sleeps on the mattress while we're on the road. We're just father and son taking in the sights."

"We'll move the supplies from your van to our storage garage. Quint and Jocko have already off-loaded."

The self-appointed major rose to his feet and strutted around the room, hands clasped behind his back Napoleon style, unwittingly calling attention to his short legs. "We're all heroes, Sergeant. Nothing is as important as what we've set out to do. Not family, not personal ambition or wealth. You understand what I'm saying?"

Properly chastised, Storm nodded.

"It's true the boy is privileged," Knox said. "In five days our group will change history. Even if we fall in the line of duty, others will follow. Perhaps it is fortunate you decided to include your son. Nothing stirs the American public like a child martyr."

Apprehension stabbed, and Strom knew he had to be careful. Most of the inner cadre was totally committed to their leader and his cause. Knox could throw Matt into the fire and none of them would blink. It had been a spur of the moment decision to bring his son along. After Lorie took up with Jake Randolph, it seemed the perfect revenge. But at times Frederick Knox bordered on bat-shit nuts. To anyone with sense, a child martyr would not further their cause.

Particularly, not his child.

There would be a martyr to the cause, all right, but it wouldn't be Matt. Knox was going down. Strom would see to it.

"We'll have to take him along," Knox continued.

"Within a few days our name will be on everyone's lips. Until then, we can't take the risk he'll talk to someone."

"Matt will stay put. He won't say anything to anyone."

"That better be true. We'll consider him a new recruit. You know what I expect from my men, Sergeant Major that includes your son."

You weren't accepted as a recruit until Knox was convinced you were absolutely loyal, absolutely trustworthy. A couple of his early recruiting mistakes vanished, and were never seen again. The group trained hard in the martial arts. All of them were crack shots and had a working knowledge of explosives.

"Can we discuss our target yet, Major?"

"When we conference with the others, I'll lay out the details. One last thing, Sergeant Major Garrison."

"Yessir?"

"No booze until we've completed our mission and we're safely tucked away in New Boston. Then I'll stand you to a weeklong drunk, if that's what you want."

CHAPTER 18

"How much longer are we going to just sit around here, Jake, and do nothing?"

"Hooker's only been on it for three days, Lorie. He'll let us know if he locates Matt. Would you rather fly back home and wait for word there?"

She whirled, fatigue and fear on her face. "Of course not. I'm never going home without Matt."

She was growing increasingly impatient, and Jake couldn't blame her. She was under terrible strain. They'd spent the past few days scouring Denver. Going to the tourist spots where Strom might have taken Matt, showing the doctored photos to attendants at the zoo, the aquarium, Elitche's amusement park. To no avail. If the father and son were still in Denver, they had gone underground.

She sobbed into her pillow at night.

"Something will break soon. The feds are mounting an all-out search for Strom."

"Do you trust this man, Dan Hooker, Jake?"

"My boss does. That's good with me."

After meeting the man, Jake trusted Hooker up to a point.

On the surface, Hooker was a typical FBI agent, impeccably dressed in a dark suit and carefully knotted tie. His light brown hair was stylishly cut, his chin closely shaven. His speech so formally polite, it bordered on cold. By appearances, a desk jockey, a man who operated by the book, but rumor had it that he was not a man to cross. In subtle ways he was different. His pale blue eyes were watchful, opaque with secrets, and he dragged more information from Jake than was given in return. Over six feet tall, he and Jake were eyeball to eyeball, and the agent was in superb shape. He moved with the leonine confidence of a man who knew his body and its capabilities.

Easy to imagine him a fellow Deltoid. Under different circumstances, Jake would have enjoyed going hand-to-hand with the man, just to test his theory. According to Cavetto, Hooker was appointed head of the Bureau's Midwest terrorist team after he returned from a prolonged leave of absence. Further rumors said there had been a trail of bodies left behind, and an FBI open investigation closed.

Hooker wrung Lorie dry of all the information she had to give, and asked to see Jake alone. He got right to the point. "If Gallagher is desperate, will he harm the boy?"

"His mother doesn't think so. I'm not so sure."

"Based on what?"

"Strom always was hot-tempered and willful. But lately he's out of control. I still can't believe he snatched the boy, and it's an indication he's gone over the edge. What have you found out about Strom's militia group?"

"Your tip was good. They have a base camp in the Flint Hills, a small farm owned by a Joseph Knox. His nephew, Frederick, is the acknowledged leader. Their camp is deserted now and the uncle claims he has no knowledge of where they've gone. He gave us a few names. We don't know what they're up to, but the fact that Garrison acquired the makings of a bomb is a serious red flag. We're searching for them throughout the Midwest and Colorado regions."

"Any leads?"

"You know I can't divulge agency business. Not even to DIA, unless the director specifically requests it."

Jake snorted a pithy expletive. "If Strom is an example, they're all dangerous. I assume you've alerted your terrorist response experts."

Hooker shrugged and Jake knew further questions were useless. Judging from the FBI's quick reaction to the evidence he and Lorie found in the motel room, it was obvious the Feds expected violence from the militia group. "You'll keep us informed. Let us know when you find him?"

"Certainly." Hooker didn't even attempt to disguise the lie. "What about Ms. Garrison? Is she in any danger from her ex-husband?"

"Not as long as I'm around."

Hooker nodded, accepting that. "Good. Because I don't have the agents to give her 24/7 protection. You have my pager number. Call me if you get a line on him?"

"I need a weapon."

"No can do." The FBI man left no room for argument on the point.

"Strom and his buddies will be armed to the teeth. I can get a weapon, but I'd prefer it was legal. Federal law mandates a seven-day waiting period and I don't have time to wait. Don't worry, I won't shoot myself or any innocent civilians."

Hooker coughed, or maybe it was a rusty laugh. "I suppose not. Les Cavetto isn't one to hand out undeserved praise. According to him, there's no one better in close-quarter combat. But no dice on the weapon, Randolph. This isn't Afghanistan."

"Isn't it? How big a hole will that much explosive leave when it's detonated? Enough to blow up the US Mint and the surrounding city block? Maybe something also vital to our country. Part of the Air Force Academy? A missile site?"

"You're too savvy by half. I should put you in lockdown until this is over."

"April nineteenth is coming up. The opening battle of the American Revolution. Then there's Waco, and Oklahoma

City. Five days from now. Not a coincidence I think. You can't afford to turn away help when it's offered, despite the fact your agency and mine have problems with cooperation. Cavetto's authority comes from the White House."

The fact that Cavetto's had endorsed him, gave Jake some clout. Unofficial, but it was there and both men knew it.

Hooker hissed in his breath. "Damn. You are trouble."

"Only to anyone who's a threat to me and mine. And my country, Hooker."

The two men eyed each other for a long minute, neither blinking. Finally, Hooker shrugged. "I'll push through the paper work licensing you to carry, and get it to the authorities by tomorrow. I don't want to know where you plan to lay your hands on a weapon."

"Appreciate it."

"And keep it low-key, or I will put you in protective custody. Lorie Garrison, too. I can't afford for any of this to leak to the press."

Jake nodded in understanding. A public panic was something the FBI would avoid at all costs. Jake intended to use his knowledge of what he knew only if necessary. If it was the only way to save Matt.

Two in the morning, and the time of dreams.

It was a small island, so small it was virtually uncharted, inhabited only by a three family settlement of native fishermen.

The terrorists were hunkered down in an abandoned WWII barracks. Heat analysis revealed eight terrorists, six guarding the hostage in the bunker, while two others constantly patrolled the camp perimeter. These were careful men.

The low-slung building brooded silently in the predawn as the twelve warriors approached. Team Delta Four had chuted into the op area in ebony blackness, a HALO insertion aided by night-vision goggles. They recconed on the rocky north shore at 0400. Every man had a specific task and had been thoroughly briefed. Eight terrorists to take down, one hostage to free. ODA (Operation Detachment Alpha), each man with his own specialty, each lethal in his own right. Their commander, Captain Downs, motioned them into position, as they surrounded the barracks. They had throat mikes and earpieces, but until the mission was complete, verbal communication was kept at a minimum.

Puma, their demolition guy and Number One, along with Fox, their Intel NCO and Number Two trooper, moved in first and vanished among the low-lying scrub that grew around the abandoned barracks. Wearing black Nomex coveralls, black Nomex hoods and gloves, their faces smeared with camouflage paint, they were invisible in the darkness. Puma could move with the silent deadliness of his Native American ancestors. He had the hearing of a great horned owl, and Jake swore the sergeant's neck could rotate in a 270-degree angle.

The plan was for Puma to blow the front door with a Mossberg 12-gauge at the same time that Jake, Number Three, and Mike Devlin, Number Four, took out the boarded-up side windows with C-4. A shotgun blast to the door lock and hinges, followed by Puma's powerful kick and the door would go down. They were all banking their lives and the life of the hostage on it.

With the windows out, Jake would toss a flash/bang grenade, to disorientate the sleeping enemy inside. The second assault element would split two and two, with Five and Six backing Puma and Weasel, and Seven and Eight coming in the windows behind Jake and Mike. Infrared reflective tape had been applied around each man's upper arms, enabling team members to spot one another in the heat of combat. In the meantime, the third assault element would secure the perimeter to assure that no terrorist would escape.

A bare whisper in Jake's ear. "Sentries down. Perimeter secure. Move!" Captain Downs' four-man sniper team had come through. Jake's adrenalin pumped while his pulse beat settled. He was in the zone now. No emotion, just do the job.

Take out the windows, quickly, efficiently.

Toss the flash/bang grenade.

The flash exploded with brief, stunning intensity. Protected by their goggles and flak jackets, and all business, the Delta men burst into the bunker. Four of the terrorists' slept with their assault rifles and were foolish enough to put themselves in play. Each was efficiently dispatched with a double-tap. Two shots to the head. The other two, confused and dazed, were quickly secured with the flexible cord handcuffs that each team member carried. If possible, take one alive, they'd been instructed.

It was over in eight seconds.

Slick as grease. A classic takedown exercise.

The hostage was tied to the far bunk. Jake's job was to release her after the terrorists were out of play. The ambassador's daughter, naked and gagged, forced to lie in her own excrement. Unconscious from pain and fear. What had those animals done to her? He unsheathed his combat knife and crept forward to cut her bonds. Until the precious cargo was secure, their mission wasn't a success.

Puma's warning shout came too late.

The flash and roar was deafening. Jake flew backward. Only his flak vest, helmet and goggles saved him from major blast injury. Nothing left of the hostage except bloody shards. A siren wail split the air. Units one and two were down, injured. Jake should have been dead. Dimly he heard Captain Downs shouting orders to the perimeter team. Those outside the bunker had escaped injury.

Jake had screwed up. He couldn't figure why he was still alive. He ate the pain, devoured the blackness.

CHAPTER 19

A warm, soft hand shook his shoulder. "Jake! Wake up."

Groggily he came out of the nightmare. "Must have been dreaming."

"A terrible dream, from the sound of it."

He'd deserved to die.

It had been a bitter lesson. Never, never approach a hostage no matter how dire the straits, until sure there was no explosive device attached to the body. In this case, the bomb was handmade, inexpertly loaded with nails and the hostage had taken the full effect of the bomb. The team walked away with minor injuries. If the device had been expertly built, they wouldn't have. Nothing could change the fact the hostage was dead.

The horror of that disastrous mistake haunted Jake every time his team set off on a mission. And his dreams were never safe. But he had learned. The debriefing that followed had been exhaustive and instructive. They'd all had their asses chewed. It was a mistake none of them would repeat.

He shook off the remainder of the nightmare. "I think I'll get up for a while. I need to run off the bogeyman."

"It's two o'clock in the morning."

"So there won't be any traffic to speak of. Go back to sleep."

To observe the proprieties, he'd worn his shorts and tee shirt to bed, while Lorie buttoned one of his long-sleeved shirts over her nightgown. A line of pillows bisected the king-size bed, serving as a reminder that he wasn't to cross over into her space. He should see about changing rooms, get one with two beds. Separate rooms weren't an option, not until Hooker located Strom, and Jake was sure she was in no danger. He avoided looking at her, knowing she would be soft and vulnerable, with the remnants of sleep still on her face.

The past days had been tough. Since Hooker made it plain that Jake and Lorie were not to leave the Denver area, the two of them had been living in each other's pockets. Bad as the days were, being close to her and unable to touch, the nights were agony.

Jake dressed quickly. With plenty of down time, he kept up his physical conditioning. He ran two miles daily, executed one-hundred pull-ups and pushups each, and used the weight-lifting equipment in the motel workout room. His body was in good shape. His psyche was not. He needed a hard run to shake off the nightmare and the ceaseless ache for sex with Lorie.

"Jake, please. Don't go."

He squeezed her shoulders. "I'll be back in forty to an hour. Don't open the door, even if someone yells Fire."

"Let me get dressed. I'll run with you."

"Later, if you want a workout, we'll run. Right now I'll be setting a pace you can't keep up with."

They'd run together several times the past few days, and always he slowed his stride for her. Her shoulders drooped. Both of them knew he could leave her in the dust anytime he wanted. The door whispered shut, closing off further argument.

Jake took a minute to do some leg stretches, his eyes raking the brightly lit parking lot. A green Chevy Impala was parked in a shadowed spot, across from their unit. Five years old and dinged up a bit, it was totally nondescript. It figured. The feds had alternated surveillance duties, sometimes in a dark blue minivan, sometimes a white Taurus. All the vehicles needed a trip through the car wash and looked like hundreds of other vehicles on the road.

Jake would have thought a lot less of Hooker if he hadn't had them watched. Why should the FBI believe their assertion that they had no idea where Strom was? In Hooker's place, Jake would have been cautious too. Jake had made no attempt to shake the tail, and the agents were discreet. The past two mornings they'd followed at a safe distance while he and Lorie jogged their two miles through the residential Westminster area of north Denver. Lorie hadn't noticed, but why should she? The shadow world was alien to her. He grinned. It was his civic duty to check out how the public servants were performing this morning.

He rapped on the driver's window. The window was rolled down and the occupant glared at him. "Yeah?"

"Just wanted you to know I'm going for a run. Alone. One of you is welcome to join me if you like, while the other stays here to keep an eye on Ms. Garrison. Agreeable with you, gentlemen?"

Swearing freely, the agent on the passenger side climbed out and shucked his suit coat and tie, while his partner reached for the mobile phone. Jake cocked his head. "Better lose the holster and piece. It'll slow you down."

The gun and holster followed the jacket onto the front seat. "Think I can't keep up? Special Forces hot dog or not, think again."

"I'll spot you a block and lose you in half-a-mile."

The guy was in better shape than Jake gave him credit for. It was close to two miles before the agent folded. Given the fact the guy wore standard Brooks Brothers' suit pants, white dress shirt and polished wingtips, and Jake had poured it on, that was a damn good showing.

Lorie heard the tremor in her voice as she asked Jake not to leave, and was ashamed of herself. Throwing the sheet aside, she switched on the bedside lamp. Sleep would be impossible. Despondently, she flicked through the shopping and news channels, searching for something to take her mind off their fruitless search for Matt. She knew they were doing all they could, but her fear grew daily. She missed her little boy to the point of pain. Missed holding him and caring for him.

Humphrey Bogart flashed across the screen in black and white. Ingrid Bergman's pure profile appeared beside him. Casablanca. The quintessential story of star-crossed lovers. How appropriate. *We'll always have Paris—*

That's how Jake found her. Propped up in bed sniveling, supported by their supply of pillows while the music swelled and the closing credits flashed across the screen.

"You've been gone over an hour," she said crossly, blowing her nose on the top sheet. "And missed a great movie."

"I can tell it elevated your mood. I hope you slobbered on your side of the bed."

She sniveled again. "I don't slobber. These are tears of appreciation for a great love story. Don't even think of crawling in here. You're all sweaty and you reek."

"Not as romantic as Bogie, huh? Remember African Queen? As I recall he was a bit scruffy in that flick."

She sighed, remembering. "Oh, that was a wonderful old movie. Two people ready to die together for a principle they believed in." She glared at his chuckle. "Do you have one romantic bone in your body, Jake Randolph?"

"Apparently not. At least they did the deed before the Nazis hung him. Ask any guy what's important."

"They didn't hang him." she said icily. "Providence intervened and saved the lovers. Sex happened off screen in those days and left it to the imagination. Maybe they didn't do the deed, as you put it."

"They did it all right, and I can imagine plenty. Like how you look under that shirt. Since I've resisted the impulse to peel it off you despite a permanent hard-on, doesn't that make me a little romantic? Waiting for you to make the first move?"

She threw a pillow at him.

Big mistake.

He was on top of her in a second, laughing and tickling, while she squealed in protest. "Not fair, you lummox."

"You started it."

He outweighed her by eighty pounds, but she was wiry and full of pent-up energy. He took a few gut punches before he captured her wrists and pinned them. "Now, my fair beauty," he sneered. "You pay the rent or I take the shirt."

She pouted and gave up the struggle. "You're supposed to be the hero, not the villain. The villain never wins!"

"I've always thought the villain had the best part. The hero was a wimp. Paying up instead of knocking the landlord on his ass."

"You have a point. Bogie always played a bit of a bad boy." She licked her pouting lips and the humor faded from his face. His brown eyes darkened; the red striations gleamed. She liked that. "Would you settle for a kiss, bad boy?"

"It's a start," he said, voice gruff with intent as he bent his head and fit his mouth with hers.

Delirium took her. Jake's kisses were narcotic and should be illegal. She could smell the tang of sweat and outdoors on his skin, could feel the heat radiating from his body. A slow burn flamed in her belly, the rich scent of him as intoxicating as brandy. She melted under the aggression of his mouth and tongue, opening herself to his assault. Pure bliss.

Was she crazy? She was in a motel room with the most gorgeous hunk of man she'd ever known, a man she'd never gotten over, and she'd erected a wall of pillows between them. No more. The wall was coming down. Her arms enclosed his neck. She arched her body under his and pressed against his arousal.

He pulled away, chest heaving. "Angel, that tasted like more."

"Lots more," she whispered.

"You're sure?"

She reached to unbutton the shirt that served as her robe and slim protection against the passion in his burning eyes. She needed desperately to feel his touch, to feel alive. To forget for a little while.

"Don't move." He pushed off the bed and headed for the bathroom, shedding his tee shirt.

She knew what he was after. He kept a box of condoms in his shaving kit. A good thing, because she felt very fertile at the moment and wanted his sex on a primitive level so deep she would have let him have her in the motel parking lot with the FBI agents lurking nearby.

The shadow men were there and had been for days, but Jake hadn't mentioned it, so she hadn't either. He was being protective. She wouldn't disillusion him, but really the man was clueless about how good she'd gotten at taking care of herself.

It was maybe the shortest shower on record. Five minutes later he emerged from the bathroom, his wet hair plastered to his skull, a towel around his waist and a box of condoms in his hand. She sat up in bed, the sheet draped loosely around her torso and watched him approach, her lower limbs heavy with anticipation. He set the condoms on the bedside stand and dropped the towel, completely unembarrassed.

Her eyes admired. His arousal was huge and heart stopping, nested in dark curls. His lean body was firm with muscle, his gut flat, and shoulders broad. Coffee-colored hair splayed across his chest, and dusted his forearms and legs. God, he was so male.

"Look all you want, angel, but lose the sheet," he said, his voice hoarse with desire. "I want to see you naked before I touch you again."

She went up on her knees and allowed the sheet to slip away. "Maybe I should get in the shower, too?"

He grunted a negative. "I love the scent of you. I'd know it anywhere. I could pick you out blindfolded, from a dozen women."

So he wasn't a Bogart with words, but his rough honesty and the raw hunger on his face tugged at her in a way pretty speeches never could. She held out her arms and he pulled her up against his chest. She melted against him and returned the kiss, matching his fervor. For now, anyway, he was hers. He lifted his head to catch a breath. She seized his ears and pulled his mouth to her breast. She would give him everything, but she would take too.

They toppled back on the bed, his mouth pressed to her breast. Moans from her, growls from him, bodies writing, and hands frantic. She clasped his erection and rubbed it against her inner thighs, riding him.

"My God! So much for foreplay." He groped on the bedstead for a condom, his hands fumbling as he tore open the foil. After sliding on the protective sheath, he tumbled her back with one sweep of his powerful forearm, spread her legs and thrust. She gritted her teeth. It wasn't pain exactly, but it wasn't pleasure either.

He groaned. "Lorie, angel, I thought you were ready. I don't want to hurt you."

"It's okay." She wiggled her bottom and spread her legs further. "I want all of you. Just go a little easy at first."

Taking deep shuddering breaths, he moved in slow increments, the effort showing in the tortured strain on his face. It had been a long time for her, and he was big.

"Enough," he gasped, pulling out. "We start over. I don't enjoy this if you don't."

"Please Jake, sweetheart—"

"Shh. In good time."

Praise God, she called him sweetheart. Long, drugging kisses were in order for that alone. He kissed her until she was limp, his hands stroking, reacquainting himself with her pleasure points. The back of her knees, her inner thighs, the hollow of her throat. Her skin was as sensitive as a rose petal. Even when they were kids, she'd responded to his touch like no other woman. How had he been fool enough to let her get away? Oh, yeah, she'd married someone else. He slid his fingers between her thighs, finding her slick with passion. She whimpered a plea, but he ignored it.

"Why did you do it?" he demanded hoarsely, his fingers merciless.

"D-Do what?" She bounced frantically under him. "Jake!"

"Marry Strom. You knew I would come for you that spring. After I graduated."

"How would I know? You never—oh, God, don't stop."

He stilled his fingers, his thumb pressed against her swollen nub of desire. "We agreed. We'd meet at spring break and hash it out. Imagine my surprise when my mother sent me the news clipping of your splashy wedding. You forgot to send my invitation."

She tried to pull away, but he held her down. He'd wanted some answers for years. At the moment he wanted answers more than he wanted sexual gratification.

"Liar," she spat, twisting under him. "What about Sugah Baby? Should I have invited her too?"

He eased his fingers away, enjoying her whimper of protest. Later she'd do more than whimper. She'd come like a roller coaster and scream her lungs out. "What the hell does that mean? What sugar baby?"

"Your sweet lil' southern grits lover. Your roommate. The one whose bed you hopped into right after we separated. You left me no choice."

"Wait a minute, my roommate at Tech? Abe was from Alabama, but he was six feet of lean mean, and a very heterosexual male."

"I called. And it wasn't any Abe-six-feet-of-male who answered. It was a woman, her voice dripping syrup. Laughing when she named me your hayseed lover. Thanks for that, Jake Randolph. Using me for pillow talk. Know what? I'm out of the mood, so get off me."

He kept her pinned. "Let's get this straight. You called me at the apartment and a woman answered. A woman with a southern accent who told you she and I were lovers?"

"Yes! Don't deny it. She answered the phone. You

played me for a fool." Her voice sounded suspiciously close to tears.

"Damn. When did you call? It had to be Rita Sue. She was a manipulative slut. She went out with Abe for a while and he must've told her I had someone at home. She made some moves on me and I ignored the invitation. There wasn't any woman after we separated, Lorie, until I heard you were married. Even if I'd been inclined, which I wasn't, I was up to my eyeballs in studies and too busy to fool around."

He rolled away and let her go, his mind spinning. Damned if it didn't sound like something Rita Sue was capable of.

She sat up, clutching the sheet. "You weren't her lover?"

"Hell, no. Never could understand what Abe saw in her."

"I don't believe you! Why didn't you call me? I wanted you to so much!"

He stroked her cheek in regret. "I should have. For one thing, I ran out of money and lost my cell service. Seems Verizon likes to be paid. For another, the professors at Tech are ruthless with their graduation standards, and I was damn busy trying to keep up my A average. And arrogant enough to believe you'd wait for me. Why didn't you?"

She bit her lip and ducked her head. No answer. Wait a minute. What had she meant, leaving me with no choice? More answers better be forthcoming, and right now. "Lorie, what else do you have to tell me? Don't turn away, because I won't let you."

She flared her nostrils. Men and their lies. Damned if she'd let him get away with it again. "Matt was born in August, six months after I was married," she snapped. "Do the math, genius. Why do you think I married so fast? Strom was past history when you and I were together and I meant to keep it that way, but you gave me no choice. What kind of man gets a woman pregnant and jumps straight into another woman's bed? And you're the one who's lying. She knew about your damn birthmark! The one on your lil' ole cute butt. Explain that, lover boy."

He hissed in a breath. "So she saw me naked. She was a sneak. You were pregnant? Not possible. We were careful. You were on the pill and I wore a condom. Double protection."

"Yes, well, not always." She shook her head. "Remember we both lied to our parents about what we were up to? I told my mother I was spending the holiday with a sorority sister. We took off for that motel in KC in such a hurry I forgot my pills. It didn't seem important with you taking precautions. But we slipped up a couple of times. You were hungry to get your hayseed lover into bed, remember? It seems we're a fertile combination. Strom couldn't get me pregnant for diamonds and pearls, and God knows he tried."

"Sweet blazing hell!" He leapt to his feet, white-faced under his tan. "You're saying Matt is mine?"

CHAPTER 20

Oh, God, what had she done? She meant to carry the secret to her grave. Never meant for Jake to know. Nor Matt. "Jake, I—I—"

The denial wouldn't come. She probably looked guilty as sin. She'd been so angry that she'd struck out with her lethal secret. The payback would be horrendous. If Strom didn't kill her, chances were good that Jake would.

He grasped her shoulders, his face taut with rage. "You are in deep trouble!"

She didn't even try to get away. His strength was overpowering. Her chin trembled as she stuck it out in defiance. "Do you plan to hit me? I'm used to a man taking his hang-ups out on me. What are a few more bruises?"

He dropped his hands from her bare shoulders like she was on fire. "Don't ever compare me to him!" He spat the words, his dark eyes narrowed. "This is hardly a hang-up. Remember this, angel. I would never, ever use my fists on a woman. No matter the provocation, I would never hit you. And since the urge to turn you over my knee is damned near overwhelming right now, you can put that worry out of your mind."

She gulped. "Okay."

"You kept my son from me! What the hell gave you the right?"

It was too late for denials. Her only defense was a fierce offense, and rolling to her feet, she went for the jugular. "I carried him in my body for nine months! I fed him with my milk. Helped him with his first steps, nursed him through teething and the croup. Were you there when he fell off his bike and broke out his front tooth? When he was baptized? When he started school? I was all he had."

His fists doubled and he turned his back on her. "You deceitful bitch. I would have been there and you know it. Did you ever intend to tell me?"

"I did phone. I suppose if you had asked me, I would have called off the wedding. But it was obvious, that is, it seemed obvious, you'd lost interest."

"So you took the word of a voice on the phone, the word of a stranger that I was playing around. Even if it was true you could have had the decency to tell me the truth. Does Strom know? That would explain him coming at me with a knife."

Fair was fair and she owed him. She owed him for the sperm that had made Matt if for nothing else. Two stupid kids with overactive libidos, who couldn't keep their hands off of each other, had made a miracle.

Warily she approached him, aching with regret. "No. At first it was best for Matt this way. Later, when Strom and I split, Matt was a little boy. I knew if I contacted you, told you, you'd want to be a part of his life and I couldn't cope with that. I deserve everything you think about me. I see how you are with him, and wish I could do some things over."

His shoulders quivered under her light touch. "Jake," she whispered. "I made a bad decision, but at the time it seemed the only road open to me."

"No more lies between us, ever. Whatever happens, no more lies."

"No more lies. I swear."

"When we find Matt, we'll tell him together. You're

right; I will be a part of his life from now on. Financially, and every other way I can manage."

How could she tell Matt? He might never forgive her. "No! We're okay the way things are. Grampa Hy buys his school clothes and pays for his karate lessons. Strom pays support monthly, even if he sometimes gets behind."

She bit her tongue. What an idiot to mention Hy's part in this, and Strom's child support. Why hadn't she left it alone? She braced herself for further fury.

It happened. He exploded in litany of curses and slammed his fist into the wall, in a reaction worse than she'd feared. Jake didn't swear much, but military life had enriched his vocabulary and he was in a towering temper.

The wallboard displayed a fist-sized dent. She refrained from mentioning it. His chest heaving, he leaned against the wall, nursed his fist and stared at her. As if seeing into her naked soul. Oh, oh. She retreated. Not fast enough. His hand shot out and grasped her elbow. He marched her to the desk and plunked her naked bottom in the chair.

"There's paper and a pen in the drawer. Write it down."

"Write what down?" She crossed her arms over her bare breasts and tried to become invisible. "And what makes you think you can order me around?"

"Because I'm taking charge. Write down every penny Strom has paid out for Matt's support. Including your maternity costs. I'll see he gets a check as soon as he reappears. If there's one man I won't be indebted to, it's Strom Garrison."

"I can't do that!"

"Matt's my kid. I pay his support. Simple as that. Write it down. I'm losing patience, so get busy."

God help her if this was his patience mode. Her hands shook as she reached for the paper and pen. "How can I remember? The past two years are pretty cut and dried, but surely you can't mean the years before? I couldn't even begin to estimate that."

"You'd better. I mean for every day of his life, everything from food to medical care to clothing. Everything."

"Jake, it would be so much! Thousands and thousands."

"I can get ninety grand for the Maserati on the east coast. I have some solid investments. The army pays me just fine and I don't spend much. I can scrape it up, whatever it comes to, so don't worry about it. Just write."

"You paid ninety-thousand dollars for a car!" She was appalled.

"What else did I have to spend money on? I used the pay I'd piled up and drove it out of the showroom two weeks ago. But you're right; it's an indulgence I can no longer afford, so the Maserati goes. Write it down, get dressed and I'll order breakfast. We have a lot to discuss and can do it better if we're not hungry and naked."

She was trapped. Jake's strength of will was formidable, and he meant business. He would insist on going public, and Strom would go berserk.

CHAPTER 21

T hat's odd."

"What?" Lorie's hands trembled as she tied the laces on her running shoes. She needed a run to mellow out. Jake had decided on a fair settlement and emailed his stockbroker to liquidate his account. He'd done it with the same slashing ruthlessness he approached any problem. It had to be done, so the sooner the better.

Her insides roiled. There'd been other demands. Partial custody. The right to have Matt for several weeks a year during summer vacation. His intent to send child support.

He was so immovable in his demands, Lorie reverted to shouting. Never happening! She'd get a lawyer! Deny the whole thing! Fine, Jake replied, his face stony and implacable. He'd demand a DNA test. That ended that argument. A DNA test would only confirm what she knew absolutely, that Matt was Jake's biological son.

While Jake saw things in black and white, Lorie was intensely aware of the grays. The problems were overwhelming. How could she tell her son that she'd lied to him for years? Strom would be out of his mind with rage, although the money might go a long way to sooth his pride. And Hy? Hy and Esther Garrison loved their only grandson fiercely. They probably wouldn't believe her when she told them the truth about Matt's heritage. Her own mother? She shuddered to think. It was a mess, and it didn't help that it was a mess of her own making.

Jake hated her. He'd made that plain.

Not that her anger was spent. She'd been abandoned ten years ago and wasn't over the pain. She tied her hair back in a ponytail and attached her water bottle to her waistband. She meant to run until her legs ached, until she dropped in exhaustion, until her mind shut down. They needed to be apart for a while.

"What's odd?" she repeated automatically.

"The feeb car is gone. Hooker has called off his dogs."

"Good. They were getting on my nerves."

He raised an eyebrow. "You knew they were there?"

"I'm not an idiot, Jake, despite my past record in the brains department. Obviously Agent Hooker suspects I know where Strom is. Or that I'm in touch with him. I just wish it was true."

He let the curtain drop. "I'll get my shoes on and run with you. Hooker must have his reasons, but I don't like this. I need to contact him."

"Do what you want, but I'm going alone. I can't be around you now and you don't want to be near me, that's obvious."

"Lorie, I may be mad at you—"

"Now there's one of Randolph's famous understatements."

"All right, I'm furious. Doesn't mean I won't get over it eventually, or that I'd leave you unprotected. So chill out until I can talk to Hooker. Eat your breakfast. You didn't touch it."

"I don't eat before I run. I'll take my key card with me so you can go anywhere you like. I'll see you when I see you." The motel walls were closing in on her.

He moved in front of her and blocked the exit. "You're not going anywhere without me, so forget it."

"Think not?" Hands on her hips, she stuck her nose up to his chin. "Move away or I scream. Good and loud, and I yell rape at the same time. Wanna put in some jail time, Randolph? How would your new boss like having to bail you out on an assault charge?"

"Damn, that does it."

He grabbed her around the waist and drowned her intended scream with a thorough kiss. The kiss was ravaging, tasting of coffee and mint toothpaste, of Jake. He was aroused again. She could feel his hard length against her belly. They'd had a horrendous fight, they were mad as hell at each other, and still he wanted her. Reality fell away. There was only the spinning glory of his mouth on hers and the burning ache deep in her gut. When they kissed she lost all commonsense. She wanted him as badly as he wanted her. No, she wanted him more. Because she loved him so much it hurt, and while he might lust after her, love wasn't in his vocabulary.

"Lorie," he rasped, holding her tight against his tall frame. It was a question; it was a prayer. She dug her fingers into his shoulders, and wrapped her legs around his, not able to get close enough. The sizzling attraction between them exploded.

"Yes," she said to his unasked question.

He tipped her onto the unmade bed and tore at her clothes, ripped off her shoes and socks, her tee shirt. Simultaneously she tugged at his shorts and found his pulsing erection, the heavy sacs between his legs. The time for talk was over. There was only this man and the fiery needs of her body. He might be motivated by primitive impulse, but she wanted him despite his motivation. She wanted it all. Within seconds he spread her legs and lunged into her, the silken liquid of her arousal smoothing his passage. Two hard thrusts and he was deep inside of her.

He propped on his elbows and took a shuddering breath. "My God. Don't move, or I'm a goner."

Waves of heat radiated from the source of her pleasure, spread to her belly, her breasts, to the tips of her fingers and toes. Just having him fill her was sending her into climax. She'd fanaticized about this for years, had thought she remembered what it was like to have him, but the reality was so much more. She arched her back and dug her fingers in his hair, sliding against his erection, rocking her hips, no longer in control of thought or action. There was only sensation and this hunger that bordered on madness.

Only him and this deep, blissful connection that fed her soul. Dimly she heard his panting growls, felt his heart pound as he slammed into her.

There always came a point with Jake's lovemaking when she lost herself. When he owned her body so completely that she floated in his arms, mindless and boneless with ecstasy. Magic. They were magic together. Her ears roared. Heat spread from her toes to her thighs to her breasts. The sensation of warmth glowed low in her belly until the orgasm speared, splintering her body into a thousand pieces. She convulsed around his hard length and sobbed with the pleasure. Seconds later he joined her and lightning lanced again, swamping her with his climax.

How could she live without this?

Why had she let this happen?

Tears leaked from her eyes. "I am such an idiot. A spineless, slutty idiot."

"Sweetheart, it's okay," he soothed, and kissed her tears. "It wasn't anyone's fault. We couldn't stop any more than we could hold back the sun. This thing between us, whatever it is, is too strong, too crazy."

"This doesn't settle anything."

"No, but it sure as hell was good."

"We didn't use protection."

"Maybe we'll get lucky and it won't take. Or maybe we'll make another kid as great as Matt. Whatever happens, I'll take care of you."

He was still planted deep inside of her and kissing her with the sweetest tenderness, when the knock on the hallway door sounded. Lorie didn't care. She wasn't ready to release him and wrapped her legs around his waist when he lifted his face, frowning. "Tell them to go away," she whispered into the hollow of his throat.

"Who is it?" he demanded gruffly, the echo reverberating from his chest. She could feel the rumble of his voice arrowing down to the cleft between her legs, and shivered in delight.

"Maid service, sir. Do you want your room cleaned? There's no *Do Not Disturb* sign out."

He looked at Lorie, then at the door. "Come back later," he growled.

"An hour," Lorie said, tugging his semi-erection deeper with her internal muscles. Instantly he spasmed and his girth increased, causing her to gasp and convulse.

Jake grinned and adjusted her closer, cupping her bottom in his palms. She dug her heels into the back of his thighs as he began to move in and out of her. Slowly. "Give it two hours," he called to the maid. "And be sure to knock."

CHAPTER 22

The phone rang and Jake groped for it, still half-asleep. Lorie snuggled closer and he wrapped his free arm around her protectively. She sighed and settled back into a deep sleep. It was the first rest she'd gotten since Matt disappeared, and he didn't want to wake her. He picked up the receiver and spoke softly. "Randolph."

The voice on the other end was that of a stranger, a remote official voice whose words didn't register at first. Easing his arm away from Lorie, he sat up. "Say again?"

"Officer Delamont. Colorado State Police, sir. I need to speak to Lorie Garrison. Regarding her missing son."

A female voice. A woman officer trying to keep her tone neutral, but not quite succeeding. Fully alert now, Jake glanced at the sleeping woman in his bed and kept his voice low. "Speak to me. I'm the boy's father."

Officer Delamont hesitated. "Well, I'm not sure. I was told—"

"I don't care what you were told," Jake snarled. "We've been searching for Matt for a week. If you have information, spit it out."

Lorie stirred and opened her eyes. "Matt?" she whispered. "Is it about Matt?"

"Shh," Jake cautioned, his full attention now on the voice

at the other end of the phone. If true, the officer's news was horrific. When Jake hung up the phone his mind was spinning. The facts were sketchy. He wasn't going to buy this until he checked it out.

"Jake?" Lorie struggled to a sitting position. "What is it?"

He took a deep breath and fought for control, trying to assimilate the news. It wouldn't do either of them any good if he lost it. "Lorie, take a quick shower and get dressed. We need to make a drive up into the mountains."

"What for?"

"I'll explain on the way." He had to organize his thoughts, to plan. My God! Their son. Their sturdy little boy, born with Lorie's stubborn chin and colorful hair. And he saw it now, with his own lanky build, cowlicks and penchant for mischief.

She clutched at him in a panic. "Something's happened to Matt!"

With the fifty-mile drive north to Loveland behind them, they headed straight west on highway thirty-four and soon were engulfed by the majesty of the Rockies. High above, glaciers peaked the mountaintops, and along the roadside the green and white of aspen groves interspersed the towering pines. Any other time Lorie would have thought the scenery breathtaking.

For several miles they climbed; the motor of the rented sedan lugged down in the effort. Jake pushed the car to its limit, squealing around curves and riding the brake. Being a total flatlander and country girl, it wasn't a drive she would want to attempt. She was too numb to be afraid. If what the state police reported was true, it wouldn't matter if they went over a cliff.

They passed backpackers and bicycle riders, some headed up, some down, but the vehicle traffic was light in either direction. They'd encountered the first roadblock a few miles back, and Jake had talked them through. No one was allowed to pass who didn't live in the area or have official business near the tragedy.

"How much further?" Lorie asked.

She was exhausted with spent emotion. Jake had held her in his arms when he told her about the tragic flash flood and the possibility of Matt being a victim. They had comforted each other. Never had she imagined that her tough soldier could break. She reached for his hand and he squeezed briefly, and released it to return his attention to the steep mountain curves as they began to head downward.

"We just passed a sign that said Big Thompson Canyon: Two Miles. We should run into another roadblock soon, and the state patrol will take us the rest of the way."

They drove alongside a torrential mountain stream that rushed through channels cut into sheer rock. He brought their rented Honda to an abrupt halt. The road ahead was obstructed with abandoned vehicles. Bewildered, Lorie shook her head. "What is it?"

"Thrill seekers. And people like us checking on loved ones. Lorie, let's keep our heads. The description the woman gave me was sketchy. I'm not convinced she had the right information. Over fifty people were victims of the flash flood."

"A young boy, the official said. Pulled out of the river from a smashed black minivan. Strom drove a black van. The license plates matched."

"Black vans are as common as flies, and there may have been a mistake about the plates. Plenty of people come here to vacation. A resort and several campgrounds were wiped out and the floodwaters have barely subsided."

Strom had loaded his van with outdoor gear before he left Kansas. It made sense he had headed for a mountain campsite. No wonder they had been unable to find a trace of him in Denver. But she kept her hope, and Jake was doubtful. There had been no definite identification of the victim.

"I guess we'll have to walk from here." She opened the passenger door and got out. Jake followed, not bothering to lock up, and abandoned the vehicle alongside the dozens of others that clogged the road.

Her heart pounded wildly. She had to be sure.

If it was true, the grief would engulf her and life would cease to matter. Everything she felt for Jake was distilled and made stronger and better in their son. Her hopes, her sweet memories. And her everlasting love. Stoically she held on to her sanity. Soon. She would know the truth soon.

A man in a state trooper's uniform approached them. He carried a clipboard and looked exhausted, his pants were grimy and damp. "Sorry, folks. Unless you have official business here, you'll have to turn back. No one allowed past this point."

"I'm Lorie Garrison. They called me. About my son."

The trouper gave a quick glance at his clipboard. "You can proceed to the next checkpoint and a vehicle will carry you to the Loveland National Guard armory, where they've set up a temporary morgue."

Lorie supposed the man was unaware of his callousness. He'd probably been at this for hours, and had gone into robot mode. Jake uttered a graphic curse and caught her to prevent her from pitching on her face. The other man stepped back, his expression even more wary.

"Sorry, ma'am. Sir, unless you're on my list, you'll have to remain behind."

Lorie put out her arm to forcefully prevent Jake from going for the trooper's throat. "Randolph," he grated. "Jake Randolph. And I don't give an effing damn about your list. I'm the boy's father."

The trooper looked doubtful. "We have a Strom Garrison on our missing, possible victim list."

"Listen, you officious bastard, we're looking for our son. Let us by."

"It's all right, officer," Lorie broke in. "He's Matt's father, I'll vouch for him."

Other vehicles approached, other car doors slammed. Other feet ran toward them. Hysterical voices screamed questions.

"Okay, proceed." The officer waved them through the rope barrier and turned his attention to the approaching mob. Jake and Lorie broke into a run, leaving his sonorous voice behind.

"Sorry, folks. No one is allowed past this point."

CHAPTER 23

Lorie had never seen such savage destruction. Floodwaters had barreled through the gorge with the power of a dozen freight trains. Piles of broken timber littered the steep sides, along with jagged pieces of buildings and ripped sections of vehicles. The waters had receded to a sluggish brown river, but ran swift and deep and carried debris. Uprooted pine trees the size of telephone poles bobbed in the lethal water. Giant boulders had been torn from the mountainside, thrown haphazardly about by the hand of God. Or the devil.

"It's unbelievable," she said.

"We got over a foot of rain in forty minutes," offered the trooper who drove them to their destination. "The mountainside was denuded last summer by a forest fire, so there wasn't enough vegetation to absorb the deluge. The water poured straight down the canyon."

Lorie took a deep breath. "Why didn't you warn people?"

"We tried, ma'am. We posted signs about the danger of a flashflood and asked visitors to move their campsites to higher ground. We broadcast warnings on television and radio. But sometimes warnings are ignored, and it came too fast for people to escape. We lost two forest rangers trying to reach the endangered campsites."

Two National Guard members dressed in green khaki fatigues stood at parade rest by the front doors of the armory. Other similarly clad soldiers were stationed around the low-slung building, insuring no curiosity seekers were admitted.

"Why are they carrying weapons?" Lorie asked. "They wouldn't shoot people!"

The state trooper, who had driven them from the flood site to the nearby town of Loveland, removed his mirrored sunglasses and tucked them in his shirt pocket. "The men on guard duty carry Tasers, a devise that disables a suspect long enough to get him in cuffs. They're not going to shoot anyone. They're here to keep order and to help out."

He and Jake exchanged glances, a soldier-to-soldier glance, and Lorie wondered about the truth of that. The men on duty might carry Tasers as the officer claimed, but many of them also sported rifles.

As they neared the hanger-like structure, the enormous side door rolled open, and two guardsmen pushed a trolley cart bearing a shrouded object toward a nearby ambulance. An elderly couple tottered alongside the wheeled stretcher, the woman sobbing, the man somber-faced and shaken. As the body was loaded into the ambulance, another was unloaded and carried into the armory.

"Oh, God, Jake," she whispered hoarsely.

Instantly he took her arm. "We'll get through this together."

The official who greeted them at the front door wore civilian clothes and a nametag identifying him as a city councilman. He carried the ubiquitous clipboard. "May I see some identification? My condolences on your loss."

The councilman had his best face on, kind, anxious. She preferred the brusque manner of the state trooper. This man was an obvious politician, and she was reminded of the greeters at Wal-Mart. How dare they make a circus of this tragedy! She trembled and Jake squeezed her hand. "Show him your driver's license, Lorie."

The man's Adam's apple bobbed. "Thank you. Everyone

in town has pitched in. We've set up a tent with coffee and sandwiches for the family members and the workers, and the pastors of our local churches are available to offer comfort to the bereaved." He made a check beside her name on his clipboard. "You may go in, Mrs. Garrison. There will be an officer inside to direct you."

Regretting her initial reaction, Lorie whispered a thank you and stepped woodenly into the building. To be greeted with the odor of death. A charnel house.

"Lorie, listen." Jake spoke softly, rapidly. "Let me do this. You stay outside and I'll come back as soon as I can."

"No! I need to. Come with me if you like, but I need to see if it's my son." He didn't argue further, simply clamped his arm across her shoulders and led her inside.

It was ordered chaos.

Row after row of shrouded bodies lined the concrete floor. Stoic National Guardsmen stood around the room, legs straddled and arms clenched behind their backs. White-coated medical personnel bent to their tasks. Two young women hovered beside one of the bodies and held each other as a medical assistant lifted the sheet. One of them crumpled to the floor, the other fell to her knees and frantically tried to revive her. A sharp command from the medical attendant and two guardsmen sprang to help, lifting her inert form to one of the empty cots alongside the cement walls. A stocky female in a nurse's uniform hurried to assist, stethoscope in hand.

The living were suffering here.

Bile rose in Lorie's throat. *Oh, please God, not Matt.* Not my son. She knew she hadn't always been a good person, but if she could have this one thing, if Matt could come home to her, she would be better. She would never ask for another thing as long as she lived. She would be more patient. Stop worrying so much if the house was clean and spend more time with her child. Go to church regularly, be a den mother—

"Lorie," Jake's voice rasped in her ear. "Sweetheart, you have to hold together a little longer."

She blinked back to reality and swallowed the grief. "Yes."

Jake spoke to the patrolman in charge, and he nodded. "This way, sir, ma'am."

Her legs moved like wooden sticks. The stench assaulted her nostrils; her eyes blurred. They halted beside a small, shrouded body, and the officer stepped back to allow the medical attendant to withdraw the sheet. Lorie lost her courage. She flung herself at Jake, shaking in terror.

A millennium passed. The only reality was Jake and the rough feel of his jacket on her cheek, the dampness of her tears, and the sick fear that racked her body.

"Lorie." He shook her gently. "It's not Matt, sweetheart."

She raised her head, really seeing him for the first time that morning. Unshaven, his hair in unruly peaks, the lines around his mouth deeper than usual. But his wet eyes were steady.

"Not Matt?" she whispered.

She had to know. She had to be sure. Pulling herself together, she looked down at the dead child. Not quite a child, at least not one as young as Matt. A boy, perhaps early teens. Long dark hair, his face the gray of a marble statue. At her gasp of horror, the attendant quickly covered the body.

The officer spoke. "We'll have to search further for the victim's ID. I'm glad for you folks. Plenty here today would like to be in your shoes."

"Before we leave," Jake said, his voice soft, but the tone lifted the hairs on Lorie's neck. "I'd like to speak to the official in charge."

The man started toward the door, leading the way. "That would be Colonel Wisenkamp of the Colorado National Guard. He's at the flood site, directing the operation. No unauthorized civilians allowed in that area. I maybe can put you in touch with one of his officers. Everyone here is swamped, as you can see."

"Not the Guard commander. Whoever is in charge of notifying a victim's family. Who's coordinating that part of the disaster effort?"

"The State Patrol set up a command post at the courthouse. If you're worried about someone else who's missing, maybe someone there could help."

"Fine." Jake stepped into the outdoors, his arm still firmly around Lorie's waist. "If someone could take us there, we'll be on our way."

The patrolman took a long look at Jake and for the first time, his impersonal manner slipped. Wariness showed on his smooth face. "There's a problem?"

"Damn right. That boy didn't come close to matching Matt's description. Why was she put through this? I realize you people are under intense pressure, but this is inexcusable. I want a talk with whoever's responsible."

Gratefully Lorie breathed in the clean mountain air. Jake was right, she realized. A horrible mistake had been made. Had other parents been needlessly exposed to this pain? Along with Jake, she wanted some answers.

The two men held eye contact, until the officer shrugged and stepped back. "I'll make a phone call."

CHAPTER 24

Jake gave the road his complete attention. Traffic intensified as they merged into highway twenty-five. The hour drive of that morning would be closer to two hours on the return. Denver rush hour was a melee of honking horns, with drivers intent on reaching their destinations. Next to him, Lorie was quiet. Too quiet. He ached for her, but said nothing, just stroked her hair occasionally, to remind her he was there. Mentally he reviewed what he had learned from the coordinator whose job was to ID the victims.

Hooker was behind it.

Hooker had notified the state patrol office that a militia group was camped in the mountains, and they were armed and dangerous. Which explained why the guardsmen were carrying weapons and were on alert for Strom's license plate number. The FBI request was given priority. When the rescue workers found the wrecked minivan with the Kansas plates, Lorie was contacted along with the FBI.

Jake had two questions he intended to ask. One: Why did Hooker suspect Strom's group was near the canyon? Two: Why had Lorie been allowed to make that horrendous journey, and where had the authorities gotten her phone number? He had no clue as to the first answer, but was pretty sure he had the answer to the second. Hooker wanted them out of the way, and this was a surefire method to accomplish it. Fed big shot or no, if that was what happened, Jake would pin the man's ears back.

Lorie shrank against the leather seat, huddled into a ball, her cheeks smudged with grime. He reached over, raised the armrests and released her seatbelt.

"C'mere," he said softly, pulling her against him. "Lay your head in my lap. You're exhausted."

She sighed and stretched out, settling her head against his thigh, her arms curled against her chest. "You haven't had any rest either. Are you okay to drive?"

He thought of forced marches that lasted two days with little sleep or food. Ordeals that involved hauling sixty pounds of gear and a heavy-barreled Remington rifle over rough terrain at a pace that would kill a horse. Of two-mile runs that had to be completed in eighteen minutes. Of river swims fully dressed in fatigues, hauling a pack and wearing boots. Delta had a tougher training regime than any of the Special Forces. A soldier did these things and did them right or washed out. Jake had learned to function through pain and exhaustion.

But that pain had been physical and easily healed. Her anguish was deeper and unrelenting. It would never go away until they found Matt. Jake would do what he could to make it easier, if only for a while.

"I'm fine. I'll wake you when we get there. Sleep, for now. We'll find him."

Jake nudged her as they pulled into the motel driveway. The blue neon sign flashed *No Vacancy*. It was deep twilight; the moon rose on the horizon. She rubbed sleep from her eyes, but didn't look rested. Her face was creased from the coarse khaki of his trousers, and there were bruised hollows under her eyes. Her thin shoulders hunched as she stared at the lodge. The windows of their room leered back at them with dark and sullen eyes. He knew that she dreaded go inside. Matt wouldn't be there, and entering their empty room would unleash another torrent of grief.

He locked the motel door behind them and led her to the bed, pulling back the covers. "Are you hungry? Do you want something to eat? I can order food."

"No." She shook her head. "I'm thirsty, but I just want to sleep."

Sleep was the last thing he would allow her that night. Her lassitude had less to do with the need for rest, and everything to do with depression and despair. Sleep would only trigger nightmares. "I'll bring you a cold drink. Use the bathroom, wash your face, brush your teeth. Shower if you like. Whatever will make you feel better, okay?"

She nodded.

Jake took the empty ice bucket to the hall alcove where the icemaker stood, stopping to feed the pop machine. In their room he loaded two glasses with frosty cubes and cola. Sounds filtered toward him: movements in the bathroom, water running, and the door opening as she shuffled back to bed. She gave him a tremulous smile as she accepted the drink and took a sip, her hands shaking.

"Thanks. I'm a total wreck. Whoever that poor child was, he wasn't—wasn't—Oh, God, Jake. I miss him so."

He knelt and removed her sandals, squeezing each bare foot gently. Her skin was cold and lifeless. "Lie down, sweetheart. I'll take care of you."

He slid her slacks down, tossed them aside and caressed her calves and ankles. He undressed her, kissing her lips, her shoulders and throat, her abdomen. His nostrils flared at the scent of mint and soap mingled with her womanly perfume. When she was stretched naked beside him he continued to stroke and comfort, until her skin warmed to his touch. She quivered and reached out to him. Quickly undressing, he crawled in beside her.

She curled trembling fingers in his chest hair. "Jake, don't leave me tonight."

"Sweetheart, I'm not going anywhere."

He spread his palm over her abdomen and captured her

mouth in a kiss, slanting his head, deepening the caress. Slow and gentle, working her lips against his. His tongue explored and tangled with hers. Wet, hot and fiery. She sighed and moved under him, but he didn't release her mouth. His hand reached lower, to probe between her legs. She was aroused, but not enough.

He turned his attention to her breasts and cupped one in each palm, tonguing the beaded buds. First one, then the other. Her sweet essence flooded his senses; his erection grew to the point of pain. Instinctively she spread her thighs and lifted her body in a bow.

Small sobs of distress erupted from her throat. "Oh, God, what are we doing? We shouldn't do this."

He lifted his head. "We're making love, angel. And yes, we should. We need this comfort."

He kissed away the salty moisture on her cheeks and soothed her with his hands, gentling her. When her tension relaxed, he rolled her on her stomach and massaged her shoulders. His hands moved down the slender column of her spine to the smooth roundness of her buttocks. No question she had the greatest ass in the world. He cupped the heart-shaped mound, kneading with his thumbs, savoring the tactile pleasure of touching her. She squirmed, clutching the pillow. "Jake, I want you."

"I know. Soon."

He turned his attention to the back of her thighs, massaged her calves, and moved down to the soles of her feet. All the while murmuring soothing sounds. When she tried to roll over, he pressed on the small of her back, pinning her. Another time she could take charge, but not tonight. Tonight he would pleasure her until she was sated, until nothing existed except the two of them. Tonight was theirs.

She beat her fist on the pillow, begging him to hurry. He slipped his finger between her thighs, slid one, then two into her. He sighed. She was wet and wild for him. He went up on his knees and entered her, pulling her firm buttocks against his belly. And almost lost it. She was a tight fist around him, slick and throbbing. This was it for him. She was his life mate and there would never be another. Not for him. He hoped not for her.

He went still and let her body ease to accommodate his girth. She gasped in surprise. They had never used this position. He liked to see her face when she came, to cover her mouth with his, to taste her breasts. But this way he could position her body for intense pleasuring. He found her center of desire, and massaged in rhythm to his strokes.

She clutched the bedcovers; cooing moans burst from her throat.

God, she felt good. For a few seconds he let his own delight spiral. Not enough to lose control, but enough to enjoy the sensations. He hadn't stopped to use protection, to sheathe himself. This was the act of love as it should be, her tender flesh pulsing around him, his hard length pressed inside her woman's heat. It didn't matter if she got pregnant. In fact, he welcomed the idea. He would take care of her as long as there was breath in his body. She and Matt would come with him to Virginia. He wanted to watch his boy grow up, for the three of them to be a family.

"Jake!" It was a shriek of urgency, a plea. He put his mind to completion and pumped fast and deep, his thumb pressed against the nub of her sex, as it hardened, became hot and grew hotter. She was very close. She shuddered internally and cried out. He was intent, thrusting deeper, the pressure of his thumb drawing out the ecstasy for her. She shuddered again and the surging climax took her. She uttered a cry and collapsed under him. When her tremors died, he kissed the nape of her neck and rolled her over to face him and cradled her, shushing her.

"Oh!" She moved against him and reached with her hand. "You didn't—"

"Not yet. Come with me again, sweetheart."

"I—I can't. It was too much."

"Not over." He entered her inch by inch, testing his control. And began again.

He refused to leave her alone for the rest of the night.

When he wasn't inside of her he was petting, kissing her. In slow tempo, he forged the physical bond between them into bands of steel. With his body he loved her. With his skill he drove the demons away and held them both on the sweet edge of ecstasy. She had come several times. Twice he'd been unable to stop himself from taking his own satisfaction. He entered her one last time in the deep of the night.

"Now," she whispered, accepting him.

"Now," he agreed. "One more time, sweetheart."

"I can't!"

"Yes. Once more." He knew her body, knew exactly how to touch her, what to stroke and tongue, when to be gentle and when to be rough. She was slick with his spent passion, a silken sheath fashioned just for him. He took her up again. She gave a last cry as her body convulsed around him and dragged him over the edge with her. The intensity of his climax swamped his senses. He could hardly breathe. Slowly he came down, his body jerking in aftershocks.

She buried her nose in his chest, shuddering. "Love—you—so much—"

Her voice was a hoarse whisper, almost inaudible. Had he heard right? Her head dropped. He lifted her chin. It lolled back against his chest. "Sweetheart?"

She was out. Sated and exhausted. Tomorrow would be soon enough to ask her, for them to make plans. He pulled the sheet around them and dove into oblivion beside his heart's mate.

CHAPTER 25

They had originally been eight.

The seven men crowded in the motel room waited for word from Major Dobie Knox. Strom stirred uneasily, and wondered if any of them had last minute doubts. Up to now they'd followed Knox without question. It was time for some answers; time to coordinate their plans and to start the final countdown. In forty-eight hours the world and three-hundred million people in the United States would know that the New Sons of Liberty were a force to reckon with.

The door to the adjoining room opened and Knox strutted in.

"At ease, soldiers. I have news. Our friend, Old-timer, has done his job. Thanks to him, the federal boyos are merging on San Francisco, convinced the Golden Gate Bridge is our target. Which means the federal cops here in the Vegas area will be at a minimum. We're green for go; countdown begins at eleven-hundred, day after tomorrow."

A cacophony of voices erupted. Questions, exclamations of triumph, laughter at the gullibility of the feds. Knox held up his hand for order.

"Early this morning, our comrade hung himself from the bars of his cell, but not before the FBI found the phony evidence he carried. It was entirely his choice to go out this way, rather than let the cancer eat him alive. We're not in the business of losing our comrades-in-arms, unless necessary. Notice of the event was sent over the AP wires, but we don't expect it to hit the national news. And if some smartass reporter sniffs around, the police and FBI will stonewall him."

Murmurs of excitement rose from the men and Knox puffed up. "Half-a-million dollars was deposited in an offshore bank account in his daughter's name. The amount all of you will receive upon the completion of our project. Our sponsor pledges that if any man goes down during this operation, his family will receive his share. Questions?"

Questions burst from all sides. Knox looked annoyed. Strom figured Knox hadn't actually meant to hear questions. He was too arrogant and enjoyed his own authority too much. Once again Strom reflected that the Sons would function better when he was in charge, instead of their unstable leader. Well, that day would come. Soon.

"In good time," Knox said snappishly. I have some questions of my own. Sergeant Major Garrison, is your son secured?"

"Yessir. We moved last night to another motel."

"No problems? No trace of your identity left behind?"

"No sir. I left the boy in the van at all times. No one saw him. I paid cash and checked out in advance."

"Your son knows nothing?"

"Nothing. I told him we were traveling again. Told him we'd stop at the Hoover Dam for a little sightseeing. He's excited about it."

"Good. You, your son and myself, will be in the van with the explosives. I'll drive, due to your incapacitated right arm. If a nosy security guard stops us, he'll see two adult tourists and a child taking in the sights. All very routine."

"I wondered about Matt—"

Knox held his hand up again. "Not now. We'll adjourn to the next room where I have a projector set up, and will continue the briefing there."

Obediently the men trooped next door and sprawled in varying positions on the bed and floor. For once, Knox seemed to ignore protocol. There was an air of expectancy on every man's face. This is what they had trained for. Knox flicked on the Dell projector, and an aerial map of the area flashed on a portable screen.

"The dam is surrounded by rocky, harsh land, mountains and desert. Make no mistake about it; there will be a massive manhunt. You have maps of your escape routes and where supplies have been stashed. Memorize the coordinates and then destroy them."

Strom knew that Knox had a different escape route planned, a copter pickup and a straight flight north. Except Strom and Matt would be aboard, and Knox would be left behind to disintegrate along with the dam. Four-Star had Okayed the change of leadership. Their sponsor was as uneasy with Knox's metal deterioration as Strom was.

Their commander's piggish eyes swept the room as every man grunted agreement. Strom thought of the dangers of scrounging for survival in the dry desert mountains, and was grateful for the copter plan. He'd head for New Boston with Matt. The bitch could burn in hell. Strom never intended to return to Kansas. There'd be willing women at the camp in New Boston. Plenty of them, and he'd have money in his jeans to live high after the heat died down. He turned his attention to the briefing.

"After the mission, make your way to New Boston," Knox continued. "As you know, it is impregnable to anything short of a nuclear bomb. Even if the feds locate us, the FBI and the ATF won't dare go that far. Waco taught them about the dangers of excessive force. We'll be hailed as heroes, men!"

A spontaneous round of applause erupted and Knox beamed.

He cleared his throat. "Sammy and Quint have cruised Lake Mead for the past five days. The people at the marina are accustomed to their rented houseboat going out every morning. How's the fishing, Quint?"

"Snagged us a couple of mermaids, yesterday," Quint leered. "Prime stuff. Drunk as skunks on wine and Retinal. A few hours of two on one even wore Sammy out." The men hooted and applauded. Sammy's success with women was highly celebrated. The boy was so good-looking, none of them were even envious. Blonde, blue-eyed, and hung like a horse. With the intelligence of tree bark.

"Good. You fit right in with the other vacationers."

Knox stroked Sammy on his shaggy platinum head, and Strom wondered anew about the relationship between their leader and the group's youngest member. Knox had no use for women, but he had a real soft spot for Sammy. It was a suspicion Strom would never voice aloud. Not if he valued his skin. Knox was a vocal homophobe.

"Now, here it is." Knox picked up a pointer stick and resumed his pompous instructor's role. "Sammy and Quint will be on the lake early. No whores this time around, boys. The suitcase will be aboard. Harry, you and Mel will be in scuba gear, and will drop anchor here." He pointed with his stick. "About a half-mile behind the dam."

"We'll make a dry run tomorrow, coordinate our timing, and be sure the scuba gear is in order. Got it, so far?"

Murmurs of agreement, nods of approval.

"At approximately 1000 hours, Harry and Mel will slip overboard, and climb on the DPVs. They will dive as close as possible to the dam, and release the bomb. Intelligence suggests that there is submerged steel-netting strung across the river above the dam, so expect that possible barrier. Use the acetylene torches if necessary. The bomb will be set to detonate at twelve-thirty hours, so you boys will need to accelerate your underwater vehicles and hightail it back to the boat. From there you're on your own. Get to shore, climb on your hogs and vamoose."

Strom was grateful he didn't have Harry and Mel's job. Driver Propulsion Vehicles were tricky to maneuver. Especially given the undercurrents in the lake depths.

"You're just vacationers having fun," Knox said. "If someone gets nosy, take them out. Strom and I will stall our vehicle on the Tillman Bridge at 1030 hours, where Jocko will pick us up. Security will eventually come to check on the van, but you and I will be long gone, Strom."

Strom interrupted, a real no-no. "Excuse me, what about my boy?"

Knox pursed his lips. "Yes, your boy. We'll have to sedate him."

Strom stirred uneasily. "Sedate him?"

"Necessary, soldier. We can't have him carrying on. We'll use enough to knock him out. You have a problem with that?"

What could her say? "No sir."

"Good. Sammy, would you get the suitcase from my closet?"

Excitement thrummed in the air amid dead silence. Strom could sense exultation, curiosity, and fear. Definitely fear. Sammy retrieved a gray case from behind the closet door. It was the size of an airplane carryon bag. How could such an innocuous device blow a hole in the earth a half-mile wide and five-hundred feet deep? The one kiloton device carried the destructive equivalent of a thousand tons of TNT.

Sammy grinned an idiot grin, and hurled the suitcase toward Jocko.

"Catch!" he chortled.

Jocko took the fifty-pound case in his midsection, the air whooshing out of his lungs. He came up with the suitcase intact, cursing Sammy with the blue language of an ex-marine, his face paper white, body shaking. Every man in the room shot to his feet, crying out in shock. Strom clawed at his belt for his Glock, his lunch a heartbeat from hurling. Sammy burst into a crazed cackle of delight.

"That's enough, Sammy!" Even Knox had a limit to the bizarre behavior he would tolerate from his favorite.

"Strom, stand down! The device is harmless as long as the timer switch is off. The suitcase is in your keeping Mel, Harry. Guard it well. For all our sakes."

Sullenly Strom holstered his weapon. Someday Sammy would go too far with his freakish pranks and get his ticket punched. From the look on Jocko's face, it wouldn't take much.

"Finally, men," Knox paused for dramatic effect, ignoring the resentful glares being sent Sammy's way. "Keep true to our motto. Strike first, strike hard, and never leave an enemy alive."

CHAPTER 26

Lorie woke with good vibes about the day. Matt was near, she could sense it. Today Jake would contact Hooker for answers. Today they would locate Matt.

Every tender part ached and memories of Jake's lovemaking returned with each throb. She looked at the digital clock by their bedside. Eight a.m. She was starving. For the first time in days, food sounded wonderful. She heard the drum of the shower and thought about joining her lover, but the shower over tub arrangement barely fit Jake's size. While she didn't plan on needing sex for another year and a half, she didn't underestimate his ability to bounce back if she rubbed against him naked.

First things first. Coffee. Eggs. Toast. Then a shower. Room service promised their breakfast would appear in thirty minutes. She cracked the bathroom door. Jake stood in front of the sink, shaving. And impressively naked.

He saw her in the mirror, lifted an eyebrow and crooked his finger, grinning. "C'mere."

"Don't even think about it, you—you sex machine." She sidled in cautiously.

He chuckled and lifted her by her elbows, depositing her bottom on the sink vanity. "Angel, I'm good, but I'm not superman. You're safe for a few hours. Come in while I shave. Did you order breakfast?"

"Uh-huh."

"How'd you sleep? You look rested."

"Mmm. What there was of it was good. You?"

"Terrific." He stretched his mouth sideways to give his wiry beard a swipe.

"Let me do that." She took the razor from his hand. "Stretch your neck back."

"So you can cut my throat?"

"You're the fearless warrior, remember? Besides, it's a safety razor." Carefully she scraped across his throat, watching his Adam's apple bob. His neck was thickly sheathed with muscle. "What's your dress shirt size?" she asked idly.

"Twenty/thirty-five," he said, tilting his chin. "Any other pertinent measurements you'd like?"

She rinsed the razor under the faucet and renewed her task. "No, I think I have that one down. It's adequate."

He snorted and pressed his soapy nose against hers. "Adequate, huh? How soon you forget."

She grabbed the can of shaving lather and squirted his chest. "Stand back, buster. I'm armed."

He retrieved his razor and the can of shaving foam. "You are a dangerous woman. I'll finish the job myself."

"I need the bathroom."

"I'll hurry. We'll be sure to get an apartment with two bathrooms." He hustled her out the door and shut it firmly.

Lorie took a deep breath. We'll be sure to get an apartment with two bathrooms? What was that about? She'd told him she loved him, but how did he feel? And did he think she'd live with him, when she had Matt to consider? She and Jake Randolph were having a serious talk. As soon as they found Matt.

Jake hung up the phone and rubbed his freshly shaven chin. "Hooker will meet us in an hour. He's not happy. Something big is in the air. I don't like it."

Lorie's optimism faded a bit. "Not something to do with Matt!"

"I don't know, but we soon will. Are you ready?"

"Almost."

Lorie pulled on jeans and a short-sleeved cotton shirt. She reached for her sandals, but at the last minute changed her mind. She could move faster in her kicks. Jake was dressed in similar fashion. He shoved his gun in the holster in back of his jeans and pulled his tee shirt over it. Hooker had come through with the gun permit, and Jake had purchased the weapon through some private source.

She finished dressing as her dread increased. The gun was a reminder that Strom and his friends were lethal, that her son was among dangerous men. Criminal men. "Jake, you're not hiding anything from me? About what agent Hooker said? About the men Strom is with? You're frightening me."

"When I know something, you'll know it."

The phone rang. Jake frowned. "Hooker better not cancel."

"It's my cell phone. In my purse." Maybe it was her mother. Maybe there was news about Matt. Not too many people had her cell phone number.

"Mom?" The quivering young boy's voice knocked her off her feet.

"Matt! Thank God, sweetheart. Where are you? Are you all right?"

"Mom, I'm scared. Can I come home?"

"Of course! Just tell me where you are! Jake and I will come get you!"

"Is Jake with you? How's Roly-poly?"

"He's fine. Listen, baby, we need to know where you are."

"A big town with lots of lights. We drive around a lot. Last night we stayed at Cowboy Pete's Motel. But we moved again. This sign has a pink bird with long legs."

"A pink bird. Did you see the name?"

"Huh-uh. It's dancing bird and part of the sign is burned out. Dad's been gone most of the night. He went to meet some friends and said he'd be back by morning. I'm really hungry."

Desperation clutched her. Her son was afraid and she was terrified for him. Who were these people Strom was involved with? Part of the militia? Matt was sturdily independent and didn't scare easily. "Listen to me, honey."

Jake mouthed the words. Tell him to get out of there!

"Matt, get out! Now! Find a policeman, or someone in charge at the motel."

"Dad said I had to stay here. He got really mad about it." Matt gulped and whispered. "He'll be mad I called you, won't he? I remembered your cell phone number, but he didn't say it was okay to call. He'll yell at me."

Feeling helpless, Lorie looked at Jake. Gently, he took the phone from her fingers. "Matt, this is Jake. Hi, kid. What've you been up to?"

Lorie pressed her ear against the receiver.

"We went to see the white tigers," Matt said. "I never saw a white tiger before. They were neat."

"Uh-huh. Sounds neat. Tell me what else you saw."

"Well," the boy's voice sounded doubtful. "A pyramid. I asked dad if we could go inside, but he said people lived there. We drove by lots of tall buildings with bright lights. But no grass or trees. I like Kansas better."

"Me, too. Did you see any other names?"

"One had a pirate ship with a skull and crossbones and it said Treasure Island. Tomorrow we're going to see a big dam named after a president. And a lake. Maybe go fishing."

"Look around the room, Matt. Do you see any stationary or match books with the motel name?"

"Huh-uh. I think Dad's coming. I gotta hang up."

Lorie grabbed the phone. "Matt, listen. I'll keep my phone with me, and you call again. Okay? Whenever your father's not around. I'll tell him not to yell at you, okay?"

"Okay." Again the voice quivered. "If I can."

The line went dead. Jake caught her and the phone.

"Oh, God, Jake! We have to find him. He's so scared."

"At least we know where he is."

"In Las Vegas."

"A dam named after a president. Hoover Dam. God, what are those crazy assholes planning?"

"Whatever is happening, my little boy is scared and all alone. And he's hungry. Damn Strom Garrison to hell!" Once the sobs started, she couldn't turn them off.

FBI agent Dan Hooker snapped off the recorder he'd used to take their statements. "We'll trace the call, Ms. Saxton. Are you sure you've told me all the boy said?"

Hooker had appeared quickly when notified of Matt's phone call. The two agents who accompanied him were stationed outside the motel room doors. Hooker occupied the only chair in the room, while Lorie sat on the hastily made bed.

Lorie nodded dully, worn out from crying and the strain of the ruthless interview. Jake paced their motel room, obviously furious. With Hooker. At the situation.

Jake whirled. "This is crap. You've had a tap on our phone since we checked in."

The FBI man nodded. "True. But not her cell. That will take some time to trace."

"Why'd you pull your guard dogs, Hooker?"

"You burned them, so what good were they?"

"Don't shag me, Hooker. You wanted me to make the tail. They weren't subtle. Lorie figured it out, too. Why pull them off? No longer concerned about Denver, right?"

Hooker looked bemused. "Any chance you'd be interested in a job at the Bureau, Randolph? The DIA will get along fine without you. Cavetto's pulled in the cream of the ex-Deltas, and it hacks me."

Lorie looked at Jake in surprise, her mouth open with a question. He shook his head. She let it go unasked. More secrets.

"I want to know what the game is," Jake said softly. "Did you bait us into that trip into the mountains?"

"The agency had nothing to do with the fiasco at Big Thompson. Some state official got his wires crossed when the Kansas license plate appeared. We think Garrison switched plates with another van. Maybe more than once."

"There's more to it. Those guardsman were heavily armed."

"Part of the militia camped near Big Thompson. They slipped through our net."

Lorie jumped to her feet. "With Matt? And you let them get away!"

"They're experienced woodsmen. Riding motorcycles and taking the back trails. We lost them. No excuse."

Jake narrowed his eyes. "If you've located that boy and haven't told us—" The unspoken threat hung in the air.

"As far as we know, the boy isn't with the bikers."

"You're lying. I don't know what the penalty is for decking a fed," Jake said. "But I'm about to find out."

Hooker gave him a measuring look. "Can't say as I blame you. Some other time, maybe. I have a plane to catch."

"That's it?" Lorie's voice shook. She was thoroughly angry. This man was a federal officer. He was supposed to help people. "How dare you! This is my child. Something awful is going on. You either give us some answers or I'll go to the police. I'll have them trace the phone call. I'll go to the newspapers and offer a reward. Jake and I will find him. I don't trust you."

"I can't let you do that, ma'am. There will be a federal officer posted outside both these doors to see that you don't do anything rash. Your phone here will be disconnected and I'll take your cell as evidence. You'll be placed in protective custody until this is over. We care about your boy, Ms. Saxton. But there are other factors to consider."

"Forget it," Jake snapped. "You're not leaving until we get some answers, and we're not going into any so-called protective custody. What are you afraid of?"

"I'm not free to discuss this. And the decision is final." Hooker started for the door, and ran into a very angry, very determined ex-Delta, blocking his path.

"You better listen to her, Hooker. You may have the power of the U.S. government behind you, but this is the boy's mother. Give her some answers."

"No. I'm sorry."

"Gulliver," Jake said.

Hooker stared. "What?"

"I made a call before we met, Hooker. Not from this phone, not from the Lorie's phone. Gulliver is a personal friend, and one of the best hackers in the business. If he doesn't hear from me every two hours for the next forty-eight, a message will be sent to all the major newspapers and television stations in the country. Exposing the Sons and the threat they pose to the Southwest. It will go out as an official bulletin from the National Security Agency. A Code Red alert. Warning the public to stay away from the following projected targets: Golden Gate Bridge, the US Mint in Denver, Hoover Dam, the Los Angeles airport—"

Hooker snarled an expletive and turned an interesting shade of purple. The FBI man took a breath, struggling with his temper. "You don't bluff, do you?"

"Bet the farm on it." Jake smiled, showing his teeth.

Hooker reached into his jacket pocket for his Sat phone and tapped in a number. The conversation that followed was brief and precise. Probably one of the few secure cell phones in the country, Jake reflected. Our tax dollars at work.

"All right," Hooker said, after he hung up. "When this is over, some folks in the FBI want a conversation with you about this Gulliver fellow. Seems he's been a thorn in their side for some time."

Puzzled, Lorie looked at Jake. He gave her a squeeze of reassurance. "I guarantee that Gulliver will no longer be a problem. He'll be out of the hacking business for good."

Hooker snorted. "If this is some teenage kid, operating out of his basement—"

How about a middle-aged Kansas farm wife? Jake had left his high-powered laptop at the farm, and his fleet-fingered-on-the-keyboard mother had been given the code to break into the secure DOD site. She was positively gleeful at the prospect.

Jake shrugged. "Let's talk. I want everything."

"What I can." Hooker loosened his tie and sat on the bed beside Lorie. "I'll give you ten minutes. Then I have to be out of here and catch a plane. I'm serious, Randolph, so don't screw with me. What do you want to know?"

"You're headed for Vegas? Is Hoover Dam the target?"

Hooker lifted a shoulder in surrender. "Matt talking about the dam clued you?"

Jake nodded.

Hooker snorted. "Here it is. The San Fran PD picked a guy up three days ago on a tip from the Golden Gate Park Police. A female officer spotted him bicycling across the bridge and taking shots with a video camera. The cops are antsy about terrorist threats these days. The guy ditched the camera, but they found it in a trash barrel. Along with some stuff which they turned over to us. He made it easy."

"What did you find?"

"Blueprints of the bridge with the main support struts and suspension pillars clearly marked. Some C4 in the right places and the entire structure would go down."

"Sounds like good police work." Jake said.

"What does it have to do with Matt? Or Las Vegas?" Lorie asked.

"The Sons have adopted the American eagle as their symbol. You can't imagine how that offends me. This guy had the perquisite eagle claw tattooed to his right ankle, which makes him one of the Sons. Do you remember a tattoo like that, Ms. Saxton?"

Lorie shook her head. "Strom and I haven't been together for over two years. I never saw a tattoo."

"It's the mark of membership. We identified the guy as a Ralph Dooley, through his service record. Served in Iraq. But he turned out to be a red herring. Frederick Knox is a devious bastard. He wants us to concentrate our attention on San Francisco. You're right, the real target is the Hoover."

Lorie gave a startled cry, and Jake hugged her close. "Holy hell, they are nuts. How'd you get the guy to talk? Drugs? Not that I care how."

A snort. "He thought he was dying of cancer. He tried to hang himself in his cell after dropping the bait. The cops took his belt and shoelaces before they put him in a cell, but he had a wire threaded through his pants seam that would have done the job. We put out a fake report that he'd succeeded in his attempt. He talked.'""

" He was going to kill himself? He's a fanatic!" Lorie's voice quavered.

"He intended to. Until our doctors gave him the correct diagnosis. He's dying all right, but not from cancer. From radiation poisoning."

"What?" Jake exclaimed. "They have a nuclear weapon?"

"Yes. This man Dooley brought the device into the U.S. through Mexico six weeks ago. In a small suitcase. Went through customs without a problem. He's kept it stored under his bed ever since. Geiger counter went wild. Everything in the bedroom was hot, the mattress, the floorboards, the bedding. The guy was being slow-cooked."

"Are you sure he's with Strom's militia?"

"Dooley admitted the connection. The man's royally pissed. Nuclear poisoning isn't a nice way to check out. To top it off, he was promised a payoff to his daughter when he died, and that turned out to be bogus."

"How the hell did the Feds let it such a fuck-up happen? A nuclear weapon coming across our borders!"

"You can believe we've tightened up our border security checks since we heard about this. From what our experts have been able to piece together, it's a small, but dangerous and dirty bomb."

"My God, Matt is near a nuclear weapon?" Lorie was beyond shock. Both men wore grim expressions that didn't ease her terror.

"Hell," Jake said, running his hand through his hair in agitation. "That border's a sieve. Everyone knows that. But how'd they get hold of a nuclear device? Even if they found a source, the Sons don't have the kind of money. It would take millions."

"Actually, it seems they do. They're a more widespread organization than we first thought. Knox just commands one small branch of it. You'll probably hear about it when you report to Langley."

"It makes convoluted sense to use a nuke. The dam is too immense for a fertilizer bomb to do much damage. But a nuclear weapon? Different story."

"Yeah, it would be a major blow to our infrastructure. The Hoover furnishes electric power throughout the southwest. Lake Mead would disappear and flood thousands of acres of farmland. That doesn't begin to cover the dam's symbolic value. The bastards chose their target well."

"Why would Garrison gather the material for a conventional explosion if they have a nuke?"

"We don't know for sure. A diversion, probably."

"When?"

"Tomorrow. April nineteenth. Sorry, Ms. Garrison, but you can see where your government's priority has to be right now. We must, and will stop these men."

Lorie stuffed her fist in her mouth to avoid crying out again. She was on the edge of hysterics. Didn't anyone understand? This was her son! "Please," she whispered. "You must help us. I beg you."

Jake stared at Hooker's face as if he was the devil. "If that's your official stand," he said, "we'll be in Vegas as soon as we can catch a plane. We'll find Matt ourselves."

"Let the pros do their job." Hooker winced. "Ah, hell, you are a pro, aren't you Randolph? If you go after the boy, will you stay out of the rest of it?"

"Absolutely."

Lorie knew that look on Jake's face, and it was an absolute lie.

"You're not to move on Garrison until we have our hands on the nuke. Or I'll keep you here and let your hacker do his worst."

"Put that way, what can I say?"

Hooker gave him a sour look. "Yeah. Page me when you get to Vegas."

"Lorie needs her phone back. Matt may try to contact her again."

"All right. Let me know immediately if that happens." The agent stepped into the hallway and motioned to the female operative guarding the door. He murmured a few words and the woman handed Lorie's cell phone back to her. The two of them swept out the door to the parking lot. No one said a friendly goodbye.

Lorie clutched her cell phone like a lifeline. *Please, Matt. Call me soon, baby.* "Why do I have the feeling he made this too easy?"

Jake ruffled her hair, smiling ruefully. "Mama Saxton didn't birth a stupid daughter. Want to bet we'll find all the flights to Vegas booked? It's a full day's drive. By the time we get there, whatever is going to happen will be over."

"So what's our plan?"

He laughed. "If Hooker only knew. You're the devious one. We'll charter a plane. Don't worry, we'll get there."

"Won't he have those blocked? Warn the private charters not to book us?"

"Not this one. He doesn't even know about it."

CHAPTER 27

The private airfield was carved out of a valley amidst the Rocky Mountains, located west of Colorado Springs. A small metal hanger, a gas pump, one plane and a short runway. A twin engine Cessna perched like a fragile bird below the snowcapped titans.

His name was Fletcher Ansari. Jake called him Puma and Lorie understood why. It was the fluid way the man moved. Not as tall as Jake, probably five-ten, lean and well-muscled. A white-toothed grin in a sun-darkened face, an air not so much of cockiness, as that of supreme self-confidence. Another warrior and a dangerous man. And one of Jake's best friends.

"It's a pleasure," Puma grinned at her as he took her hand, the grin transforming his hard face. "Don't break my heart. Tell me this thing between you and Jayhawker is temporary madness. I'm willing to wait five whole minutes for you to end my misery. We'll get married. Have two-point-five kids. A dog. Drive a minivan—"

Okay, maybe it was cockiness.

"We've got to get you laid, Ansari," Jake said amiably. "It's way past time for you to lose your virginity."

"I'm so agreeing," Puma said solemnly, his hand on his heart. "If the lady is willing?"

Lorie cleared her throat. "Ahh—no. Sorry. I think."

"Flyboys," Jake said. "Crazy, but you gotta love 'em. Is this puddle jumper of yours trustworthy? Or is the duct tape all that holds it together?"

"Please, you wound me. It's in as good shape as the bird mechanics at the Air Force Academy can keep it. Which is pretty damn good, if I do say so."

"I thought the academy was jets and supersonic bombers and such," Lorie said.

"If they want me to instruct their greenies in survival techniques, they let me fly in. No way I'm driving highway 25 during rush hour. That's dangerous."

"This from a guy who jumps out of airplanes to fight forest fires," Jake said.

"You teach at the academy?" Lorie asked. "Jake said you worked for the U.S. Forestry. Smoke jumping."

"During the fire season. April through September. When the snow comes, the fires fizzle out. I get some vacation time, work at my ranch, and for a few weeks show the straight-arrow boys a piece of the real world. They keep my Cessna in shape and sometimes I hitch a ride in one of their metal chariots. It works out."

Jake shrugged. "Former 82nd Airborne. Still in the reserves. What can I say? They're all wacky."

"Smoke jumping sounds—ah, like an exciting life," Lorie said. Actually it sounded terrifying. "I'm sure we're in good hands to get us to Vegas."

"Problem is," Puma said, totally deadpan. "I only have two parachutes."

He was kidding. At least Lorie hoped so. "Really? What will you do if Jake and I have to bail out? Maybe you just flap your arms and fly?"

Her lover burst into laughter and Puma grinned. "Sharp-tongued lady," he commented to Jake. "I like that. Where'd you find her?"

"Kindergarten," said Jake. "And she's wearing my brand, buckaroo."

"Much as I'm enjoying this—" Lorie said.

Just like that the tomfoolery shut down.

"You're in a hurry," Puma nodded. "Jake filled me in. Tough about your kid. I didn't file a flight plan, because we won't land at Vegas. I've got a buddy who owns a few thousand acres fifteen miles north of the dam, on the Nevada side. Has an airstrip cut into the desert. Jericho Okayed us to land there, and he'll have an all-terrain vehicle ready. He faxed me maps."

"I owe you big time, Puma," Jake said. "Did you get a hold of the stuff I need?"

"Ruger-14 rifle. Custom optic sight. Accurate to a hair. I tested it myself. You picked up the Beretta in Denver?"

"Thanks. Good price. Nice weight and I did some test shooting. No jamming, no misfires. A serviceable weapon, so no complaints. It'll do."

"You still want the NVGs?"

"Yeah, just in case."

"Jake? What's that?"

"Night Vision Goggles. Amplifies star and moonlight so you can get around in the dark," Jake answered.

"I don't understand," Lorie said nervously. They were talking a foreign language and she didn't like the strange vibes between the two men. "We're just going to grab Matt and run. Why do you need a rifle? And the NVG things?"

"Lorie, these men are lunatics. We know they have high-tech weapons. They have a terrorist attack planned. That's the FBI's job, but I have no idea the situation we'll find Matt in. I believe in being prepared."

She pressed her hands on his chest. He avoided her eyes, totally focused inward. It was unnerving. She had seen him in many moods, but never this one. "I'm not just afraid for Matt, but for you. Maybe Hooker is right."

"Matt's in serious trouble. Don't expect me to step back. It might be a matter of loading him up and taking him home. I sure as hell hope so."

Abruptly, he turned toward Puma and changed the subject. "Got any sandwich stuff, Puma? Bottled water? We should get going. It's a four-hour flight and we haven't had much food today."

"Sure. In the kitchen. Take whatever you need and put it in the cooler on the cupboard."

Lorie gave up. Neither man would listen, and she had no right to be upset. This was what she'd asked Jake to do. To find her son and bring him back to her. She knew one thing. Strom would never put Matt in danger, so this Rambo preparation was unnecessary.

"I'll do it," she said. "Isn't that traditional? The women make sandwiches and the men do the macho stuff?" She stalked off toward the rustic bungalow that was Puma's home.

Puma pulled his boonie cap over his eyes and whistled. "Nice ass."

"It's a great ass."

"I'll bet she's a challenge."

"She's under a lot of pressure. Matt's been gone for over a week. He called her this morning and hung up when Strom appeared. Wants to come home."

Never again would he refer to Strom as Matt's father. The man didn't deserve it, either biologically or by his actions. It remained to be seen whether Jake would earn the right. That would be up to Matt, but Jake had a damn good role model to follow. If Matt would give him the chance.

He watched Lorie enter the house and slam the screen door behind her. "Strom and the New Sons are deadly, and completely off the rails. Whether she'll admit it or not, she knows it. The setup sucks big time."

"How bad is it?"

"Worse even than I told you. They have a nuke."

Puma winced. "Hell. Do the feds have a handle on it?"

"They're on it."

"You're expecting trouble. Otherwise you wouldn't need all the firepower."

Unsteadily Jake swiped at his hair. There had been another bomb in the past. One that had exploded and destroyed an innocent life. He was heartsick at the thought of Matt being held as a hostage. And terrified his son would suffer the same fate. "There'll be trouble. Far as I can tell, Matt is in the proximity of enough explosive to level a square mile. God, I better get it right this time."

"Jake, you didn't kill that woman. Ortega and his band of thugs did that."

"I screwed up. We both know it."

"It could've been anyone of us. It happened to be you. Let it go, Jayhawker."

Jake muttered a curse. "We're running out of time."

He squatted to fieldstrip the rifle and used the kit Puma handed him to lubricate its components. He trusted his Delta buddy, but took care of his own weapons. Puma began the same process with his M40 and his own handgun. They fell into the familiar routine of soldiers preparing for battle.

"What kind of ammo?"

Jake paused in his task. "Not your military sniper issue. A non-jacketed hollow point. One that explodes on contact."

"That'll limit your range."

"You're the long-range hotshot. I don't plan to be over a hundred meters away if I have to shoot."

"Eight, maybe ten guys, you said. I'm backing you," Puma said. "Don't argue."

Jake grunted acknowledgement. "Don't intend to. Appreciate it."

"How do you plan to find the boy?"

"Matt said there was a pink neon bird flashing on the motel sign. I checked with Vegas directory assistance. There's a motel listed as The Frolicking Flamingo. If Strom and Matt have moved on, we go to the dam site, recon and wait."

"If they hold the boy hostage? Use him for a shield?"

Jake thinned his mouth. "They give him up or die."

CHAPTER 28

T he kid had phoned the bitch.

Strom had never hit Matt before, but damn it infuriated him that the kid had pulled such a stupid stunt. It had been a major goof on Strom's part to leave his cell where the kid could get ahold of it, but who the hell would figure Matt knew enough to insert the SIM card and call the bitch?

Matt had finally stopped crying, and lay huddled on the bed, nursing a fat lip. If he valued his hide he wouldn't try it again. Matt had displayed a rebellious streak lately and was hard to deal with. He'd scrubbed out the black hair dye Strom had applied in Denver, and the result was a weird shade of purple. Maybe Knox was right. Kids were a liability when you had serious business going.

The good thing was Matt hadn't told Lorie where they were. At least that's what he claimed after Strom slapped him a few times. Bawled like a baby calf that lost its mama's teat. But Matt could read just fine, so maybe he knew the name of their motel, and he'd admitted to blabbing about the sightseeing. Knowing Lorie she'd hotfoot it to Vegas, maybe enlist the local cops. Which meant they had to move again. Immediately.

Strom threw their possessions in a duffle bag. Didn't take

long. They were traveling light. They'd spend the night in the SUV, and drive to the storage shed early in the morning, where the Sons would load the explosives. One more day and they'd be gone from the Vegas area. Lorie was still in Kansas, so it would take her a while to get here, and by the time she did, the feds would be crawling all over the region. Security would be so tight she'd run into a brick wall, and Matt would be gone forever. She'd never find them. He chuckled at the pain Matt's disappearance would cause his ex. She deserved it. No need to mention this to Knox. Everything would be fine. Fine as frog's hair.

Jake exited the backroads from Jeremiah's ranch, headed south on US 93 toward the Hoover. Nothing pretty about the drive once they entered the highway. The roadsides were interspersed with motels, ratty buildings and trash. Hundreds of electrical towers were strung along the route, carrying electricity from the dam site to Vegas and points north. The scenery improved once the entered the Black Canyon area; there the highway was booked by sheer stone walls that looked like they'd been white-washed, and was strung with rocks the colors of rust and lead. Deep shadows shrouded the craggy peaks, and even in daylight the hills appeared black. Ubiquitous electrical towers still staggered along the route, a reminder of the dam's real purpose, to provide power to a civilization totally dependent on its manufacture.

Five miles from the dam site, Jake pulled over and Lorie took the wheel, continuing on at a more subdued pace. At Exit 2 they left US 93 and turned onto NV 172. From there it was a four-mile trip to the dam, and traffic had slowed despite the early morning hour. They'd been warned that there would be delays getting through security, and the earlier they approached the dam site the better.

The checkpoint site was crawling with Feebs. The government men were discreet, but Jake knew a Feeb when he saw one. Blue and whites were parked everywhere, and the cops in dark uniforms were armed. And no one could tell him the check they were running at the entrance to the dam was the usual procedure. Hoover security cops were usually unarmed. Every vehicle was stopped. Any that raised suspicions was waved aside for a detailed search. As he'd feared, they were using dogs. Jake and Puma had removed the spare tire from the trunk and stowed Jake's weapons in the emptied well. Ripped bags of coffee beans were stowed beside the ammo. Hopefully, the strong scent would confuse the dogs. Covered by the trunk mat with their luggage piled on top, the guns were invisible without a thorough search. Courtesy of Puma's buddy, they were driving a late-model Jaguar sedan that screamed power and sporty style.

Easing up to the mandated checkpoint, Lorie lowered the automatic window, blinked her hazel eyes, fluffed her mass of auburn curls and smiled at the trooper who stopped them. "My BF would rather have stayed at the casinos, but I talked him into a trip to see the dam, and for once he let me drive. Where is the best place to take photos?"

After an envious glance inside the luxury vehicle, the man leaned in. "You can get good shots from the observation deck in the visitor Center, both of Lake Mead and the Bypass Bridge. The dam is closed to vehicle traffic, but you can park and walk across it. The most specular photo-op is from the north walkway of the bypass bridge. From there it's a full-frontal view of the dam, and absolutely spectacular. If the rain holds off, it'll be a fine sight today. When you leave the dam site, backtrack to 93 on ramp, and take the exit to the bridge parking lot. From there you can walk up the ramp or take the steps to the bridge walkway.

"Can't we view the dam as we drive along the bridge bypass road?"

"Sorry, no. The walls along the sides of the bridge were built too high to allow sightseeing from the highway, and traffic is forbidden to stop anywhere on the bridge. But if you don't mind heights, I'd recommend you investigate the walkway. The bridge crosses the canyon nine-hundred feet above the Colorado and is almost two-thousand feet long, a remarkable engineering feat."

Jake made a Let's Get On with it growl, and the officer stepped back and after a last appreciative glance at Lorie, waved them on. Jake did his best to look bored and sulky, his eyes hidden behind dark glasses, his unspoken message Tell Me Again Why we're doing this? He slouched under the floppy Hawaiian print shirt that Puma dug out of his closet. The cop barely glanced his way.

It would have been a different story if Puma had been along. Cops noticed Puma.

One look at him and their eyes grew wary, their muscles tensed. Sometimes they'd loosen their weapon in the holster, just to be sure it was readily available. Not that Puma did anything to warrant the suspicion. He just was who he was.

Puma wasn't with them because he'd gone cross-country on his borrowed dirt bike at 0400 hours. He'd be crouched down somewhere amid the rocks and sparse vegetation that loomed over both sides of the dam site. With the skill to move as silently as his namesake, he'd have passed unseen by any sentries the Feebs had posted. Dressed in desert camo pants and a sleeveless black tee shirt, with skin almost the hue of the red-bronze cliffs, he would disappear into the scenery. He had the NVGs. Probably not necessary. Puma could see in the dark just fine.

"We're almost onsite," Jake spoke quietly into the throat mike he wore under the buttoned collar of the gaudy shirt. "Where are you?"

"Hunkered down on the Nevada side, on a rocky outcrop halfway between the dam and the bridge. I hope this doesn't take all day. I'll be sitting in a frying pan once the sun heats up these rocks. And damn, that wind is howling fierce."

"Yeah, we can feel it swaying the car. How much of a factor will the wind be if you have to shoot?" Jake craned his neck. He'd have sworn a mountain goat couldn't manage that climb. Puma carried enough water and booster bars to stay put for twelve hours. If need be he could rappel down the cliffs in minutes.

"Not your worry, Jayhawker."

"Okay. We're headed for the dam site. A few cars and a tour bus ahead of us. Traffic is slow moving, and security is rousting every vehicle. Far as we know, Garrison is still driving his black van. We'll find a vantage point and wait. You've got a bird's eye view with the Bushnell's?"

"Roger that. I'm sweeping the area now and will watch for your vehicle. Hard to miss a cherry red Jaguar. It's an awesome machine."

"Yeah, built like a gorgeous woman. 'Preciate your buddy being so generous. Loaning us the Jag and you the bike."

"Jeremiah has more money than an Arab sheik. Park as close as you can to the exit in case you have to leave fast, and I'll keep an eye out for the black van. Shouldn't be over—say a couple hundred of them appear today?"

"It's a Jeep Cherokee with a luggage rack on top, probably loaded with camping gear. That help?"

"Every little bit helps, Jayhawker. Don't be a stranger."

"Roger and out," Jake acknowledged softly. "We'll be in touch."

CHAPTER 29

L orie drove down the winding highway along Black Canyon.

Hoover Dam lay in the valley before them.

It was an amazing sight, a dazzling white blaze in the hot desert sun. Lorie had seen pictures, but nothing had prepared her for the reality. Puma had gathered maps and information about the dam site, and she and Jake had studied them during the flight from Colorado Springs. All part of Jake's Be Prepared philosophy, and it kept Lorie's mind from the fact that they were winging over some of the most desolate terrain on earth, bouncing around the sky in a shoebox. She was convinced only the hand of God had kept them from plummeting to the rocks below.

The massive curve of the dam spanned from canyon wall to canyon wall, connecting the states of Arizona and Nevada and reached seven-hundred feet in height. Behind the imposing curved structure lay Lake Mead. The water was sapphire blue and untold fathoms deep. Quite a panorama, as they drove toward it.

"It rains maybe five inches a year here, and it chooses today." Jake spoke into his throat mike. "How's the visibility up there? Getting wet, Puma?"

"Nothing to worry about, Jayhawker. See anything

interesting? What about that black van I spotted a few minutes ago?"

"Minnesota plates, and two kids waved at us from the back seat. Neither of them Matt. We're going to check out the dam site on foot."

"Roger that and out."

"Jake, I don't get it," Lorie said. "Now that I see this place, see how huge it is, could anything destroy it? Short of a ten-point on the Richter scale earthquake? Maybe not even that. Certainly not the amount of explosive that Strom could carry in his van."

"You're right. It would take a loaded semi of dynamite to do much damage. Which is why they long ago diverted eighteen-wheeler traffic to another highway. But a nuclear weapon would be disastrous. What I don't get is why Hooker didn't shut everything down today. Pull over into this parking area, and I'll take a look. Wait here."

Where was Hooker? He and his men had to be somewhere.

Lorie pulled up and Jake jumped out, slinging the binocular strap around his neck and strode toward the pedestrian walkway that edged the dam. She slammed the car door and trotted after him, determination in every step. He shook his head and took her hand. At least this way he knew what she was up to.

It was a brilliant view. The concrete and stone wall that ran along the top of the dam was several feet high, but the scene from the footpath was unimpeded. A quarter mile upstream a string of marker buoys stretched across the lake, warning watercraft to proceed no further. The deep blue of Lake Mead slammed against the north side of the dam, eddying currents swirling around the intake towers. Looking south was the bridge, a soaring steel archway, backed by buttermilk clouds and a blustery sky. The structure seemed to be a bird in flight, defying gravity. Truly a marvel of engineering.

Lorie took a deep breath. "Jake! What if the bridge is Strom's target?"

Jake took off on a dead run, pulling Lorie behind.

Adrenalin poured through Strom's veins. This was it. The destruction of Hoover Dam was the perfect choice to demonstrate the Sons' rising power. He'd had a few bad moments when a state patrolman motioned them off the road and rapped on their window. Evidently they were doing random stops along the 93 entrance to the Bypass Bridge. But Knox had been cool. Rolled down the window and yakked with the guy about the weather. Maybe it was going to rain. Too bad, because his brother and nephew had been looking forward to this visit.

Matt lay curled up in back, sawing logs and dreaming chemical dreams. The kid stubbornly wouldn't eat breakfast, but drank the chocolate milk laced with barbiturates. A ton of explosives was stashed under the mattress where he was sleeping, but there was no official checkpoint or vehicle search required to enter the bridge. It was considered a safe bypass of the dam and a quick route into Arizona.

The cop glanced at their license plate. Checking the number? Maybe, but Strom had done a running switch with plates in various motel parking lots over the past several days. This one listed California as their home state. They'd repainted the black Cherokee a neutral beige, and it blended right into the tourist landscape. If there was an APB out on Strom's van, it was worthless.

They would stall their vehicle on the bridge and set the timer. The bomb was wired to explode thirty minutes after their getaway, an event guaranteed to divert attention from the main entertainment, and the nuclear fusion powerful enough to bring down the dam. As a side benefit, the bridge would suffer irreparable damage.

After they dropped the nuke, Mel and Harry would escape underwater on the DPVs, re-board the houseboat and dump the underwater vehicles. Sammy and Quint would navigate to the cove where they'd stashed their Harleys, and the four of them would swamp the boat, split up and make their way to Montana where a half-million payoff awaited each of them. Mel and Harry had the tricky job. If they got too near the intake towers, they'd be sucked into the current and atomized along with the dam.

Strom glanced at his watch. Coming up on 1130 hours. They had to get into position, because timing was crucial. The nuke was set to go off at 1230 hours. That didn't give them a lot of time to blow the van and get out of there. They were to be the decoy. A task Strom didn't relish, but the escape plan had been set up carefully. They'd be miles from the dam site when the time came for the big bang.

One deviation from the plan that Knox was unaware of. When the van exploded, Knox would be dead behind the wheel, and Strom and Matt would be long gone. Headed toward Kingman, where a copter pickup had been arranged. Once in Montana, Strom would take over leadership of the Sons.

"Your boy better not start crying again," commented Knox. "There's still a chance we could be stopped."

"I gave him enough sedative to put him out for a couple of hours. He won't cause a problem. We're lucky he was along. Probably kept the cop from being suspicious."

Jake and Lorie drove onto the O'Callaghan-Tillman bypass bridge that spanned the tumultuous river. Once on the bridge, the thick walls were built so high that the dam vanished from sight. Pedestrians with cameras clicking would be walking along the northern pathway meant specifically for sightseers. With Lorie at the wheel, they made a slow trip across, and reached the east side and Arizona territory with no sight of the van that Strom drove. Fifteen-hundred feet upstream, the lower portals of the dam discharged Mead's thunderous outflow. Far below them the Colorado River surged wild and free on its way to Mexico. A hundred feet above, high voltage wires hummed.

"Okay," Jake said. "We need to reverse."

They headed back toward the Nevada side. Fierce winds buffeted their vehicle as they steered west. Traffic flowed steadily on both sides of the bridge highway. Still no Strom. Nothing to do now but turn around and drive east again.

"It's sprinkling harder," Lorie said. "Should I park so we can get a better look?"

"Not yet. Pull over to the side, but leave the motor running. I don't want to be caught here if we spot Strom's Cherokee."

Still no sign of their quarry. Jake climbed out of the auto and swept the horizon with his binoculars. "Puma." Jake spoke softly, his unease getting stronger.

"I hear ya', Jayhawker. Where are you?"

"Pulled over on the Nevada side to take a look-see and off-load the firearms. My gut tells me I need them. We'll head back to the Arizona side. You're closer to the dam than we are. Sweep the lake with your glasses. What do you see?"

"Not much. Been bothering me. No sailboats or water skiers. A houseboat anchored in the middle of the lake maybe a half-click back, but damn little water traffic. A light shower wouldn't keep a real fisherman on shore."

"It's too quiet. Where in the hell are Hooker's men?"

Puma whistled. "I spot a patrol boat, Jake, coming in fast. Can't make out the markings. Wait a minute, NPS. That'd be National Park Service. Damn, here comes another one! No, three! They're pulling up to the houseboat. There're gonna board her!"

"I don't like this."

"Nor do I, buddy."

Lorie tugged at his shirt. "Jake? What's going on?"

"I hope our friend Hooker's not too late. Where would a nuclear explosion do the most damage? In a car, crossing the bridge, or below?"

"Below! At the base of the dam. My God!"

Jake whirled, his chest squeezing. "Lorie, I'm staying; you head west. Fast. Take the road that leads back to where Puma's friend lives. He pilots his own plane. Tell him to evacuate. Take his family. You, too. Let me think, where—

Las Vegas? No, Denver. I'll meet you at the motel where we stayed. Are you getting this, Puma?"

"I'm already on the horn. Jericho's wife just picked up. I'll fill her in. You take off, Jake. Keep your lady safe."

"You didn't hire on to be a hero, Puma. Get out while you can!"

Jake let the binoculars drop against his chest. Whatever was happening out in the lake was beyond his control. But Matt and Strom were here somewhere, and he had to find them. There was nothing on this side of the bridge, but Strom's vehicle had to be heading this way. That had to be it. If a car bomb went off near the center of the bridge, all hell would break loose. Perfect cover for the killing blast that would follow. The one that would take the dam down.

"Lorie, get going! Now!"

"No! You can't make me!"

He caught her wrist. "Dammit, Lorie. There's nothing you can do here. I know what I'm doing. Trust me. I'll find Matt, I swear it."

"And then what, Jake Randolph? You'll find him, then what!"

"I'll get him away from Strom. To safety."

"How?" She screamed the question and jerked from his grasp. "If I take the Jag, how will you go anywhere? Can you outrun a nuclear blast? You need the wheels, and whether you admit it or not, you need me. I'm staying!"

Puma's voice crackled in Jake's ear. "Whatever you do, Jayhawker, do it quick. The feds are tying the houseboat to a towline. Looks like she was abandoned and drifting. Which could mean the suitcase we're concerned with maybe lies a hundred fathoms down under. In which case the pooch is screwed, white brother."

"See any evidence of divers?"

"Water's too deep near the dam, with dangerous undercurrents. Sure death to a diver. What's the plan?"

"You get out. Where'd you stow the bike?"

"Two clicks across country. I'm hangin', Jayhawker, right where I am. You need a spotter, and that's me."

Jake didn't argue. Puma didn't budge when his mind was set. "Okay, then, do this." He rattled off Hooker's pager number. "This guy will know what's going on. When he calls back get some answers. We may not have much time."

"Less than you think. Hear the sirens? There're trooper cars closing in from both sides of the dam. Maybe a mile away. And unmarked oversize vans. Two Blackhawk copters above. You know what that means."

Unmarked oversize vans and Blackhawks meant the Feds. Jake opened the trunk and retrieved his rifle and sidearm. "Get on the horn to Hooker. Tell him where we are and what we're driving. Last thing I need is to have the FBI shooting at us."

Knox approached the west entrance of the bridge and slowed. A few cars were ahead of them and a recreation vehicle followed behind. "Call Jocko and Fillmore and tell them we're starting across. After you blow the tire, I'll pull over to let the traffic go by. Jocko will pick us up, and we'll take Route 93 east."

"Done," Strom grunted. He wiped the sweat from his palms. "They're on the way."

"It might play out a little different than our trial run yesterday." Knox gave a yellow-toothed smirk as he gunned onto the bridge. "Things never go as planned. Nothing we can't handle, right?"

You have no idea, you egomaniac freak.

"Right." Strom smirked back.

They neared the center of the bridge. Traffic flow was light. Which was good. A bottleneck was the last thing they needed. "Blow the tire!" hissed Knox. "We're halfway and the pickup's only a few cars behind,"

The bang was immediate. The SUV slid sideways, the brakes squealed and the vehicle almost stood on its front bumper as it was flung against the south wall of the bridge. The airbags let loose with a bang. Loud honking ensued, as the cars behind them switched lanes to avoid a pileup. Neatly done, as planned.

"Okay?" Knox asked, leaning against the steering wheel, gasping for breath as the airbags slowly receded.

"Okay," Strom said, swiping at the powdery dust sifting through the cab. He reached into his boot for his K-bar. The blade was razor sharp, and one thrust between the ribs, an upward cut to pierce the heart and Knox would die instantly. Bloody, but quick, silent and efficient. Strom would set the timer, hoist Matt on his shoulder and jump into the pickup. In thirty minutes time, bang. No more Knox, a big fricking hole in the top of the dam bypass, and they were out of there.

Jocko and Fillmore knew the drill. They were as ready to get rid of Knox as he was. Jocko had been promised a piece of pretty boy Sammy as part of his reward for switching sides. Strom's hand froze, fingers curled around the knife handle. He'd do this left-handed. His right arm wasn't up to full strength yet, damn Randolph's hide. He'd get back at him for that humiliation someday. Something to look forward to.

Dobie turned toward him, a strange smile on his face.

There was no mistaking the click. The click as the trigger was pulled on Dobie's Glock. The dull plunk of a silenced pistol hitting a target. Strom stared in disbelief at the red splotch widening across his abdomen. No pain, just a swirling, encompassing blackness. Another plunk. "Wha—what—-" He clutched his side and stared at Knox, his eyesight dimming. Knox pressed his lips against Strom's ear, in the gesture of a lover. "Nothing personal, Sergeant Major," he whispered. "Strike first, strike hard, and never leave an enemy alive."

Blackness, then nothing.

CHAPTER 30

Jake tossed Lorie into the passenger seat and jackknifed behind the wheel. Her heart pounded after their frantic sprint across the blacktop. The world had gone mad. She'd heard only one side of the conversation between the two men, but enough to understand that the situation had turned deadly. That perhaps the nuclear weapon already rested deep in the water against the dam.

Her instincts screamed. Jake meant to get rid of her because of the danger. Matt was nearby. Jake was not ditching her! Wherever Matt was, wherever Jake went, whatever happened, she'd be there too.

"Where're we headed?"

"Back across. The law is on the way with sirens blasting, which means the militia crazies could panic. Maybe blow the bomb earlier than planned. Strom must be here somewhere. We have to find him."

"Jake!" Puma's voice roared in his ear. "On the bridge! Three o'clock! Van had a blowout and plowed headfirst into a stanchion. Jeep Cherokee with a luggage rack on top. It's tan, not black."

Swearing, Jake threw the Jag into reverse and wheeled into a sharp turn. "Lorie, Puma spotted a van in the middle of the bridge. Front end smashed. Does it look familiar? It's tan, not black, but it could be Strom's vehicle."

The tires spun, spraying dust, as he hit the accelerator hard. Lorie hung on the dash and craned her neck to see ahead. The militiamen weren't stupid. Vicious, but not stupid. It made sense they'd repaint Strom's van.

"Yes! I'm sure of it. The luggage rack on top is like Strom's! He had it custom made to hold his camping gear. Jake, Matt must be inside!"

Jake barreled toward the disabled van, rapidly processing what was happening. Had Strom blown the tire deliberately, or was it an ill-timed accident? It made a difference and Jake wished he knew. Were the explosives loaded in the van? Where were the other members of the militia? They had to be more nearby.

With his eyes intent on the road ahead, disaster came from behind and out of nowhere. The glass in the rear window shattered; the Jag bucked violently. Jake fought the wheel, hit the brake and steered into the spin. Effing hell, what was that!

Lorie screamed and flew forward, slamming toward the dash as they went into a skid. They'd been going fast. The tires squealed in violent protest. The vehicle spun sideways, did a complete three-sixty. But it held to the road and jerked to a stop, the engine still throbbing. Dust from the deflated airbags hovered in the air.

They'd been rammed. A heavy-duty pickup with oversize tires. A real Bigfoot brute. The truck roared around them, heading east.

"Lorie! Are you all right? God, he came out of nowhere."

She took her hands from her bruised face. "Yes, yes, I'm okay. Just find Matt. Go, please. Please, Jake. I'm okay."

Thank God they were driving a sturdy vehicle, or they would have been fileted. Drivers behind them laid on their horns, swerving around their stalled auto. Some adventurous pedestrians had climbed on the walkway wall and were gaping in shock. Jake heard the sirens, some distance away. Whatever help was coming would be too late.

"Puma! We were rammed! Black monster pickup!" Jake wheeled the Jag eastward and stomped the accelerator. The superb machine responded and roared after the speeding truck.

"Got him, Jayhawker. It stopped by the disabled Cherokee. Short guy wearing camo just hopped out of the driver's seat and jumped into the truck bed. Holy hell, you won't believe this. Little bastard has a video camera and is recording the scene."

"I'm there, Puma," Jake said, glancing Lorie's way. She was stony-faced, with a knot on her forehead, her chin quivering in determination. He came to a fast halt beside the wrecked van, throwing the gears into park. It appeared empty.

Not waiting for a complete stop, Lorie leapt out and raced toward Strom's van. A split second behind her, Jake yelled, "Wait, Lorie!"

She ignored his bellowed warning. Or didn't hear him.

The flashback staggered him, the memory buckled his knees. Blinding light—a deafening roar—Jake blown off his feet, saved only by his body armor, the hostage reduced to bloody shards.

Her hand clawed at the door handle.

Oh, God! Not again. Not Lorie.

"Lorie! No!"

"Matt!" she screamed. "He's inside!"

The back door was locked. She lurched for the other door. Jake hit her in a flying tackle, knocking her to the ground. She screamed again and kicked frantically, as he pressed her against the pavement.

"Let me go! Matt's in back, not moving! He's unconscious—let me go!"

"Lorie!" He shook her. "Listen to me! There could be a tripwire!"

She froze. "A tripwire?"

"I know how to disarm it. I'll let you up. Just don't—touch the door again, okay?"

"Yes, yes. Jake, for God's sake, do something!"

"I will. Please. Stay away from the van until I check."

He rose to his feet and scanned the back of the van. Matt lay there senseless, his freckles standing out on his pale face. Breathing, thank God, but far too still. Drugged.

Lorie struggled to her feet and hovered beside him, but kept her hands from the door handle. There wouldn't be a tripwire on the driver's side. That was the exit the militant had taken. Jake could safely open that door.

Holy mother. Strom!

Slumped down in the passenger seat, blood soaking his chest and abdomen. Mouth slack, eyes open and blank. Dead, or nearly so. The driver had shot him before he bailed.

He turned his back on Lorie and spoke softly into the mike. "Puma, we have another problem. Strom Garrison's been gut shot. Whoever escaped in the pickup did him. Can you stop it from up there?"

Five-hundred yards above them, Puma had the advantage of height. He could pump lead down onto the truck until the motor blew or the driver took a hit.

"Got it!" Puma's voice rang in his ears. "They're at the east end of the bridge and moving fast. Little bastard is still standing in the back. That section is clear of traffic. I'm taking a shot."

"Do it!"

Dimly Jake heard the whine of a high-powered bullet, then the crack of Puma's rifle as sound caught up with the projectile. Another. Two more. Squealing tires, followed by a violent crash. Puma didn't miss.

"Got him." Puma's voice crackled in Jake's ear.

Jake grunted a satisfied acknowledgement and wrenched open the driver's door. Analytically he sorted the data in front of him. Matt was sprawled on the mattress in back, still as death. No visible tripwire. The raw petroleum smell assaulted his nostrils. The mattress was soaked with fuel oil. An empty gallon can had been tossed beside his son's inert body.

Strom groaned. Astonished, Jake glanced at the wounded

man. He was still alive. All that blood meant it wouldn't be long. Not even a medic could save him at this point. He snapped his focus back to Matt. If there were a tripwire, it could be attached to Matt. He prayed. Don't move, son. Please, God, don't let him move. Give me a chance.

"Jake!" Lorie shrieked from behind him. "What is it? Hurry!"

Strom groaned again and whispered. "Lorie?"

Lorie swung her attention from Matt to the front seat, and screamed at the sight of her ex-husband covered in blood. "Strom! My God!"

"Stay back, Lorie," Jake snapped. "There's nothing anyone can do for him."

Heedless, and before Jake realized her intent, she rushed to the front passenger side and jerked open the door.

That answered one question. No tripwire on the passenger side.

"Lorie," Strom whispered. "Get Matt. No time." His head lolled back, wheezing gasps escaping his chest.

Lorie tore off her shirt, crumpled it and pressed it tightly against Strom's wound. "Hold on, Strom! We'll get a doctor! Jake, get Matt out of there!"

Jake leaned over Strom, his voice low and urgent. "Strom, can you hear me?"

Strom opened his eyes. "Randolph?"

"Yes. Is there a tripwire? Under Matt? Somewhere?"

Shallow breathy gasps. "No tripwire. Timer."

"Where? Dammit, man, where is the timer?"

"See you—in hell." A spew of blood poured from the wounded man's mouth. There would be no more answers.

Lorie sobbed in disbelief. "Is he—is he—"

"He's gone. Lorie, you have to get Matt out of here."

He leapt into the backseat, checking carefully for a wire. Even dying men had been known to lie.

No wire, but Matt's clothing was soaked with fuel oil. A cup of the stuff equaled fifteen sticks of dynamite. In cold rage he accepted what that meant. Someone would pay.

He threw the door open and cradled the boy in his arms,

lifting him out of the van. Matt stirred and sighed.

"Get behind the wheel of the Jag, Lorie. The key fob is in the well. You'll have to drive. Now, dammit!"

She blocked the way. "Let me see him. I have to touch him. Oh God, he's so still!" She kissed and stroked Matt's white cheek. "Please, baby, wake up."

"He's been drugged. Get him away from here, fast. That's your job. As soon as you get to safety, have a doctor look at him."

Sobbing in agreement, she ran to the vehicle and climbed into the driver's side. The back of the vehicle was caved inward and plastered with shards of glass. Matt would have to ride in front, next to his mother. Jake smoothed the hair from the boy's white face and fastened the seatbelt around his son, Thank God, he was breathing, even if it was ragged and raspy. Lorie pumped the gas and the motor roared to life.

"Jake! Jump in back!"

"I can't. Go now, and fast." Jake reached for the rifle in the car's backseat and leapt out of the vehicle. Urgency overwhelmed him. There wasn't even time to kiss his son and the woman he loved goodbye.

"Jake, for God's sake! Let someone else take care of it!"

Jake slapped the roof of the Jag. "Go! Think of our son. There's no time, Lorie."

"Don't do this! Don't you dammit do this to us! Don't you die!"

"Lorie, there're people in danger here. I'll be okay. I'll meet you at Puma's ranch. He'll be right behind you. Puma?"

"You got it, Jayhawker. Soon as you'n me disarm that pesky little sucker, I'm on my way cross-country. Just talked to your friend, Hooker. Grouchy fellow. Don't look now, but the feds are closing in."

There was no time to argue. Somehow he had to convince his pintsized lioness to get to safety. To leave him behind to do his job.

"Lorie, do you trust me?"

"Yes, of course. I love you."

"Then go, sweetheart. I love you, too. I'll be okay. Take care of our son."

She gave him a last searching look, a look that held terror as well as baffled anger, and wheeled the Jag forward, taking off to the Arizona side of the dam.

Jake laid the rifle across the roof of Strom's vehicle. It was worthless for now. He had to find the timer. Chances were good it was under the front seat.

"Puma, I found the timing mechanism. Damn, looks like we have less than twelve. Talk to me, brother."

"Describe it. Where are the wires?"

"It looks like a kitchen timer. Really, really low tech. Two wires lead under the seat to a suitcase in the back of the van. Must hold the detonator. Next to the sacks of ammonium nitrate. Petrel fumes are damn near overwhelming. That can't be good."

Eight minutes.

"You're right there, Jayhawker. Do you have a knife? Sharper the better."

He'd left his combat knife at home. Airline restrictions were tough. And he hadn't gotten another from Puma. "No knife. I have my pistol. I don't suppose I could shoot—no, bad idea."

"Real bad."

"Damn, this isn't like any device I've ever seen. I cut one wire, right? Which one?"

"Either. You want to break the circuit. Maybe you should get out of there, Jake."

The glove compartment! Maybe there was a cutting tool in the glove compartment. Gently he put the timer down and reached across Strom's body, wrenching open the compartment's hinged door. Maps. Driver's manual. Church key. Nothing else.

Five minutes.

Alternate plan. Two more minutes and he'd have to hurl his ass behind the nearest cement stanchion and pray.

"Puma, I have a beer can opener. Can I—"

"Nada. You need a clean cut. Jake, search Garrison."

Damn, his head wasn't working. Strom's K-bar. The one he carried in his boot.

"Got it!"

Three minutes.

"One clean cut, Jake. One wire. Don't hesitate. Slice straight across."

"Puma, if something happens, help Lorie through it."

"We'll see ya' at the ranch, Jayhawker."

That was Puma. Probably had moved out two minutes ago, figuring Jake either made it or he didn't.

Counting down.

Now!

He slashed. The wire split cleanly.

The timer stopped.

Jake laid the timer mechanism aside and stood. His chest ached in delayed reaction. That was as close as he ever wanted to come.

CHAPTER 31

Sirens were on top of him. Better late than never. Official vehicles converged from both sides of the dam. They surrounded the pickup that had smashed against the bridge abutment, courtesy of Puma's marksmanship. The front end was crumpled and the hood sprung open, emitting steam. Warning shouts. Men poured out of the vehicles, but no gunfire. Nothing moved inside the smoldering wreck of the pickup.

Several state patrol cars screeched to a halt beside the Cherokee, sirens at full blast. The whacking sound of helicopter propellers beat the air above. Closing in. Two copters. One circled the lake; the other hovered over the steep rock formations surrounding the visitor's center.

"Keep your hands up! Keep your hands in sight at all times!"

A bullhorn blared from the lead car. Jake sighed and lifted his hands high. Great. Wouldn't it be fine to have a trigger-happy trouper do him in? Men wearing body vests marked FBI, poured out of a large enclosed truck. Carrying semiautomatics. The FBI SWAT team. The way they spread out told Jake they knew what they were doing.

The bullhorn barked again. "Hit the deck, pal! On your knees, hands above you head. We're not fooling around here."

Jake knelt and raised his hands and didn't twitch a muscle.

He spoke calmly, projecting his voice. "It wouldn't be a good idea to shoot. The van's loaded with explosives. I've disconnected the timer."

The uniform in the lead stopped. "Explosives? We were told—"

"I don't care what you were told. The van's loaded with explosives. So keep your finger easy on the trigger, pal."

"It's okay, Jake. No one's taking a shot at you."

Hooker's voice this time. Jake watched the FBI man climb out of an unmarked Crown Vic and head his way. Finally, some answers.

"Did you get the nuke?" Jake asked.

"Got it. Disarmed, and headed for Langley by Air Force courier jet."

There was a genuine grin on the agent's face. First grin Jake had ever seen crack Hooker's stoic facade. The group of armed men stood down, muttering, easing their weapons to their sides.

Jake raised an eyebrow and slowly lowered his arms. "Sounds like a story. Buy me a beer, and we'll trade yarns."

"You got it." Hooker lifted his voice. "Get the bomb squad over here! The rest of you sweep the area. We're missing two suspects. This isn't one of 'em."

"Who got away?"

"For one, a guy named Mel Albertson. Slipped away underwater in scuba gear. We're looking for him."

"The nuke was on the houseboat you boarded?"

"Yeah. We've been monitoring the marinas and water traffic, expecting a strike at the dam from the lakeside. Three other guys were on the houseboat. Two went down. We have the third in custody. A male blonde bimbo. He sang like Tweetie Bird after two of my female undercover agents got a hold of him. If he stops talking, I put him back in a locked room with Haggerty and Howe."

"How un-FBI like. I'm shocked you allowed it."

"The guy and his partners made the mistake of thinking they were hookers. Got them out on the middle of the lake and drugged them. My agents had to take the abuse or blow their cover. It was payback time."

"You said two got away. Who else?"

"The leader, Frederick Knox."

"What does he look like?"

"Description we have is a bandy-legged guy, about five-eight, shaved head."

"Wearing camo?"

"Always. Loves to play soldier."

"He was in the back of the pickup when it crashed. He must be the one who killed Strom Garrison."

"Yeah, we got that much from your buddy, the one who paged me. Two guys inside the wrecked pickup are in bad shape, but Knox was thrown free. We'll get him, thanks to your pal stopping their getaway vehicle. Your shooter was perched up on those rocks above the Visitors' Center, right? Hell of a shot. Must be seven-hundred meters."

"I wouldn't know. I've been busy."

"We want to talk to him."

"Good luck."

By now Puma would be astride his dirt bike. Staying under the cover of rocks and brush. Headed across country toward Jericho's ranch where he'd hangered his plane. Not even the copter had a prayer of spotting him.

"Is your lady safe? The boy?"

About time the agent showed some concern in that direction. "They're okay. Matt was drugged. Lorie's getting him to a doctor. Thanks for caring."

Hooker grinned again as if he enjoyed the sarcasm. "Don't get your shorts in a twist, Randolph. I had a job to do. Looks like you did yours, too."

"Agent Hooker, better come here." One of the bomb squad members called out. "There's a dead guy in the front seat."

Hooker shot Jake a searching look. "Garrison, right?"

"Knox meant for Strom and Matt to go up with the van. I

want five minutes alone with that pig bastard when you catch him. Professional courtesy, Hooker."

"Much as I'd like to oblige, we need the guy alive. There's someone behind this mess, someone with major bucks, and him I want bad."

"Have any idea who?"

"Not exactly. But we know the money is coming from overseas. That puts you and Cavetto squarely in the ballgame with us."

They exchanged glances for a long moment, while Jake processed what the FBI man implied. "Al-Qaida" he guessed softly. "Jihadists? They're pitting local militants against us? Our own citizens?" He shook his head. "I can't believe Strom would go along with that group of fanatics."

Hooker winced. "Since when do people like the New Sons use any common sense? Skinheads, anti-Semitic groups, survivalists, the fringe militia group in general. Someone is organizing them. And likely they have no idea where the money is coming from. It's going to be a long, cold war Jake, rooting out the enemy within."

"My God."

This wasn't just bad news. It was catastrophic.

"Indeed," Hooker nodded. "We intend to cut off the Hydra's head."

Jake held up a hand to halt their conversation, the honed six-sense of armed combat alerting him to a movement in his peripheral vision.

Knox.

Fifty feet away. Standing atop the concrete wall that bordered the south side of the bridge. His camo outfit hung in dirty rags. His face was bloody, one arm lay limp at his side. Fanaticism alone must have sustained him.

"This doesn't end here! You'll never defeat us!" The terrorist's voice was high-pitched, almost squeaky. He aimed a pistol toward Hooker, the look on his face maniacal. The pistol is his hand wavered.

Jake caught his breath. The FBI men all wore bulletproof vests, but Hooker stood directly in front of the disabled van. If a stray bullet hit, they'd all end up molecular parts of the environment.

Warning shouts from the FBI team. Running feet. Guns drawn. Hooker screaming at his men. For God's sake don't shoot in this direction!

Processing as he reacted, Jake seized the rifle he'd put on top of Strom's van. It didn't have the range of Puma's M40, but it was accurate.

"For flag and country!" Knox screamed, leveling the gun.

To Jake, the sounds were no more than the buzzing of a gnat. Instinct. Swing the rifle. Squeeze the trigger. Again. Reminiscent of the days when he and his dad went hunting and bagged their limit. A quail covey didn't wait for you to take careful aim.

Knox's chest exploded. His head disappeared. The pistol flew. Up. Over the stanchion, into the waters of the Colorado River far below. The militiaman's legs buckled in death. The limp body toppled and followed the path of the pistol. A slow slide into oblivion.

Fish food.

CHAPTER 32

Lorie sped down the highway, her foot heavy on the accelerator. If she got stopped by a cop, so much the better. When her cell phone rang, she snatched it up one-handed, praying.

"How's Matt?" Jake's voice.

Relief flooded her. He was alive. She'd put the unthinkable alternative aside while she concentrated on getting her son to safety.

"Jake! You're all right?"

"I'm fine. Hooker's team disabled the nuke and Puma and I took care of the car bomb. We still have some cleanup work, and the FBI wants a debriefing. How about you and Matt?"

"I don't like the sound of his breathing, really ragged and shallow. And it's getting worse. He must have inhaled some toxic fumes. And he still won't wake up. He's in and out of consciousness."

"Where are you? Near Kingman yet?" His calm voice didn't fool her. Jake had some medic training. He knew how dangerous noxious fumes were to a child's lungs.

"I passed the turnoff five miles back and kept going toward Kingman. I need to get to a hospital, and it's the nearest town. I called 911 and they gave me directions."

"Good thinking. How far are you out from the hospital?"

"Maybe thirty miles. Headed south fast as I can drive. I'm really worried, Jake. Does anyone there have medical training and could give me some advice?"

"Wait a minute, I'll check with Hooker."

He was back on line almost immediately.

"Lorie, the FBI will send a copter to pick you up and carry you to the hospital. I'll be on board. Keep driving down the highway. We'll spot you from the air and land. A medic will be with us."

"Yes. Hurry, Jake."

"On the way, sweetheart. Hang in there."

"Jake?"

"What will happen—what will they do with—"

"Strom?"

She heaved a sigh. She'd been unable to ask, especially with Matt semi-conscious in the front seat. "Yes. Someone will have to call his parents."

"The FBI will take care of it. And, Lorie?"

"Yes, I'm here.

"Until we touch base, don't discuss what happened with anyone. When the doctor asks, Matt accidentally swallowed a barbiturate, and was exposed to spilled gasoline fumes. We found the bottle of sleeping pills in Strom's luggage. Ambien."

"This is my child. What are you asking?"

"I'm appealing to your commonsense. If you want our part in this to end here, say nothing."

"I don't understand. We have Matt back. Strom is gone."

"There are more of these crazies running loose, Lorie. From what Hooker said, the conspiracy is widespread and well-financed. I want you and Matt out of it."

Her son slept peacefully. Not the comatose stupor of before, but a restful sleep.

Lorie sat by his bedside and held his hand, while life-giving oxygen pumped into his lungs and an intravenous drip diluted the drug in his system. He'd be kept in the hospital for observation, but the doctor thought he would be well enough to leave the next day.

"He's been so brave, Jake. He feels terrible, but he smiled at me. When he high-fived you, I almost lost it."

"He's a great kid. Tough."

"Like his father. Jake, how can I tell him what happened? There's—so much."

"Can we leave him for a while, sweetheart? You could use a hot drink and some rest. And we have to talk."

Reluctantly she let go of Matt's hand. "I know. But I haven't seen him for so long. I want to be here when he wakes up. I don't want him to be afraid."

"He'll sleep for hours. We'll come back and check soon."

She leaned over and kissed Matt on the cheek. "Take care, son. I'll be right back."

Pain flickered across Jake's face. "Can I kiss him? Would you mind? I never got to hold him when he was a baby."

Guilt rushed in, and she was overloaded with it already. "Oh, Jake, of course."

Jake knelt by the bedside and brushed aside the tousled hair. His mouth curved in a smile as he touched his lips to Matt's forehead. "God, he's special. I can't wait to throw the football with him, take him fishing. Teach him to ride."

"Jake, I'm so sorry," she whispered, interrupting the dangerous turn of his thoughts. She couldn't swallow. The lump in her throat was enormous.

"I love him, Lorie."

"I know. That's what makes this so hard. We both love him, and I love you. You love me. I'm being torn apart."

She was. Literally. The pain of what she had to do was searing. He'd forgiven her twice. He wouldn't again. Not Jake. She prayed the right words would come. Words that would at least help him understand.

"We need to make some plans." He took her wrist and led her across the hall, toward a rest area set aside for visitors.

Gratefully she sank into one of the plastic-covered armchairs. "I may fall asleep sitting up. I'm exhausted."

"Stress does that. There's a vending machine nearby. What would you like?"

"Something hot. And chocolate if possible. I need to recharge."

She pulled his garish shirt tighter around her chest, feeling the chill of the canned hospital air. Jake wore only his tight-fitting tee shirt. He'd given her his shirt, or rather Puma's shirt after they climbed into the FBI helo that carried them to the hospital. She'd used her blouse to staunch Strom's wounds, and her upper body had been exposed except for a skimpy bra.

She couldn't bear to think of Strom. Of what had almost happened to Matt. Of the danger he was in, even now. Of the repercussions ahead.

Jake looked at her with concern. "Coming up. A hot drink will do you good."

He came back with two steaming cups, handed her the cocoa and pulled another chair next to hers. "No one else is around, and the nurses mind their own business. This is as good a place as any. Be careful of that drink. It's hot as blazes."

She took a careful sip and sighed. "Ambrosia. Thank you."

"You're welcome. Do you want to start this, or should I?"

"Me, I guess. Jake, I know you think we'll stay together, but it won't work."

Unbelievable. She'd said it in one flat sentence. The words sounded harsh, even to her. The softness she'd seen on Jake's face when he kissed Matt, disappeared. His eyes gleamed flint, and his nostrils flared. She took a swallow and scalded her tongue.

He set his cup aside and stared at her. "I can't believe it. You're dumping me? Haven't we been through this before?"

"Please, don't think that way. I have my son back and I'm eternally grateful to you. It's a debt I can never repay."

"Our son, you mean. What else?"

"You're an adventurer, Jake. A gypsy. I'm a nest builder. Can't you see what a shaky foundation that makes for anything permanent? And how bad that would be for Matt's future?"

"My wandering days are pretty much over. This new job—"

"With the Defense Intelligence Agency. I heard Hooker say you were working for them. Don't tell me it isn't dangerous. Every time you left in the morning I'd wonder if you were coming back." The memory of the shadow of death that had touched them made her shudder. All three of them inches from annihilation. He might have nerves of ice, but she didn't.

He shrugged. "There's danger when you cross the street. I'm careful."

"Don't blow this off! You know what I mean."

"All right," he said. "There's less hazardous work. Since when did life come with a guarantee? I know how to do my job. It's necessary and I'm good at it."

"No doubt of that. What happened after you waved goodbye to Matt and me on the bridge? With a live, ticking bomb six feet away? Not your usual 'I may be late getting home for dinner, honey' scenario."

He shifted in his seat. "What do you want to know? I disarmed the bomb. Hooker came and took over. End of story."

"Dammit, Jake!"

He grinned. "Okay, there's a little more. Someday—"

"Know what? I don't want to hear about it. Not now, not someday. Not ever."

The grin disappeared. "You're serious. I have to choose between my work and you. That's what you're saying."

"Would you stay in Nokeah? Let us build a family together there?"

"You know I can't. You want me to pump gas for a living? Help dad out at the farm? The land barely produces enough for my folks to live on. I make good money at what I do. I can take care of you and Matt just fine. What I do, the DIA? What we do, is important, Crucial. I wouldn't be worth loving if I left this job unfinished."

"In D.C. Away from Matt's friends, his school and his family. You can't expect me to pull up his roots like that."

"We'll be his roots. Maybe we should ask him."

"No. He's too young to make these decisions. I'm his mother. It's my choice."

She twisted the paper cup in her hand and discarded it in a nearby receptacle, avoiding his piercing gaze. She was a coward. She knew it. But it was how she felt and she couldn't help that. As much as she loved Jake, as much as she wanted to melt into his arms at that moment. Matt had been through too much. He needed peace. He needed stability. And so, by God, did she.

His mouth thinned. "Your choice? I don't think so. No one is taking my son from me again."

CHAPTER 33

H e stood and towered over her. His anger was under control. It was the steely determination that frightened her. Her heart faltered. She wasn't sure she had the strength to fight him. She braced herself against the slick support of the chair, and struggled to keep desperation from her voice.

"You can see him whenever you come home. As soon as he recovers from Strom's death, I'll tell him about us."

"No, you will not. I'll tell him. Before I leave."

"But when are you leaving? I need some time."

"I'll stay until Matt is well. Until he can walk out of here on his own feet. Then I need to report. But I'll be back soon. Believe that, Lorie. And be prepared for some unpleasant surprises."

He sounded so hard, so bitter. "Please, Jake. Let's don't quarrel. That won't solve anything. I want us to stay—"

"—friends?" he finished, mocking her with a lifted eyebrow. "How convenient for you. I can see Matt on your terms. We'll hop into bed now and then, when you get the itch. That may be what you want, angel, but it's not my plan. It won't go your way this time."

He cupped her face in his big hands and lifted her chin, stroking his calloused thumb across her lower lip. The sensation shivered her toes. *Watch yourself, Lorie.* She couldn't stop him from touching her, but she didn't have to make it a pleasant experience. Not while they were so at odds. She clamped her jaw.

"Let go," she hissed. "I bite."

He chuckled. A low sound of intent. "Sounds like fun. And I bite back."

He pulled her up into his arms and his mouth came down on hers. Not hard. If he'd forced his will on her she could have resisted. He kissed one corner of her mouth gently, then the other. Quick soft kisses, gentle caresses of his lips. Kisses, like the patter of raindrops and just as sweet, just as life giving. She tasted coffee and the wild flavor of Jake. More kisses. These not as quick. Lingering kisses that drugged her senses and clouded her mind. His mouth moved to the hollow of her throat, brushed across her neck. The sharp stab of pleasure pierced the core of her being.

"Jake, please!"

"Please, what?" he asked softly, nibbling her earlobe.

He had her face captured in one hand. The other streaked her back, wandered down and squeezed her buttocks. Damn him, he knew just how to seduce her, how to make her wild. She wanted his hands on her breasts. She wanted his sex against hers. He rubbed their noses, his mouth hovering. She felt his heat and inhaled his heady scent.

"Open your mouth for me," he said roughly. "You know you want this."

She did. She wanted his deep kiss, and oh God, she got it. His mouth slanted, fitted to hers. Her knees buckled as her lips parted, and he took her to their sweet special place. She spiraled into the honeyed abyss that was Jake. Where she wanted to stay forever.

When he pulled his mouth away, her back was slap up against the cool stucco of the wall and they were plastered chest to groin to thigh. His erection thrust into the vee of her thighs. Her softness yielded to his hardness. She wanted his mouth back, and fought the impulse to grab him, to pull him into another kiss. She buried her face in his chest and clung like ivy to oak.

He clamped her shoulders. "Look at me, Lorie."

She couldn't. She shook her head, her nose still buried in his chest, her arms hugged his waist. He cradled her chin, forcing her to meet his intent gaze.

"I could take you right here. Up against this wall, and you wouldn't stop me. Not if a troop of nuns walked by. Admit it."

She shuddered in surrender. "No, I wouldn't stop you. Is that what you want?"

"Now? God, yes, it's what I want. But not what I want for the long haul. Marry me. Give us a chance. Let me be your lifetime lover and my son's fulltime dad."

"I can't!"

Abruptly he released her and stepped back. She sagged against the wall. The throbbing ache between her legs was intense. A hunger that only Jake could feed.

He looked her over like he was rejecting a piece of shoddy goods. "I'm going to sit with my son. Tomorrow, I intend to tell him the truth. You can be there or not, that's up to you. We don't have to profess undying love for each other, but by God, we'll be civil around that boy. Do you understand?"

She shuddered at the iron in his voice. Of course she wanted that for Matt. It was part of what she hoped for. It was so damn confusing. She knew Jake was hurting as much as she was. Who could blame him when she'd thrown his love back at him so brutally? Yet she was doing the right thing, she was convinced of it.

He regarded her coldly. "If you're pregnant, we get married. Period. No discussion."

Her own anger stirred, and she welcomed it. Damn, he was arrogant. If she were angry, it would be easier. If she got mad enough, the painful need would ebb. He couldn't force her to marry him. Her chin jutted out. "I'm not pregnant. Any more orders, sir?"

He laughed. A bitter, hateful sound. Not the joyful full-throated laugh she loved to hear. "A few. First, you'll be available to me for sex whenever I find it convenient."

"The hell I will!"

"You owe me, remember? That debt you can never repay? I intend to collect. I'll let you know when the books balance."

"Damn your rotten soul to hell, Jake Randolph."

"If I catch another man in your bed, you'll regret it. Are you taking notes?"

As if there could ever be another man. As if she would admit that, she had her pride. "You have no right to demand fidelity! What about you?"

"Don't try me. Second, I'll be back frequently and carry Matt out to the farm for the weekend. My parents deserve some time with their grandson."

She swallowed and this time the lump went down. Maybe it was the best solution possible. She wanted Matt and Jake to get to know each other better. Matt needed a man in his life and Jake was the best man she knew. Certainly Mary and Wil would make wonderful grandparents, and Matt would love the farm. She searched for the risks and found them acceptable.

"But—the logistics—and won't it be expensive?"

"I'll manage. There's a redeye flight that leaves Friday nights from Dulles, and a straight flight back on Sunday afternoons. I'll visit the folks Friday, and stay at your place Saturday night while Matt's at the farm. Expect me to be hungry." His glance flicked over her again. "We may or may not go out to dinner first. Depending on my appetite."

Did he think that would scare her? An occasional night with Jake was a thousand times better than nothing. "All right. I agree to that."

For the first time he looked amused. "I thought you might. When I'm there, we'll go to church on Sunday. You, Matt and I will sit together as a family. Next to my folks."

Her antenna went up. Damn him, he intended to make them a public display. It wouldn't take long for everyone in town to figure it out. "You—you want to humiliate me? Matt looks more like you every day."

"Oh, I don't think I need to humiliate you, Lorie. I think

you'll do a good job of that yourself. But I intend to claim my rights. Legally. You'll sign a paper agreeing to joint custody, or I'll go to court and it becomes a public fight. Those are the terms."

"There's no need for that! I swear you can see Matt as often as you want. And—the rest of it, too. We can make it work, Jake."

"Maybe you can understand I don't trust you. We'll do it my way this time. You'll sign papers."

Apprehension caught in her throat. Was this the first step to take Matt away from her? But she had no other option. Jake didn't make idle threats. "You're a bastard."

"No question. But I earned the title. What choice are you giving our son?"

The force of his words shattered what was left of her composure. Her legs gave out and she staggered into the nearby chair. Tears trickled down her cheeks. Was he right? Was her plan to keep Matt comfortable and safe a good one? Or merely misguided? Jake lifted her chin again. Not a tender gesture. His eyes were hooded, brooding. Nothing loving there.

"Think about it. I won't ask again. You'll have to come to me. Now, let's go see if Matt's awake."

CHAPTER 34

If there was one thing Lorie knew how to do, it was to survive. She stiffened her spine and went on, and the bad memories began to fade. Surprisingly, she grieved for Strom. He'd been a part of her life for so many years. Now that he was gone, she found herself remembering the good times, before alcoholism and hatred took over his life, when they'd been young and carefree and the world stretched out before them.

The story of the terrorist attack on Boulder Dam never became public. The Nokeah Journal reported that Strom died in a car accident, and condolences poured in. Hy and Esther Garrison were devastated. They clung to Matt during the funeral like he was their lifeline. The FBI visited the Garrisons. Afterward, Hy seemed to shrink; his robust frame dwindled into a skeletal wraith.

Something bad had happened between Strom and Matt. Her son didn't talk about Strom anymore. He hadn't shed a tear at the funeral.

Jake.

For seven months, she and Jake and Matt had lived in limbo. Four times Jake had been back. Each time it was harder to see him leave. Even Matt's natural exuberance dimmed the days after his father left. She did her best to keep her life in order. To go to work each day, tend to her house, feed and care for Matt. But she was on autopilot. Jake was handling it better than she was.

So was Matt.

Matt knew the truth of his heritage. Even Jake agreed it was best not to confide in others. His family, her mother and Matt knew, and that was enough for him. It would leak out, but hopefully the talk would die eventually.

She smiled when the storm door banged admitting her son. At this rate, Jake would have another repair job next time he came home. Matt stomped into the house, and Roly-poly immediately bumped at his heels. The cat had become Matt's shadow, and wasn't a kitten anymore.

"Take off your boots. Where've you been? It's dark outside. I was worried."

"Jeff and I built a snow lady in his front yard. His mom gave us a carrot for her nose and one of her old hats and a big purse. She's neat."

"Hang up your coat. A snow lady, huh?"

"If it snows again, we're making the snow dad tomorrow. And a couple of kids."

"Awesome."

"I have to check my email," Matt announced, heading straight for the refrigerator. "Dad hasn't written me for over a week."

When had Matt started calling Jake, Dad? It had been a gradual thing, but both males accepted it as a natural progression in their relationship. And last week, Matt had started signing his school papers "Matt Randolph". Jake had bought Matt the computer and set up an email account the first time he'd been back. A few short lessons, and Matt had taken to technology like a baby bird took wing. No problem, just fly.

"Okay," she smiled. "Let me know what he says."

Usually she didn't probe about the communication between father and son. But if Jake hadn't been in touch with Matt for a week, it meant only one thing. He'd gone on a mission. God only knew where. And chances were good that wherever it was, it was dangerous.

"I think he's away somewhere," Matt said. "He's never skipped a week before."

"He's probably just busy."

"Naw," Matt said, wiping the milk mustache from his mouth. "Gotta be more than that. He told me sometimes he'd be going away and doin' stuff. You know, spy stuff."

"Matt! Your father, ah, Jake told you that!"

"'Course not," he said scornfully. "I figured it out. What can I have for a snack?"

"Not now," she responded automatically, chilled by her son's matter-of-fact acceptance of Jake's line of work. *Don't you dammit die on us, Jake!* "Dinner in ten minutes. Tuna and noodle casserole."

"Yuk."

My God. This was why she'd refused to marry the man she loved, why she lived with the pain of life without him. To shelter Matt from the harsh reality of Jake's world.

Jake's world had found them.

She was very afraid.

"Matt, go ahead and check your email. I'm stepping out on the porch for a minute to get some fresh air."

"It's real cold out, Mom."

"November in Kansas usually is. It's supposed to snow again tomorrow. I hope it does. We can use the moisture."

She turned off the oven and stepped outside. The searing cold shimmered off the driveway and sidewalk. Icy patches dotted the street. She sat on the front steps, and huddled in her coat, hugging her knees.

This was her world.

The lawn lay brown and withered under the crust of icy snow. Because of the drought, no one in town had watered their grass last summer. The farmers were suffering. She wondered how Jake's folks would survive this year. She had heard Wil say there would be some belt-tightening. And she knew Dex had taken on extra rodeoing and auctioneering, trying to fatten the family coffers. Mary had a job in town, teaching computer classes at the community college.

She couldn't imagine Wil and Mary giving up. They accepted uncertainties. They endured. That's what farm folk did. No one could control the weather. Love, either.

She thought this the safest place in the world, but suffering and hardship existed here. And death. Death had found Strom here.

She remembered Jake's last email to Matt.

You asked me why I do what I do._Maybe when you see Washington D.C., you'll understand why I can't come back to Kansas and find another job. Someday, when you come to visit, I'll take you to the Vietnam Wall. It's a monument dedicated to soldiers who died in a terrible war. All the names are there, many of them were not much older than you. It makes you sad, but proud, too. Maybe they didn't want to go to war, but they did. Because it was their duty, and their country asked them to. We'll visit Gettysburg and the Arlington National Cemetery. The Capital building is a must see, and the Washington and Lincoln monuments are wonderful sights. There's so much history here, Matt. We stand on the shoulders of giants, men and women who dedicated their lives to make this the best country in the world. It's my turn on watch, son.

How could you not love a man like that?

The message had been as much for her as Matt.

Matt's holler woke her from the reverie.

"Mom! Come quick! Hurry!"

She rushed into his bedroom. "What? For goodness sake, calm down. You scared me to death."

"Look! Dad's bought a house. He sent a picture."

Lorie stared at the screen. A white frame house. Two-story, almost buried behind mature trees and juniper bushes. Paint peeling, a shutter or two missing.

"Good grief," she whispered. "He really bought this house? Where is it?"

"Yeah. Read his message."

Dear Matt,

I just bought this house. It's in Virginia, not too far from where I work. It's on an acreage with lots of trees and a horse barn and corral. It needs work, but is a solid house. Want to come and help me during Thanksgiving vacation? Tell your mother I'll send a plane ticket. Love, Dad

PS: Click on the next picture to see your early Christmas present. His name is Barnaby and he's waiting for you to ride him.

"Want to see the next picture, Mom?"

"Of course."

Despite her determination to live life without him, she'd nursed the hope Jake would change his mind. That he'd quit and return to Kansas to be with them. A foolish dream. He'd bought a house. That meant permanency. What had he said? Since when did life come with a guarantee?

She had never felt lonelier in her life.

"Look, Mom. Isn't he beautiful? I'm going to print him out."

"Yes," she murmured. "Beautiful."

But she wasn't looking at the sturdy palomino on the computer screen. She was looking at the man who held the pony's bridle and grinned at the camera. It wasn't exactly a thunderbolt that hit her. She supposed she'd known this was her fate for months. But would Jake still want her?

She wouldn't give him the chance to say no.

She'd beg if she had to.

The printer began clacking, echoing Matt's excited chatter at the prospect of having his own horse.

"Matt," she said, "What would you think of moving to Virginia?"

CHAPTER 35

Jake pulled into the driveway of his home. Funny, after a month he already thought of it as home. There was a lot to do. The roof sagged and needed to be re-shingled, and a paint job was imperative. That had to wait until spring. The house had good bones. When the repair work was done and the overgrown thatch of greenery that surrounded it was hacked out, it would be a comfortable house for a family.

The fact it was in such disrepair was why he'd been able to afford the place. Property in Virginia was sky-high. And to get an acreage with a house—that was unbelievable luck. When he finished the outside work, he'd start on the inside. Cosmetic stuff mostly. Something he wasn't good at. It needed a woman's touch. Lorie's touch. He'd seen her home and what she could accomplish on a spaghetti budget.

There wasn't much furniture yet. He'd bought a king-size bed for the master bedroom, and bunk beds for Matt. A kitchen table and bare appliances. That was it. Not even a TV. The house had four bedrooms. Plenty of room for a family.

As soon as his master plan worked out.

The last time he'd been back, he'd thought Lorie was weakening. She'd cried when he left. Matt's chin had quivered. Jake wasn't above using his son as a lever. Like they said, desperate times call for desperate measures.

His four-part plan was simple.

First, become indispensable.

There were always repair jobs around her house, and her car needed constant attention. He took care of those things when he went back. He cut her grass and shoveled snow. Lorie's mother had even warmed to him, no small miracle.

And not to visit too often.

He didn't want Lorie comfortable with the status quo. He wanted her to miss him when he was gone.

To indulge her in long, slow nights of lovemaking.

He grinned. Not that that was a chore. They damn near scorched the sheets every time they were in bed together.

And to be the best father he knew how to Matt.

Eventually, he'd wear her down. Or Matt would. The palomino was a masterstroke. Matt loved to ride when he visited the farm, and Dex was teaching him. Jake could teach his son many things, but Dex was the expert with horses. He'd have to buy two more mounts eventually. Lorie could ride well enough.

Yep, it was working.

She'd crack soon.

He'd give her until Christmas. Then he'd go to Plan B. Which he hadn't perfected yet. His Celtic ancestors had stolen their brides. Maybe he should kidnap her and shackle her to his bedpost.

His son was due tomorrow for a week visit. Jake hoped when Matt returned to Kansas and told Lorie about Virginia, she'd be intrigued enough to visit. It was a beautiful state. And blessed with more rugged countryside than people in the Midwest realized. He had his own little world right here. He just needed his family.

Damn, he missed them.

The palomino whinnied as he climbed out of the five-year-old SUV he'd traded the Maserati for. He'd gotten a boatload of cash for the import. Added to what he had in savings, it was enough for a down payment on the property

and some left over for repair. He walked over to the corral
and patted Barnaby's velvet nose. The pony lipped at his
hand, looking for a treat.

"We'll go for a ride, boy. Would you like an apple or a
carrot?"

Barbary whinnied, and pawed the ground, bobbing his
head. "Both, huh? We'll have to see about that."

"Dad!"

He wheeled in astonishment. "Matt! How did you—"

"We're here! We're here!" His son gave a whoop and
leaped. Jake caught him and staggered backwards.

"Whoa, kid. You'll knock your old man on his tail."

"Naw, you're pretty strong. Is that my horse? Wow! Can
I ride him?"

"Sure. Ah, who's we? How did you get here from the
airport?"

"By bus and taxi. You should hear Mom complain. She
said it was two month's groceries and we're having tuna
casserole forever. I don't care! Can I ride now?"

He swept his son up on his shoulders, his heart thudding
in anticipation. Was Lorie actually here? "How about this
for a start. Matt, your mother—"

"I'm here, Jake. On the back porch."

God, he couldn't believe it. She stepped carefully as she
walked toward him. The porch floorboards were on his
Needing Repair list.

"Lorie," he whispered hoarsely. She carried Roly-poly in
his crate. They were going to stay! She had come to him, to
be with him.

"Hello, Jake," she said, stopping a few feet away, as if
she wasn't sure of herself. "Could I have a hug, too?"

EPILOGUE

◆

Lorie cuddled next to Jake as the last flames flickered in the stone fireplace. This was her favorite time. When the soft curtain of night embraced them and she could look forward to sleeping with her husband. A year of marriage hadn't lessoned their passion. Nor had the rounded belly of her pregnancy. If anything, she desired him more.

The day's chores were done and Matt was sleeping peacefully in his bedroom above them. The only light in their comfortable living room came from the glowing coals of the fire and the six-foot evergreen standing in the corner, its branches heavy with sparkling ornaments and stars of colored lights. The scent of fresh pine and burning apple wood permeated the air.

Jake stroked her hair. "Want me to add another log?"

She tightened her grip around his chest. "Huh-uh. I don't want you to leave this couch. Let's snuggle here until the music stops playing. I love Christmas music. Christmas Eve is magic."

He stretched out an arm and snagged the afghan lying across the back of the couch, wrapping it around her. "I turned the thermostat down. You'll catch a chill."

"Mmm, not a chance. You're like an oven wrapped around me. My red-hot lover."

He chuckled and kissed her. "Merry Christmas, sweetheart. You're sure you don't mind us staying in Virginia, instead of going home for the holidays?"

"We couldn't get Matt away from Lily with a blowtorch. We're not going to be able to go anywhere until that puppy grows up enough to behave herself in a kennel."

"How do you suppose he came up with that name? If the size of her feet is an indication, that dog is going to end up nose to nose with Barnaby. Hardly a delicate lily."

"She's a collie-borzoi mix. And a doll. We have lots of space for a big dog and a boy to romp in." She caught his chin and planted a fervent kiss on his mouth. "Thanks."

He returned the kiss and it turned into a production. A low hum of satisfaction rumbled in his chest. "Let's go to bed," he murmured, nibbling on the sensitive spot under her chin. "I'll give you your Christmas present early. You can thank me then."

"Thanks for being you. For loving me," she whispered. "And this is home. Wherever you are is home."

That earned her another kiss, one full of promise. He cupped her rounded belly. "We'll visit this spring. After the baby is born."

"We'll have to. Three grandparents and one uncle are waiting to spoil her."

"You're right there. My mom would be on the plane for the birth, if her teaching job at the college didn't keep her tied down. She's over the moon at the promise of a granddaughter."

"You probably shouldn't have told her. Ultrasounds are occasionally off."

"Won't matter. Boy or girl, she'll go nuts. Is your mom still coming for the birth?"

"Uh-huh. You will behave yourself, right?"

"Of course," he said blandly. "I'm her favorite son-in-law, remember?"

"Ha! You're her only son-in-law."

"That, too."

She rearranged the afghan so it covered both of them.

"What do like most about being married to me?"

"Steady sex," he replied promptly. "Speaking of which—"

She punched his shoulder. "Wrong answer. Try again."

He seemed to consider. "Great steady sex?"

"Just for that, I get to be on top."

He flopped on his back, arranging her thighs to straddle his. "Take me, I'm yours."

They lingered over the lovemaking. He was gentle, but thorough. Afterward he wrapped the coverlet around them again. His mouth curled in amusement. "Told you you'd thank me."

"Mphh," she managed, her face buried in his naked chest. "Smugness is one of your least endearing traits."

"We should get to bed. Matt will be up at dawn."

She sighed. "I know. I can't believe the size of that pile of presents with his name on them."

"I'm afraid Hy equates material goods with love."

"You don't mind he and Esther still consider Matt their grandson?"

"That would be foolish. And cruel. They lost their only son. I wouldn't take Matt away from them, too."

They were very quiet. Strom was gone, but not forgotten. He never would be. He was woven into the fabric of their lives. "You're a good man, Jake Randolph," she said softly. "I'm so lucky you're finally mine."

"Honey, you've had me from eighth grade. Can we go to bed now?"

They pulled on enough clothes to be decent and walked arm in arm to their bedroom. Lorie's heart brimmed with gratitude. Gratitude that she'd found the courage to step into the unknown, and accept that life had risks. That the risks were nothing compared to the rewards.

*Turn the page for an
excerpt from*

FIRESTORM

I'm Your Man Series
Book Three

Blaine Kistler

FBI agent, Rachel Cortez, is ambitious and daring to the point of recklessness. Puma Ansari, ex-Delta and skilled smokejumper, prefers soft and compliant women. Turn the page for the beginning of their story, Book Three of the I'm Your Man series, Firestorm.

CHAPTER 1

Puma stripped and stepped in the shower, grateful to ease his stiff muscles under the steaming water. The rugged workout had left him regretting the winter's excesses. Too much food and soft living. Fat season, the smokejumpers called it, and he had less than a month to get in shape. Failing the annual fitness test meant turning in your gear.

The doorbell chimed over the drum of the sluicing water.

He shut it off and slid back the shower door, narrowed his eyes and listened. It was late. Almost midnight, and his ranch lay a mile from the nearest neighbor. Not that someone after his scalp would enter by the front door, but uninvited guests didn't venture near Sundance. If a snarled warning didn't suffice, the German Shepard could knock a two-hundred pound man flat and keep him there.

Why wasn't the dog barking?

Puma toweled off quickly and pulled on his jeans. His inner eye served him well, and the instincts inherited from his shaman grandfather warned trouble lurked behind the door. He yanked it open, ready to take someone's head off.

"Yeah?"

The woman stood in the shadows, her face concealed in the depths of his porch. Her tawny hair gleamed under the artificial light. Like the moonlight. No, not moonlight. The shaggy tumble over her shoulders was too warm for that. Not the coolness of moonlight, but the dappled bronze-gilt of sunlight streaming through an aspen grove. Her clothing blended into the night and added to the illusion of a faceless phantom. Black trousers, a black tee shirt under a jacket of muted tweed. She wore arrogance like perfume.

His heart thumped in his chest.

He'd had no warning, no premonition of this. Nothing to prepare him for the sexual reaction that sliced his gut. The sensuality emanating from the phantom woman staggered him. He pitched his voice low, to a growl of menace.

"Who are you? Show yourself."

She stepped into the light. "Sorry. I know it's late. I'm Rachel Cortez."

Her face shimmered into focus and became a beautiful woman. Creamy skin, brilliant emerald eyes. Her light scent hovered just out of reach. Sweet clover, maybe. Again, he endured a clutch to his gut. He'd preferred the phantom to reality. It made no sense. She wasn't his type of woman at all.

She was tall and thin, almost bony. Only the luxuriant, amber hair softened the image. She wore boots with high heels and the two of them stood eye to eye. He favored small women, dark-haired and dark-eyed. Cuddly, submissive women. Women that he could tuck under his chin, who would follow his lead in bed. He'd never been emotionally unfaithful to Sadie. Even ten years after his wife's death, he had a woman only when his sexual appetite clawed so fiercely that he gave in to it or lost his sanity.

Always he took soft, Rubenesque women.

This woman was not soft.

He swept cold eyes in her direction. "State your business."

"Could I come in? It's personal. That is, it's business and personal."

"FBI business is never personal."

Her lips curved. "They told me you were good. What gave me away?"

"Other than the pistol holstered on your belt? The attitude, lady. I've dealt with you people before. Let's see your badge."

Still smiling, she palmed the badge from her jacket pocket. "Can I come in now, Mr. Ansari?"

"We weren't introduced. How do you know who I am?"

She looked him up and down, the smile replaced by a dispassionate stare. "Fletcher, aka Puma, Ansari. Thirty-four years old," she recited. "Ex-Delta, expert smokejumper. Five-foot ten and a half inches tall. That gives you a half-inch on me. Weighs in at one-sixty-five. Dark hair. Bronze-skinned from one side of his family tree, blue-eyed from the other. Meaner looking than the file photo. Cheekbones that could cut ice. A sensual mouth—"

She bit her lip, shutting off the speech with an unladylike mutter.

He folded his arms over his bare chest, amused despite his distrust. "I doubt all of that is in my file. Why should I let you in?"

"Talk about attitude."

He laughed. Couldn't help it. "You nailed me."

"I brought an old friend who wants to talk."

Ah, now it made sense. "So, is Hooker lurking in the vicinity?"

The voice came from ten feet away, the man cloaked in the darkness of night. Puma knew the voice. Crisp, authoritative. "Here, Ansari. Let the lady in. She has a case to state, and it needs to be done in private."

Grudgingly, Puma opened the door. There weren't many men he respected enough to overlook his instincts for self-preservation. Dan Hooker was one.

She stepped inside, bringing her female scent into his house. Hooker followed. The hair rose on the back of

Puma's neck as she brushed past his shoulder. He was crazy to let her get within ten feet. He'd listen politely, and then hustle them out the door.

He remembered his duties as host. "Could I get you something to drink? Coffee? Soda?"

"I'd take a beer." Hooker's deep voice rumbled as he shrugged out of a leather jacket and tossed it on a nearby armchair. Dan Hooker taking a drink? And out of his usual three-piece tailored suit? Puma's inner voice screamed again. Whatever the pair's business, it wasn't official.

"Nothing for me," Rachel said. "Shall we get down to it?"

The tone of a woman used to taking charge. If his instincts weren't so busy shouting at him, Puma would have found that an amusing challenge.

Puma glared at the long-legged woman prowling the perimeter of his living room, his temper at low boil. "Absolutely not. I won't even debate this. She'd never stand up under the physical demands."

He wasn't having much luck in getting his uninvited guests to leave. Hooker was settled into the most comfortable chair in the room, and looked like he planned to grow roots there.

The FBI man took a deliberate swallow of his beer. "She's a quick study, Puma. And tougher than she looks. She'll do."

Puma jumped up from the couch and began his own pacing. "Dammit, Hooker, do you know what you're asking? It takes months of training to master the techniques of smokejumping and firefighting. And it never stops being dangerous."

The woman, Rachel, halted and faced him. "I'm not a doormat here. Include me in this discussion, please. I can perform any task necessary, Ansari."

Puma hadn't bothered to don a shirt to answer the door. Why should he? It was his house, and he was decently covered. Still, her scathing glare made him feel naked, and he wished he'd taken time to pull on a tee shirt. And boots. She irritated him. She was too tall and too flinty for a woman. Too snippy. And her buddy-buddy way of referring to him by his last name annoyed him. Even more annoying was the fact that Sundance was crouched in the corner of the room, tail thumping expectantly. When Rachel bent to scratch his ear, Sundance quivered and whined, his brown eyes mooning over the sexy witch. Damn worthless dog was in love.

No question the woman radiated sensual heat. It made a man wonder if she'd take that same energy to bed. He fantasized tangling his fingers in that tawny mass of curls and shutting that lush, smart-alecky mouth with a thorough kiss. Of suckling those delicate breasts until she moaned with pleasure. There's a woman somewhere under that hard-ass exterior. Bet you wouldn't be so snarky flat on your back, baby. It would be fun to break her to saddle.

Dangerous thoughts. He had to get rid of her.

Puma turned his attention to the FBI man who watched them both with amusement he didn't bother to conceal. "Send me a man to train, Dan. I'll do it if you send me a man."

Hooker raised his eyebrows. "A woman is less likely to be suspected as a plant. Rachel's worked undercover before, and she's good at it. This is important, Puma, or I wouldn't ask. I need her to establish a credible cover in three weeks, and I can't go through regular channels."

"Why?"

"You figure it out." The FBI man's face darkened.

"You have a leak? Where? In the Denver office?"

Hooker waggled his beer bottle. A gesture that could mean yes or no, but he wasn't going to discuss it further. "Just take my word for it. Washington Okayed going off the books for this one, so we're covered. You know I wouldn't shag you, Puma. And you owe me."

"You never proved a thing with that Hoover Dam business. I was a tourist tooling around the desert on my dirt bike. Nothing illegal about that."

Hooker barked the sound he called a laugh. "Caught on the bluff overlooking the dam, carrying a recently fired M40 rifle. The same caliber that took out the terrorists' pickup. Personally I'd have pinned a medal on you, but you know those boys in Washington. By-the-book types and starchy about civilians interfering with fed business. You and your Delta pal left a lot of bodies behind."

"Not all our work. Your people did their share," Puma said. "If the nuke had destroyed the dam, the body count would have been hundreds higher. And a disaster to our country."

"The Bureau took responsibility. We kept you out of it."

"A dead terrorist is better that a live one any day."

"No argument. That's why I'm here. We need to establish how deep this latest conspiracy goes and crush it."

"I know you're working with the FBI anti-terrorist task force, Dan. So whatever this is about, it isn't local."

"We think our old pals, the New Sons of Liberty, have reorganized. This time they're going after our forests, planning to burn and destroy as much property and as many lives as possible in the process."

Puma shook his head. There had been devastating fires earlier than normal this season, but the experts, and Puma was considered one of them, blamed it on the drought and unusual high winds. After two years of inadequate rainfall, much of the natural forest system was tinderbox dry.

"A small number of fires we deal with are arson, no question," Puma conceded. "But most are natural phenomena, lightning strikes, spontaneous combustion, and some are purely manmade carelessness. You have evidence there's a terrorist conspiracy to burn the forests in Colorado?"

"Not just here. California. Arizona. Oregon."

"Whoa! You're talking about something that widespread?"

"Yes," Hooker nodded. Hooker never used two words where one would do.

This was troubling. Dan Hooker was a good agent, one

who believed in solid evidence before he made an arrest. Given the proper motivation and weapon, Puma could knock a squirrel from a tree at 700 meters. Call it frontier justice, if terrorists were burning his forests, Puma would find them and bring them down.

He didn't need the woman for that.

He shifted his attention to her again. "What's her angle?"

"She's usually based in New York. No one around here knows her, which is a definite plus."

"I don't know her, Dan. I won't baby-sit a rookie who could get herself killed on my watch. Send me a man to train, give me six weeks to get it done, and I'll pay off that favor."

Baby-sit! Rachel's temper slipped into the red zone. She'd been letting the two males duke it out, but enough was enough. She hissed a protest. "If I might have a word, gentlemen?"

Hooker shot her a warning look, which Rachel ignored. So he was her superior and her boss. He was getting nowhere with the stubborn Mr. Ansari and this was too important. Her career was on the line. The FBI promotion system guaranteed equal treatment of the sexes, but if she were turned down for this assignment because she was a woman, there would be consequences. Subtle, but nonetheless damaging, and her personal ambitions would be scotched.

She walked toward Fletcher Ansari and pursed her lips, turning on the sugar, appealing to his reason. "Look, why don't you hear me out? I'll make you a deal."

The half-naked savage glared at her and stepped closer, threatening her by force of his personality. "What deal? The only deal I want is for you to leave."

Rachel swallowed. Damn, the man intimidated her. An aura of menace shimmered around him like body heat. She was used to working with dangerous men, but this one was in a class by himself. She'd read his records and knew he'd performed deeds that were legendary while in the service, that he'd volunteered for missions no one else would consider. He was a loner with his own code of honor and as far as anyone knew, incorruptible. Also, it seemed, unbendable.

She would have to be very careful.

Fear wasn't in this man's makeup, and he would have no patience with it in others. He would be contemptuous if he knew of her terror of fire. She needed to keep her secret close. Perhaps facing her old nightmare would conquer it.

"Hooker thinks if anyone can get me ready in three weeks, you can."

"I didn't say I couldn't. I said I wouldn't."

"Because I'm a woman."

He hesitated. "Yeah. Because you're a woman."

"There're women firefighters. There's one on your duty list." Thank God she'd done her homework. He'd have to find a better reason than her gender to refuse Hooker's request.

"Jeanette? She's a pro. You're not."

"But you could turn me into one."

"Not in that amount of time. Do you have any idea what's involved?"

Good, she had him talking. That was progress.

Out of her side vision she saw Dan Hooker lean back and relax. Her boss intended to let her run with the ball, at least for a while. She looked the firefighter in his Viking eyes, and felt a stir in her belly when his pupils warmed and darkened. Any woman breathing would've been attracted to him. The superb body, the sensual mouth, and the subtle bad boy mystique that presented an unspoken dare to a female. *Tame me if you can. Wouldn't it be fun to try?*

He smelled of freshly showered male and carnal knowledge. She itched to tangle her fingers in the damp hair, to soften that hard, whiskered jaw with a brush of her lips. No question it would be stimulating. She took a breath and shook off the thought. She wasn't here to play with the man, tempting as the idea was. She'd go with humility. "You're right, I don't know what's involved. So tell me."

"You need a valid red card to get a job with any firefighting unit."

"No problem. Hooker can get me one."

"Not a legit one. If you want me to sign off on your red card and place you on my team, you earn it."

"How?"

"Three months of class work. A year in the field. That will qualify you for certain positions. Not smokejumper. That calls for more extensive training."

She brushed that aside. "I don't plan to do this fulltime. Just long enough to catch the psychos who're setting these fires. All I need is enough basic knowledge to carry off my cover story."

"Just enough to make you dangerous, you mean. I have my people to think of, and we're a team. One rotten link could endanger us all."

"I'll work hard. Do what it takes to pull my weight."

He stared at her like she was a lower life form. "You'd ruin your manicure, sweetheart. Wouldn't want that, would we?"

She looked down at her hands. Her hands were one of her few vanities and she kept them creamed and the nails polished. Her breasts were small, her legs too long and ugly, but she had pretty hands. "To hell with my manicure. All I'm asking is a week. If I can't cut it in a week, I'll back off and let Hooker recruit someone else. A man."

"A week? How about a day?"

"Try me."

———◆———

FIRESTORM

available in print and ebook
Coming 2018

THE
I'M YOUR MAN
SERIES

Illusions
Homecoming
Firestorm

ABOUT BLAINE KISTLER

After a twenty-year career of teaching the language Arts, I'm pursuing my dream of writing stories. I write the kind of relationship stories I find intriguing and passionate. Hopefully my readers will enjoy the *I'm Your Man* series, because stories are meaningful only if they have an audience.

The most important thing in my life is family. I grew up the oldest of six girls, and while we live widely separated, our love keeps us close in heart. After writing, I enjoy reading, swimming and cooking. I love flowers and animals of all kinds. Flowers give us beauty and animals give undemanding love, asking in return only that we are kindly caretakers.

As my characters are on a journey of discovery, so too am I.

You can contact me through my website
www.blainekistler.com